Spytime

ALSO BY WILLIAM F. BUCKLEY JR.

God and Man at Yale

McCarthy and His Enemies
  (With L. Brent Bozell)

Up From Liberalism

Rumbles Left and Right

The Unmaking of a Mayor

The Jeweler's Eye

The Governor Listeth

Cruising Speed

Inveighing We Will Go

Four Reforms

United Nations Journal:
  A Delegate's Odyssey

Execution Eve

Saving the Queen

Airborne

Stained Glass

A Hymnal:
  The Controversial Arts

Who's On First

Marco Polo, If You Can

Atlantic High: A Celebration

Overdrive: A Personal
  Documentary

The Story of Henri Tod

See You Later Alligator

Right Reason

The Temptation of
  Wilfred Malachey

High Jinx

Mongoose, R.I.P.

Racing Through Paradise

On the Firing Line: The Public
  Life of Our Public Figures

Gratitude: Reflections on What
  We Owe to Our Country

Tucker's Last Stand

In Search of Anti-Semitism

WindFall

Happy Days Were Here Again:
  Reflections of a Libertarian
  Journalist

A Very Private Plot

Brothers No More

The Blackford Oakes Reader

The Right Word

Nearer, My God

The Redhunter

Spytime

The Undoing of James Jesus Angleton

A NOVEL BY

William F. Buckley Jr.

HARCOURT, INC.

New York   San Diego   London

Library of Congress Cataloging-in-Publication Data
Buckley, William F. (William Frank), 1925–
Spytime: the undoing of James Jesus Angleton: a novel/
by William F. Buckley Jr. — 1st ed.
p.   cm.
ISBN 0-15-100513-3
I. Title
PS3552.U344 S6 2000
813'.54—dc21   99-054977

Designed by Kaelin Chappell
Text set in Electra
Printed in the United States of America
First edition
J I H G F E D C B A

For Lucy Gregg Buckley

Acknowledgments

This is a book of fiction, though it is very roughly based on the career of James Jesus Angleton of the Central Intelligence Agency. Liberties have been taken with historical events.

I am indebted, in my own office, to Tony Savage, who manicured the manuscripts, and to Frances Bronson, who supervises everything. To Ms. Rachel Myers at Harcourt for her fine copy editing backed by her extraordinary scholarship. Any anachronism or chronological ineptitude is done athwart her advice.

My thanks also to James Panero, who served as a research assistant and labored diligently and intelligently on the project during the whole of the writing of the manuscript.

I am grateful to friends and family who read the manuscript, including Priscilla and Reid Buckley, my wife Pat, and my son Christopher; and Evan Galbraith, Chester Wolford, and Thomas Wendel.

I am not permitted by my editor Samuel Vaughan to expatiate again on his brilliant and resourceful and devoted editing, and therefore I will not do so.

I am indebted also to Mr. André Bernard of Harcourt for his encouragement and his fine editorial ideas.

I have read the following books, which helped me in writing my own:

Kim Philby, *My Silent War*, London, MacGibbon and Kee, 1968

Genrikh Borovik, *The Philby Files*, Boston, Little Brown and Company, 1994

Tom Mangold, *Cold Warrior*, New York, Simon and Schuster, 1991

Aaron Latham, *Orchids for Mother*, Boston, Little Brown, 1977

Kai Bird, *The Color of Truth*, New York, Simon and Schuster, 1998

David C. Martin, *Wilderness of Mirrors*, New York, Harper and Row, 1980

Robin Winks, *Cloak and Gown*, New York, William Morrow and Company, 1987

Allen Weinstein and Alexander Vassiliev, *The Haunted Wood*, New York, Random House, 1999

Edward J. Epstein, *Deception*, New York, Simon and Schuster, 1989

Frances Stonor Saunders, *Who Paid the Piper?*, London, Granta Publications, 1999

W. F. B.
Stamford, Connecticut
November 1999

Spytime

BOOK ONE

Chapter One

September, 1974

CASA NOGALES

My name is James Jesus Angleton, he wrote. And then spoke the lines out. "Yes, that's J-e-s-u-s. For most of my professional life I went out of my way to suppress my middle name." He would explain that: "One picks up quirky inhibitions, when young, inhibitions we have no reason to be proud of. One of mine was to hide my middle name." He sipped from his glass, fought briefly what had proved was a losing battle — his onetime resolution not to write a journal of any kind. He closed his eyes and summoned his determination to do what he thought his duty. To himself.

How is it I came by such a name, you might wonder?

I was given that name by my Mexican mother. She was seventeen when my father, Hugh, married her, in Nogales, Arizona. "Na--CI-- en la fronTERa / A-CAAA--d'este LA-do . . ." She used to sing that to me. *Born-n-n over he-eeer, / On this si-i-i-de of the border.* Sounds better in Spanish. For a long while they (Mum and Dad) spoke to each other mostly in Spanish (my father learned how to do that while fighting in Mexico under General Pershing, chasing after Pancho Villa). Pancho Villa. A popularized rogue, I pause to remark. My father, when I was very young, let me in on the true character of that wild-west hero, and I tucked it away. A piece of intelligence.

Tucked it away where? Tucked it away in my memory, which is copious. In Mexico the name *Jesús* is quite commonly given to a son, especially as a middle name. The spoken use of it isn't disruptive, unlike here, this side of a barroom. I'm not pretending I know a lot about barroom palaver, though I know something about what saloons stock. In the Latin-speaking world you might hear a formal old lady remark, *"Jesús, María, José, cómo habla esa señora!"* Commonplace, but you would not expect a well-mannered woman in America (outside of an asylum), to go about saying, "Jesus, Mary, and Joseph, how that lady runs on!"

You will guess, with the launch of these few lines, that I have got about a bit in my life. That is so, I have. We lived briefly in Idaho and when I was still a boy, my father and mother moved the family (I had a younger brother and two sisters, also younger) to Milan where he practiced his trade. He was an executive of the National Cash Register Company.

Then I went to a British public school, about which there is also, as in Pancho Villa, a set of public attitudes, namely that such schools are all centers of vice and sadism. (I never had sex with one of my fellow students, nor was proffered sex, notwithstanding that I was an egregiously handsome boy and young man. I was beaten exactly twice. I should have been beaten six times. But, very young, I was acquiring those skills that have taken me to the top of the profession from which they now propose to disengage me. I learned something about guile, in my school, something about maneuvering around the rules. No skill is more important in the practice of counterintelligence.)

Then there was Yale. As a student I was undistinguished. I took comfort (though gave none to my father) by reminding myself from time to time that if academic eminence was what I wanted to achieve, I'd have taken the pains to achieve it. If you want to be the first boy in the class who knows when the Punic wars were fought, go ahead. And if I had had trouble penetrating *The Cantos*, I wouldn't have looked for a trot, I'd have asked Ez what it was he was being abstruse about; because I came to know Ezra Pound when, as an undergraduate, I pursued poetry in the special way I have pursued poetry ever since. I did go on to Harvard Law School, but going there was never disguised as other than filial docility. I never plumbed the motives of competent young men who labor with the law and spend whole lives arguing with one another in behalf, as often as not, of moneyed men and women they would not wish the company of at dinner. So when the war came I quit law school, eschewing the immunity I'd have had from the draft if I had stayed on in Cambridge. I then discovered that my eyesight was below the GI margin, but had no trouble devising a way of faking a test.

So I went to war. Something about my background had been uncovered by an unruly corporal at the processing center who took more than the usual ten seconds to examine the qualifications of incoming soldiers. He discovered that I was fluent in Italian and passed the word up. So I was marked for intelligence work and sent to London. There I did clerical work on the Brits' supersecret Ultra but only briefly. They needed agents in Italy.

My qualifications as a linguist were augmented by analytical skills I must have been born with. In the spring of 1945 it had become a practical necessity to establish, by the application of skills in detection and surmise, which of those Italian Fascists put into camps as the Allies approached victory were enthusiastic creatures of the grisly partnership of Hitler and Mussolini, who were simply doing as instructed to do by their superiors. My research resulted in not a few Italians executed, but resulted also in not a few Italians who, but for me, would have been shot, settling down, instead, for detention, until the war ended.

I made lively contacts in Italy, with the Resistance, of course, but also with the diaspora. These were Jews who had two goals in mind, the immediate goal of defeating Hitler and the Zionist goal of establishing a homeland. Except that practically everything I have done in my life is shrouded in secrecy it would be known internationally what I accomplished in the way of expediting the passage of Jewish exiles into Palestine well before the partition, what I have done for them in the two decades since then, in the way of channeling to Jerusalem information vital to the state's welfare and, indeed, its survival. I have to admit that my mood tonight takes me to the outer edge of propriety, where I pose willingly for the grateful orisons of history, hoping for some little measure of what is owing to me.

It is distasteful to dwell on it, but I cannot help from recording tonight — en passant — in my journal —

My journal! An exception: spies aren't supposed to keep journals. I am not, technically, a spy. I am a *counterspy.* Counterintelligence has been my business. There: I said it. It *has been* my business, because today I have concluded that what they intend to do is to — *fire me.* That would be a most extraordinary feat of bravura, to *fire* me, James Jesus Angleton. The mind strains for a comparable act of national self-mutilation. I would not liken it to turning down Winston Churchill, as the British voters did in 1945, because Churchill was, of course, a chief of government. I was — I *am,* I suppose, until the door closes finally . . . the principal intelligence officer in the West. Will they actually remove the keys to my office? Ha! As though they could keep *me* from the office, if I set out to enter it.

(Angleton went back to the punctuation and reworded the phrase with an exclamation point.)

. . . if I set out to enter it! I do not conceal that anything Houdini was capable of, mutatis mutandis, I am capable of —

But I was describing — to whom, ultimately? Perhaps only to myself. Describing my formal position. I am and have been for twenty years Chief of Counterintelligence for the CIA, the Central Intelligence Agency. It is my responsibility to winnow the information that comes in from the one thousand sources we woo, generate, stimulate, reward, punish, encourage, for the purpose of recommending counteraction at the operating levels of government. Counteraction can involve everything from a surgical nuclear strike to escorting an alien to an airship and telling him never again to step foot on American soil.

Many journalistic observers have described what it is the CIA does, this side of recommending a nuclear strike yet a little brawnier than merely chauffeuring a spy or a courier to Dulles Airport. They will never catch up. The spy profession, including its language, is always on the move; changing; adapting. I leave it here, in this—so far—discreet appearance as an autobiographer that nobody—*nobody*—has seen all the things that I have seen. And now that fool Colby, I suspect he's behind it all, actually proposes to close me out of my office! Close me out of my office and the recesses of my office. Recesses no other human being has examined. (It was only Anatoliy I gave access to my deeper files, and then only when I was with him, of course.) Anatoliy... Golitsyn. He wouldn't believe it possible, if Colby goes through with it.

James Angleton rested his pen on the broad red blotting board on his mahogany desk with the withered old Italian golden braid along the edges. He took the pen up again. His features seemed gaunt now, as he concentrated, allowing his hand to work along the lined paper pad as if transcribing what was passing through his mind. He refilled the liqueur glass.

He could go to the President.

I've never liked meetings with the President. Wherever the President is, he is conspicuous. There is no such thing as a furtive meeting with the President of the United States, at least not for an official in government.

An old friend once begged me to plead with President Kennedy that he agree to meet, however briefly, with Don Juan, Count of Barcelona, claimant to the throne of Spain, while Kennedy was on his illustrious visit to Paris in 1961. I had to explain it to him — grand dukes do not understand relatively simple things. I said to him that *any* meeting with the President while in Paris, with one thousand authorized cameras focused on him and ten clandestine cameras focused on him, ruled out any secret encounter with a rival contender to Spanish primacy. Prime Minister Franco *would learn about it.* If Franco's *ambassador* had requested the audience, in behalf of the Count of Barcelona, it would be granted; otherwise, the President would be thought to be conniving with the restoration movement behind Franco's back. . . .

No, I doubt I'll go to the President, even assuming Dr. Kissinger would permit me in the Oval Office. Though I would not want to think that at age fifty-six I am without the resources simply to materialize in the Oval Office, if I set my mind to it. But I suspect I have got gabby, *chiacchierone.* The result, no doubt, of that second B & B (whom am I deceiving by saying that? *Moi.*) — that *fourth* B & B. But I will do something about this crazy situation. Something *éclatant.*

He half smiled. Maybe I'll tell them I've figured out who the Fifth Man is.

Chapter Two

Early April, 1945

The decision to make James J. Angleton a deep-cover agent and post him to Italy was Allen Dulles's, no less, the Director, U.S. Office of Strategic Services in Europe. Dulles monitored, from his eyrie in Bern, the movements of resistance fighters in Italy, France, and Germany. When in the London dispatch on personnel movements he came across Angleton's name, he didn't need to shake his memory very hard. Allen Dulles had known the boy's father, Hugh Angleton, well. The senior Angleton, a veteran of the First World War, was an enterprising businessman with the National Cash Register Company, and he lived, with his family, in Italy until the war broke out.

Dulles had a specific memory of young Jim Angleton. At the time a lawyer with Sullivan and Cromwell, Dulles visited the Angleton's country house outside Milan. He remembered vividly the lanky, muscular teenager, taking his summer vacation with his family, on "hols" from his English school. An iced tea in hand, Dulles had sat that sunny day in 1936 on a webbed outdoor chair alongside Hugh at the family tennis court where young Jim was energetically competing with a neighbor's boy of the same age.

It was a noisy game. They spoke to each other after every point and often in midplay — jibes, oracular threats, squeaks of satisfaction, sighs of pain, according as the point had gone well or badly.

Dulles, ever attentive, was dressed in light brown slacks; a braided red belt, a dark blue, red-striped cotton sports shirt; his habitual corncob pipe in hand. He leaned over to his host. "You wouldn't know which one of those boys was Italian, which American."

Hugh Angleton answered matter-of-factly: "What would you expect, Allen? Jim's lived in Italy since he was what, fourteen?"

Seven years later Dulles instructed his aide. "Have Angleton sent to Valerio in Milan. Deep-cover status."

Major Gruber frowned on hearing about Angleton's background. "Milan? Isn't there a chance he'd be recognized in Milan?"

"You have a point, but I don't think there's much risk. The Angletons pulled out of Italy in 1941. And anyway, the family lived mostly in the country. It was Hugh — the old man — who spent time in the city."

"How tall would he be now?" Major Gruber persisted.

"Well, unless he shrank while at Yale" — Dulles's impatience was surfacing — "he would have to be the same height as when I saw him playing tennis. Maybe six feet two. Stop fretting. Rome is central, obviously, but Milan is where the Germans and what's left of the Mussolini Italians will make their final stand, I reckon."

Dulles often ended one of his declarations in that way. It had the effect of muting the sense he gave off of absolute self-assurance in all matters. "I'll have apple pie, I reckon" suggested to subordinates dining with him that it was safe for others to order peach pie. He made a notation and said to Gruber, "Tell London to have Angleton grow a beard."

The orders were received in London and James Angleton leaned over the desk at the crowded quarters of the Office of Strategic Services, which shared the old building at West End Ryder Street with

MI6. He studied it closely. His name did not appear anywhere on it, at least no name he'd have recognized as his own. And the source of the dispatch was similarly obscured. He learned that he'd be going to Milan, which lay in enemy territory, well up from the military front line that was pounding its way north in uneven thrusts. He learned that he would not wear a uniform, which meant that he would be shot if detected, and learned that he was to grow a beard.

He wondered how he could accomplish a credible beard, if indeed he was to set sail the following Tuesday aboard the British submarine in Southampton. For Angleton, such questions were a matter of five minutes' research: How fast does human hair grow? The answer (he discovered in the *Book of Knowledge*, at the library next to the refectory) was one-half inch per month. Inasmuch as passage by submarine, Southampton to Naples, would take only five days, if he began tomorrow on his disguise by skipping the morning shave, he would have eight days to work toward a beard. How well would he have fared? *Quickly now . . .* One-sixteenth of an inch of hair. Stubble, really, but effective, he acknowledged, toward the end of concealment.

He was given intensive instruction on the war scene in Italy and then a carefully documented biography. James J. Angleton was now "Nicola Paone," orphaned native of Como. If he knew now his identity, he knew nothing about his assignment. His instructions were to transmit a particular message to a particular radio channel when he knew within an hour or two the time at which the admiralty would permit the submarine *Duluth* to rise into the Bay of Naples and sidle over to the abandoned submarine shed. Somebody would be waiting for him on the dock. "Look for someone carrying a guitar case."

There wasn't much danger from enemy bombers or fighters. The Nazi line in Italy, embedded in the Po River Valley, had been static, 250 miles north of Rome. It was thin and porous, and such air support as the Germans could spare from the massive requirements on the Western Front at Belgium and the cascading Eastern Front at the Polish border was deployed well north of Rome. The Luftwaffe left the skies over southern Italy to the seemingly indomitable Allied forces. There was left only the occasional hit-and-run bomber coming in from Yugoslavia. But nighttime security procedures were strictly observed.

Jim Angleton had never before seen a submarine, let alone traveled in one. This was a U.S. Gato-class sub, the USS *Duluth*. At the dispatch center in Southampton, a staff sergeant wearing two battle decorations took Angleton into a cubicle, one of several secreted in the huge waterfront shed that housed the ordnance and bureaucracy of war. He drew the curtain and and told him to strip naked and to empty everything in his seabag on the left end of the bed. On the right end were normal supplies — toiletries, mostly — for one man.

"I know the general purpose of stripping naked," Angleton permitted himself to say to the sergeant standing just inside the drawn curtain, "but I hope you're not going to do a strip search."

The sergeant replied, "What I'm doing is what we do on the eve of a covert operation. In a way it's symbolic. On the other hand sometimes there's a tattoo that needs — attention. If you were one of *them* — an enemy falling into our hands — a strip search is exactly what we'd do next. But now" — he turned to the bed — "we just look for anything traceable to a foreign manufacturer. Everything you have here at that end of the bed has been made in Italy. The GI-wear you'll use in the submarine will be left on your bunk when you disembark. You will probably be the first man off the ship, and you know who to look out for. You will be in the hands of Caruso. Caruso as in Enrico Caruso."

The sergeant completed his examination of the bag, paying special attention to a worn leather briefcase ("you can go ahead and dress now"), and turned his eyes to the wallet. Nicola Paone's wallet contained a modest supply of lire, a St. Christopher medal, an Italian draft card stamped FERITO IN AZIONE, CON CERTIFICATO D'ONORE ("Wounded in Action, with Certificate of Commendation"), and a tourist's map of Italy, of the kind available at Italian bookstores. In a separate plastic case he had six packages of Italian Maxima cigarettes. They would pose considerable temptation to Angleton, who smoked compulsively, but if he consumed these — he was once again reminded — he would be consuming the equivalent of cash. And, finally, a handshake. "I don't know what it's all about, Nicola, but I wish you luck."

Late that night he was led to the submarine tower. He found the descent down the narrow tower awkward. It was convenient that James Angleton was skinny. But he was broad-shouldered and felt the tightness of the cylinder. In seconds he found himself in the brightly lit command station, face-to-face with all those navigational devices he had seen in photographs and in movies. He was eager to examine the whole ship, inch by inch, but he quickly noticed that no one was chatting. All conversation was utilitarian. An orderly of some sort examined the paper handed him by the captain and led Angleton through the ship's catacombs to a bunk. Angleton had anticipated the fright with which, dreading a negative answer, he'd be asking the question, "Is it OK to read?" But the mate nodded, flicking on a reading light by the bunk. "Store your gear under the mattress."

Angleton drew from his seabag a package of Italian newspapers and magazines. He had inserted into his leather case a paperback of *The Divine Comedy*, in the original, noble Italian of the fourteenth century. He remembered with amusement Professor Lipari's opening lecture at Yale. "In the unlikely event that any of you go on to a doctorate in Italian literature, I now violate the rules that forbid any tipping off to an aspirant of test questions. I will tell you what will be the first question asked by me, who if I live that long will be senior in the panel of examiners. My question will be: 'Give the dates of the great Dante.' The answer is: 1265–1321. Do yourselves the favor of committing those holy dates to memory."

A problem arose the first morning, at the mess hall. Carrying an aluminum tray, a young seaman turned to him: "Well I'll be damned — Jim Angleton!" They had known each other at Yale. Angleton confronted the very first security problem he had ever been challenged by. His mind worked quickly. He could exclaim that the seaman was mistaken, he was not "Jim Angleton." But that would give rise to a problem: He was dealing with Eric Stevenson, who had been a sophomore of dogged habits, Angleton knew from his experiences on the Yale *Lit*, for which Stevenson aspired to write. He could pretend to choke over his cereal, diverting attention from the scene — but that would merely postpone the problem.

What he did was raise his index finger to his lips, the universal sign of, *Silence!* Stevenson reacted well, sitting down with his tray and engaging another sailor in conversation. After breakfast Angleton approached him. "Eric, I'm on a covert mission. Pretend we never knew each other. OK?" Eric Stevenson nodded and gave an elaborate theatrical wink.

Chapter Three

His briefing in Rome was exhilarating, Angleton confessed to Enrico Caruso, his security contact, the only man with whom he had official communication, the law of the deep-cover agent, at their fourth and final meeting. The contact, a middle-aged man with a bony face and a patch over one eye was, simply, "Bob." The minute was quickly approaching when Angleton would leave him, descend the stairs of the safe house at 23 Bartolome, and leave the building through the ground-floor coffee shop. He would start down at exactly 6:53. It was now 6:51. Angleton felt a keen attachment to this stranger, who had sketched exactly what Angleton's movements would now be, carefully instructing him on details and emergency procedures.

"That's all I have to say, Nicola. God be with you."

"You know, Bob," Angleton said, his eyes bright with anticipation, "here in Rome you feel the pulsations of—of—"

"Victory."

"Yes."

"I feel them, too. But then I force myself to ask: How many

people who are alive today will be dead when victory finally comes? How many Italians, how many Germans? How many Americans? You may well be one of them but not, I hope, from any act of recklessness." Enrico looked at him. "You have" — he glanced at his watch — "less than an hour."

Angleton extended his hand and then walked to the door, went down the stairs and out into the street. He started the short walk to the bus station. As he neared it he heard the organ music throbbing out from the church. He turned impetuously and opened the doors. A funeral, passionately felt by the organist. Might he have been grieving his brother? His father? His child? Angleton knelt in the back pew and thought to pray. His mind traveled to his family, to some classmates; he prayed, too, for Ezra Pound — what would they *do* to that aberrant genius, already under investigation on charges of treason? Then the great prelude was ending, and Angleton thought to say a final prayer for Bob. But it was possible he would never see anyone again whom he had known in the days since leaving Southampton.

At the station he boarded the bus to Viareggio, on the Ligurian Sea.

Arrived there, he was one hundred miles from Milan, eighty-five miles of them under enemy control. He walked to an address he had memorized, gave his code identification, was brought into a shipyard's electrical store and given bread and soup. Although it was still light, he was counseled to sleep. "It is a very long walk to Cavriago." His guide spoke of the small town south of Parma. To get there meant crossing enemy lines. They would go over a mountain range to limit their exposure. "It will be cold, but not crowded," Giuseppe, his host, said, wryly.

It *was* cold, and even colder after they mounted the two mules at a site before the steeper part of the journey. Twenty miles later they left the mules, at Giuseppe's contact point; another ten-mile walk and then, before dawn, Angleton was once again given shelter. He was very tired and very cold and very hungry. This host was an elderly woman who gave her name simply as Maria. She did ask, after they ate coarse bread with warm milk and a teaspoon each of honey, "Do you, Nicola, by any chance have a cigarette?"

Angleton was not given to impulsive gestures. His mother, he knew, would without a thought have turned over to his host the entire supply. Angleton reached cautiously into his bag, angling his body to conceal from the gaze of Maria the stupendous horde of cigarettes he carried. He drew out two cigarettes from the same pack he had opened on leaving the submarine, where cigarettes were abundant and free. It was half full. He placed two cigarettes delicately on the bread tray and handed them to her. Her eyes blazed with delight. She asked whether Nicola would like another slice from the loaf of bread.

Again they traveled at night. Before dawn he could make out first the glow of Milan, and then the lights. Over the last two hours they had heard the thud of artillery in the northeast. Maria described, using the local map he carried, the route he had to take. From now on—he shook the hand she stuck out at him, resisting her initiative to a hug—he was on his own. He would report to Colonel Valerio. If interrogated between here and his destination, he would show his wounded-in-action discharge certificate and mimeographed commendation from an adjutant of Mussolini's Seventy-second Brigade, stamped on the fifth day of the great Arno offensive the preceding year.

Otherwise, his instructions were spare. He was to sit on the park bench directly opposite the La Scala Opera House, scanning a section of the day's *Corriere della Sera*. Get to the bench at five minutes before noon and stay until a passerby asks if he may have the discarded part of the newspaper.

"You are to say: 'Will you share it with Stella?' He will reply, 'Follow me, Nicola.'"

———

"Follow me, Nicola."

Five years had passed since Angleton had seen Milan, a city he knew more intimately than any other. He had spent the hundreds of idle hours that are the special perquisites of growing boys wandering about its lively precincts. He remembered especially Justo, on the back of whose bicycle Angleton would manage, his legs held up, to dart into the alleyways and chase, and be chased by, rivals. The great sport was to scoop up a piece of fruit on biking by the markets. There is always life where there are Italians, he reflected.

But the war's devastating presence was everywhere. There had been bombing, and there were scars on almost every surface from fires lit and doused. The stores were open but there were no displays in the windows. At the end of the Via Manzoni, down which he was led, always spruce in memory with the brick and the trimmed ivy, there was now what seemed to be a huge infirmary. Angleton lowered his head as he sidestepped the file of wounded coming out of the bus for medical care.

He hoped his guide would arrive soon at their destination. He did, two blocks away, on the Via Monte Napoleone. The guide used a key to enter one in that long series of dull row houses. The door closed, his guide made a gesture. Nicola responded by putting down his backpack, taking off his coat, and handing it to him.

"*Molte grazie. Fa freddo.*" Many thanks. It is quite cold.

"*Le vado a prendere un tè.*" The thought of the tea being offered was welcome.

He was led into a small living room. The appointments were conventional. The green-felted armchair, dappled gray couch, the coffee table stained almost black. James Angleton thought back to when he had been invited for tea at the house of his mother's cook. Now his guide brought tea and left it on the table. For a moment he was alone.

Then Valerio came. His eyes told the story: he was in charge.

Big, heavy, the collar of his khaki shirt buttoned at the neck, a black cap tilted down obscuring his forehead. He extended his large hand, then sat down in the armchair.

Angleton cleared his throat. He thought it best to say immediately what he now knew would be necessary to say.

"Colonel —"

"Emilio." The voice was sharp. The syllables unmodulated.

"Emilio, I wish you to know that I am an American. I spent my boyhood in Italy. Here. I am a member of the armed forces attached to the intelligence arm."

Valerio's face began with surprise, edged briefly to suspicion, then settled in indignation. He was offended by the underperformance of his own intelligence. "My people checked you out. We had you *ferito in azione, con certificato d'onore.*"

"I know you did. But I was not wounded in action and do not have a certificate of commendation. . . . We took special precautions. My assignment is to aid your movement. The resistance movement. To do that most usefully I will need access to a radio." London had instructed Angleton to get to a radio at whatever cost. "With the radio I can signal the Fifteenth Army Air Force for special strikes at planned targets."

Emilio Valerio stood up and rested his large arm on the mantelpiece. "I have never heard the like of it. A total stranger comes through the lines, sheltered by my people, walks into my headquarters, and tells me he wishes a radio! Do you also, *paesano*, want the names, dates of birth, and present location of all the members of the Resistance?"

Angleton's face was entirely serious. But it had been a long day and he said, "Emilio, I have saved a few cigarettes and would like to smoke one now, if that isn't inconvenient."

Valerio laughed. "Are you like the prisoner who wishes a cigarette before his execution?"

Angleton managed a smile. He bent over to his bag and pulled out the open pack. He offered a cigarette to Valerio, who gladly accepted it but did not light it. He didn't smoke.

Angleton drew deeply on the cigarette. Obviously the Comitati di Liberazione Nazionale would require confirmation of his credentials. "Now let's get very serious. I am here to participate in resistance missions and also—by radio—to request surgical strikes aimed at *your* targets. Let's perhaps go over the map"—he pointed to the mantelpiece. "I am one week behind you, Emilio. Please catch me up on the military situation."

Valerio's outfit—a subdivision of the Comitati di Liberazione Nazionale with its critical base in Milan—had been singled out by the OSS from the half-dozen other resistance units operating in enemy territory. It had accomplished the most effective acts of sabotage during the last four months, the period of the great January offensive of the Allies. The group's identity was now a national story. The CLN operatives, whenever possible, would leave a calling card to memorialize their gory initiatives. Most often a mere "N," a circle—drawn by pencil, pen, paintbrush—around it, left somewhere on the wreckage of the bridge, or pasted on the door of the victimized house or hotel or on the body of the army officer.

"Colonel" Valerio was not technically in command of the CLN, deferring by the tables of organization to a General Vecchione. Valerio was in his thirties, a stocky, fair-haired northern Italian from mountainous Torino, fifty miles to the west. He wore a thick mustache and regularly bared his teeth giving what Angleton concluded was a practiced smile of defiance. Suddenly, as they examined the war map pinned above the mantelpiece, Valerio seemed to have abandoned any security reservations about Nicola Paone. The prospect of air strikes done at Valerio's demand was exulting. "*Grandioso!*" On the broad question—how was the war going on the Italian front?—he was authoritative. "The Fascists are in retreat. They will not last through the spring." He looked up at the map and with a pencil sketched the progress the Allies had

made since January. "Soon their line—our line—will advance
even more, north and west."

He displayed his defiant smile and then spoke somberly. "The
bad news is that the Fascist police and military are desperate. They
take orders directly from the Nazis. Mussolini's puppet government is not even consulted. Nobody knows where Il Duce is. Almost certainly in hiding. The police do not bother anymore to
interrogate suspects. Their only problem is that they can't shoot all
of them right away, they need to keep the torturers employed!—I
have a good list of them, Nicola. *My reward* for all of this"—he
drew his outstretched finger across his throat—"will be to supervise personally the end of Fabrizio Sabini, Victor Tabacchini,
Bruno Andolini, Giacomo Gabanelli, Federico della Serra,
Michale Lombardo, Giuseppi Enzo, and Massimo Dambroso."
He pronounced the names in the somber accents of a judge sentencing defendants to hang. "But the police now, they just"—he
lifted his right hand, turned his head to the left as if aiming a
rifle—"shoot. On the other hand, you know, Nicola, there is something to be said for direct action."

"Yes, of course."

"That is the specialty of the CLN."

Angleton let pass the invitation to discuss summary justice. He
got down to urgent business. "I must have one hour's rest—"

"An hour's rest? You will need a night's rest."

"I do not need more than one hour. I will be ready for an
assignment."

"You wish to participate in tonight's sortie?" Valerio sounded a
bit surprised.

"I am here to engage in the direct action of your resistance
movement." Angleton told Valerio that he was not to be insulated
as a mere radio operator. Valerio understood.

Nicola Paone was given the rank of corporal and assigned to a
unit of four partisans whose daily exercise was to carry explosives to

critical junctures along the military front and detonate them at ex-pedient moments. The unit's targets varied. Small bridges were frequently waylaid, holding up provisioning convoys and also the movements of retreating Nazi forces. More frequent now, the er-ratic movements of the enemy having confused the military front, the Resistance was engaged in assassinations.

Chapter Four

In two weeks Angleton engaged in four missions. The fifth was canceled — air force bombers had got to that army installation ahead of the CLN. Indeed, it was running short of manageable stationary targets, a tribute to the relentless bombardment by the Allied air fleet based in Rome. The Allies had taken out most of the substantial bridges, with one or two conspicuous exceptions. Northern Italy being a latticework of rivers, mostly running west to east, Valerio called adamantly for assault on the incremental bridge. *"There is always another bridge to blow up!"* His finger pointed at Urbano Lazzaro, the slim young, beardless platoon leader of "the Puecher detachment of the Fifty-second Partisan Brigade," as he frequently reminded those of his fellow partisans given to abbreviating its name.

"All right, Colonel," Lazzaro said, "we can find more bridges, but if they are very small, the Fascists rebuild them quickly. If they are larger" — he pointed on the map to the bridge leading to Mantua — "they are not easy to approach because every... every malingerer... in the Italian army, I think, wants to do guard duty! — it

keeps them away from the front. But it also means big concentra-
tions of watchdogs surrounding the bridges and installations. So it
is very difficult to take on Mantua unless you want a major operation. To destroy that bridge we would need four machine guns delivering sustained fire, and fast, before a German 88 turns around
and sizes us up."

Colonel Valerio looked over at Angleton, sitting at the corner of
the room, his head tilted down, his thick eyeglasses blurring his
sleepy brown eyes. Valerio had told "Bill" something about the special resources of Nicola Paone. Urbano Lazzaro's nickname was
Bill, named by his mother after Buffalo Bill. Mama Lazzaro had
seen the movie *With Buffalo Bill on the U.P. Trail* the night before
Urbano Lazzaro was born, nearly twenty years earlier.

What Valerio had told Bill was that Nicola Paone, who had
joined forces with them only a fortnight ago, had mysterious com-
munion with St. Jude, celebrated in Milan as Mediator of the
Impossible.

"I will talk with Nicola about the Mantua bridge," he said, with
mysterious intonations. "He will need, of course, to know the exact
location of it, to the one-tenth of one second, so be very careful
when you bring me the coordinates from the atlas." Then he dismissed Bill from the headquarters office and said to Angleton, "Get
up, Nicola. Come here and look at the map."

Angleton had twice validated, to the satisfaction of Valerio, his
claims as a forward scout of the Allied air force. He knew that
Nicola was on the level, but knew also that a requested bombing
from Nicola did not always bring results. The two spot-bombings
on CLN targets of the week before were two compliances out of six
requests. Baker Baker Delta Baker, after receiving a bombing request, did not say to Nicola, "Yes, the Allies will dispatch a plane,"
or "No, the Allies cannot spare a plane." Valerio smiled fatalisti-
cally and said "*San Juda è molto misterioso.*"

St. Jude might be very mysterious, but Nicola filed the Mantua
bridge request and was surprised that the dispatcher told him to

open the line up again in twelve minutes: he had a message to give out in "Code April Fool plus 23." Twelve minutes later Angleton wrote down the request: the Allied powers wanted something in addition from the little resistance group, CLN.

It was urgently needed by Operation Trident, as the offensive against the north had been dubbed, that a flare signal be lit on the southern face of the mountain between Varese and Como, on April 27 at 0700, at elevation 7300 feet or higher. "Confirm if possible within one hour."

Valerio read Nicola's notes and paused for only an instant. "*Le dica che sta bene.*" Tell them OK. And added, "Ask them again about the Mantua bridge."

A five-man squad was detached from the Puecher platoon under the command of Buffalo Bill. He was to take Nicola Paone with him. Valerio and Angleton coordinated their deception — only Valerio knew the special uses of a radio in the hands of Paone. Nicola Paone was known among his comrades only as a discharged Italian corporal. Valerio entrusted one of the three Vecchio army radios in the inventory of the CLN to Nicola. To Bill: "Paone is skilled in the use of radio." The radio would be useful for quick contacts with CLN headquarters, which was all that Buffalo Bill imagined it would be used for. Concealed within the bulky Vecchio radio was a radio model U.S. BC-611.

The five commandos were given an address in the outskirts of Domaso on Lake Como where they would assemble. Angleton reminded himself that he was ostensibly a native of the area. Soon after the sun set, bringing back the alpine cold of early spring, they filed into the little house off the street in Domaso. Their hosts were as hospitable as they could be, after five years of life in disputed territory. Alfonso had lost a leg in Abyssinia; Sieta worked during the day at the rehabilitation center. The partisans ate bread and cheese and each drank a half liter of native wine. They reviewed their

equipment and heard advice from their hosts about how to bend
the flare elbow to guard against the southeasterly wind gusts. Nearing midnight they set out for Monte Bregagno.

They had only to follow the narrow trail, now laced with snow
and ice, after coming on the westerly fork in the road, two hours
out. Buffalo Bill knew the mountain from his summer trips as a
boy. Some minutes before four in the morning they came upon the
hut, used during the summer by picnickers and Boy Scouts. Its
shutters were closed but cold drafts raced through the hut's single
room. The partisans made adroit use of their coats and gathered
pine needles to help insulate themselves during the cold hours before dawn and, later, the cold hours before Flare-Time.

"Are you going to radio that we're here?" Bill asked Nicola.

"No. No transmissions until one hour before the signal flare.
Then we will tell them that the Puecher detachment of the Fifty-
second Brigade is doing its work." Angleton—Nicola—enjoyed his
new, institutional status. There had been nobody at Yale to give orders to, except the printer's messenger, and the young man rather
enjoyed telling people what to do, a satisfaction with a particular
flavor when he was confident that he knew best what it was that
should be done. Which was most of the time.

At 0630 the next morning he used the radio to speak with Valerio:
The flare for the Allies, he reported, was in place and would go off
at the designated time. He needed to know now whether the squad
members should proceed directly back to Milan or whether there
was an intermediate mission.

Colonel Valerio was not in a passive frame of mind. He barked
back in code so quickly Nicola had to resort to improvised abbreviations in his notebook. "A German detachment is headed north from
Menaggio, toward Dongo. The detachment has three hundred
soldiers in thirty truck columns, an Italian armored truck, and a German anti-aircraft unit. Plus a dozen civilian cars. Proceed immedi-

ately to any convenient point south of Dongo and erect a blockade. Am dispatching six partisans who will assist. They will proceed north on Mongono Road toward Dongo until they find you."

Nicola transmitted the order to Bill, who looked at it, struggled with the abbreviations, read it again, and then asked Nicola to read it out loud.

"Very well. We'll head down as soon as the signal lights have been fired." He paused then, positioning the top half of his overcoat over his head to shield the light of his cigarette from prying eyes. Then after a minute his head emerged from the coat, under which he cared lovingly for his cigarette.

"You know something, Nicola?" He grinned. "It is a very good sign that German units are moving north. But now that they want to leave Italy, we'll just prevent them from going without first tasting our hospitality!" He returned to his cigarette.

One hour later the compacted tar and kerosene let off a huge signal light. Bill acknowledged that he was tempted to stay by it for a few minutes, just to warm up. But no. *"Presto, presto, dobbiamo andare giù a Dongo."* Yes, quickly, quickly, they must proceed toward Dongo.

They walked carefully, silently, descending the trail, straining to see any electrical light or hear any sound of human activity. When the sun finally rose they had reached the valley, three miles from Dongo, the lofty mountains on their left, the emerald lake on their right. The surface water quivered, yielding its haze to the balm of the early sun of April 27. The lake gave off a special brilliance, Angleton reflected, lost for a moment in his own thoughts, sensing for the first time since his arrival in Italy an unwelcome detachment from his American, homegrown military enterprise. He uttered a prayer to St. Jude, the line he remembered from his English school: "Pray for me, I am so helpless and alone."

Chapter Five

Two dozen partisans had assembled at the roadblock south of Dongo when the German column came into view several miles away and traveling slowly. Bill had supervised the construction of a bulwark of rocks, plentiful at the foot of the mountains, and barbed wire, appropriated from a neighboring farm, stretching fifty feet beyond the road on both sides. Ten riflemen and two machine gunners waited behind the rocks and protrusions that provided cover. The other partisans hid in and about the farm shed, behind individual trees—seemingly everywhere; but that, Bill said, deploying his meager force, was the impression he wished to give the Germans. He instructed the guerrillas to await his first shot and then to fire away at the military units of the column. It was for the Resistance a suicidal mission, they knew—two dozen riflemen against armored cars and three hundred soldiers. At the end of the ambush, when out of ammunition, Bill had said to them, "Depending on where you are, dive into the lake or climb up into the mountains, and hope they are in too much of a hurry to pursue us."

Bill waited until the slow armored carrier in the lead was fifty meters from the roadblock. The partisans' fire then exploded, a relentless fusillade lasting a full minute.

"Then I saw," Buffalo Bill Urbano Lazzaro later remembered, "what I never dreamed of seeing. No, what I only *dreamed* of seeing. *Santo cielo!* A white flag! Attached to what seemed a broom handle sticking out of the lead truck.

"I proceeded warily, of course. I shouted out, *Cease Fire!* Then I got up off the ground and signaled to Nicola to come with me with his radio. We walked together up to the lead car. We depended heavily on the enemy's believing there was a battalion, or at least a company, not merely a platoon, hidden behind the trees and rocks.

"It was deadly silent as we walked forty, fifty paces toward the white flag. A German officer in a Nazi uniform, pale and unshaven, a helmet pushed back over his head, came out from the armored truck. He was holding the flagpole himself, with his own hands. He didn't motion to us. He just stood there.

"We reached him. I said, 'Who are you?'

"He answered in broken Italian. 'I am Major Eichner, Eighty-first German Tank Division. We have instructions to surrender.'"

Bill simply stared at the major. Then he turned to Nicola. "Nicola," he whispered. "What do we do, now?"

Angleton counseled that he assemble the partisans and disarm the military. He, Nicola, would radio to Milan.

He managed to get through, the radio speaker in hand, the radio on his backpack, while walking down the German column, past the anti-aircraft unit, past the three hundred soldiers, stacking their arms at the instructions of the partisans, as if doing so in their sleep. A senior officer of the partisans had arrived now by motorcycle from Dongo. He was "Pedro." Bill knew Pedro and gratefully turned over command of the partisan operation to him. Pedro — Count Pier Luigi Bellini delle Stelle, he gave his full name to Nicola — would now give instructions.

Angleton was joyfully receiving the news, in bits and pieces — the Italians and Germans were surrendering right across the north

Italian plain. Suddenly Marcello, one of the partisans, hit him
hard on the shoulder.

"Nicola! We have here *el crapun!*" The big cheese.

Angleton, the radio clinging to him only by its strap, ran toward
the truck the partisan was pointing at. He climbed up the back
steps, Marcello on his heels. A dozen elderly men and women
were seated along the right, another dozen on the left, their backs
against the guardrail, their eyes downcast.

He spotted him instantly.

He didn't accost him, he just stared at him, perhaps the second-
most-famous face in the world, after Hitler. Benito Mussolini wore
a German army helmet over his baldness. His paunchy face angled
down on his chest. He showed no sign of life.

"I think," Marcello said slowly, almost reverently, "I think that Il
Duce is drunk."

Angleton picked up the humming radio and heard the voice saying "*Goddamn it goddamn it you hear me Beta Alpha Beta Beta I've
been Beta Alpha Beta Alpha Beta-ing — you hear me I've been talking to nothing — to nobody — for five fucking minutes!*"

Angleton spoke into the receiver in hoarse tones: "Mussolini is
here."

There was silence. London Radio Zeta Prime had cut off the
transmission. Angleton placed a second call, this one to Colonel
Valerio. Quickly, he gave Valerio the news.

Pedro had made a quick bargain. The partisans would remove the
roadblock, permitting the Germans to proceed toward their destination — Germany. But all the Italians in the caravan would remain, prisoners of the CLN.

Pedro posted six riflemen to surround the Italian part of the caravan. To Bill he gave the orders: "Detain Mussolini in the truck —
off-load everybody else. Mussolini and his woman. Handcuff them
and drive them to the Dongo Hotel — you know it?"

Buffalo Bill nodded.

"Put them in a room there, do not remove the handcuffs. Guard the room, take Nicola and Marcello. Await further instructions."

The other Italians, most of them members of Mussolini's cabinet, were ordered out to the side of the road. An aide interrupted Bill. "I think Pedro would like to know that car number four has more gold than in all of South Africa. I didn't know that much gold existed!"

"Notify Pedro," Bill ordered, swinging himself up to the driver's seat, Nicola at his side. They drove the fourteen miles to Dongo with their silent passengers, protected from public view by the canvas overhang of the truck. Bill told the clerk only that they had important prisoners of war. Mussolini now had on dark glasses and a fedora tilted well forward. Claretta Pettaci, his dowdy mistress, kept her eyes tightly closed through it all. Bill led them into a suite on the second floor and handcuffed Il Duce to the brass headboard, his mistress to a bedpost in the adjoining room.

Angleton breathed deeply. His face puckered in concentration. Suddenly he bolted out to the hallway, racing down the steps to the street. He needed air; needed to think. At that point Valerio roared in on a jeep with three heavily armed partisans, dusty from their drive at full speed from Milan.

"Are we taking them to Milan?" Angleton asked.

"No." Colonel Valerio spoke sharply. "The CLN has ruled that the prisoners shall be immediately executed. We await only the arrival of General Vecchione. Now, Nicola. Where are they?" Angleton pointed to the stairs. "Room 204." Valerio and his partisans ran up the staircase.

Angleton walked across the street into the shade of the movie house opposite. He spoke into the radio, contacting the now-familiar voice at Zeta Prime.

"Valerio and the CLN detachment," he spoke hurriedly into the little speaker, "are going to execute the prisoner. As soon as the general arrives."

Zeta Prime told him to hang on. "Hang on hang on hang on," the voice repeated. "We have to go to Washington on this." Angleton waited, hoping anxiously the radio's battery would hold up. It was two full minutes later that he heard a voice different from his dispatcher's. Angleton recognized it, but the voice identified itself.

"This is Allen Dulles. Do you read me?"

"Yes, sir."

"This is James Angleton?"

"Yes, sir."

"Angleton: Under *no circumstances* are you to allow summary execution if there is any means of preventing it, including the use of force. That is all I can tell you. Did you hear me, Alpha Beta Alpha?"

"Yes sir, Zeta Prime."

He heard the radio go dead. His batteries had given out.

Angleton looked about. Where might he get batteries? The crowd was thickening and now armed partisans were guarding the door of the hotel. He walked over to the stall where the young girl with the fire-engine-red lips was selling tickets to the movie, *Amapola.* "*Mi scusi, bella signorina,* can you tell me where I can buy some batteries for my radio?"

She replied that she had not seen batteries for sale in over a year. But perhaps at the corner, over there—she pointed. Angleton tore down to the end of the block. It was a book and stationery store: Did they have a 1.5-volt dry cell battery?

No, but the clerk would take his name down for the next shipment, if he wished.

Angleton kept hearing the words in his mind. *Under no circumstances . . . summary execution . . . use force if necessary.*

He strode back to the hotel entrance. Marcello waved him in past the guard. He bounded up the stairs to the second floor. Valerio was conferring outside room 204 with a partisan Angleton didn't recognize. He would try to argue. He interrupted their conversation.

"Listen, Valerio, Mussolini's going to hang, I mean, nobody in the *world* questions that. But why not give the Allies the satisfaction of *trying him* ... of exposing all that he did—"

"Exposing *all* he did? That would require opening two million graves."

"I see your point. But Valerio, if he is just ... shot ... here ... it will lose all the ... all the solemnity of a trial and execution. The satisfaction you would get is *fleeting*. Imagine him with a tribunal staring into a camera for a few days—"

Valerio wanted to hear no more. He turned and resumed his conversation with his confederate.

What to do now?

Angleton drew himself up to his full length. He slapped his hands together to arrest the conversation. "Colonel Valerio, I have instructions from the Supreme Commander of the Allied Forces in Europe to detain the prisoner Mussolini and bring him to Milan as a prisoner."

Valerio turned, his mouth still open. His expression was at first explosively indignant ... then, suddenly, propitiatory. "Nicola, you have done a fine job. Now the war is over. Mussolini is an Italian. You are not an Italian. You are an American. Go try your own people, string *them* up. Leave ours to us."

There was a clamor on the ground floor. Valerio peered down inquisitively and then, with his companion, went quickly down to the lobby. Angleton opened the bedroom door.

Benito Mussolini was staring up at the ceiling. He spotted Angleton. "*Mi porti al bagno!*" I need to go to the toilet. Cautiously, Angleton tripped the double lock of the handcuffs fastened on the bedpost. Mussolini, wrists manacled behind his back, lunged forward on the bed to try to get on his feet. Angleton helped him up and thrust him forward into the toilet closet at the other end of the room. "*Mi abbassi la chiusura lampo.*" Lower my zipper, he moaned. Angleton was suddenly the poet. He fancied that the expression on his face was that of Ezra Pound's forlorn Malatesta. He reached with his left hand into Il Duce's pants and pulled out his penis.

The door opened.

"What in the name of God are you up to!" Valerio bellowed.

Angleton pointed to the figure crouched over the toilet.

Valerio turned to a partisan. "Bring the whore from the bed."

He himself grabbed Mussolini's handcuffs and pushed him out through the bedroom door into the hallway. The staircase was lined with armed partisans who created a macabre ceremonial column that filed down to the truck, still outside, that had brought them from the military caravan yesterday.

Mussolini and Claretta Petacci were shoved down the stairs, out into the street, and up into the back of the truck. There was a great clamor from the swelling crowd. Angleton grabbed a seat opposite the prisoners and in a roar to Bill, seated next to him, asked, "Where are we going?"

"Valerio has an address he cares about. I tried to tell him no, that's not how to do it."

"Where? What address?"

"Right here in Dongo."

The partisans moved the crowd away. Valerio at the wheel, the truck began to move.

The sound from the crowd was now deafening. Valerio had to plow through the shrieking bodies, but the truck picked up speed and moved a few blocks to number 14 on Via Massio, one in a row of wooden houses of dirty yellow stucco.

Valerio stopped the truck and motioned to the guards.

"Put them up against the wall there. Face them *toward* the wall." Claretta Petacci fell on the ground but was pulled to her feet.

The prisoners were dragged to the wall and propped upright in the ignominious position—backs to the executioners. The guards quickly separated. The crowd was suddenly mute.

Valerio signaled to the machine gunner at the rear of the truck to stand by. He then raised his own pistol, taking a long, voluptuous sight on the back of the big bald head of Il Duce, and fired.

The machine gunner picked up the signal, and did his work.

The corpses were removed, back to the truck. The drive to Milan would be less than one hour. By sunset, Mussolini and his mistress were hanging by their heels outside a gas station, for all the world to see.

BOOK TWO

Chapter Six

September, 1975

CASA NOGALES

There was the whole Mussolini business and the strange fuss Colby has been making of it lately, attempting to ascribe to me a pattern of misbehavior, technical and philosophical, dating back to 1945. Here is Colby's line: I had been told, on April 27, 1945, by radio, by Allen Dulles himself, that the high command wanted Mussolini alive. I will not now, thirty years later, come up with: "What was I supposed to do?" In the first place I don't like the expression. It is too often used to excuse inaction. "What was I supposed to do about Pearl Harbor?" Mr. Roosevelt might have said. Answer: Keep it from happening.

It is true that I was authorized to use force. I won't waste time by elaborating on the obvious mismatch that day at Dongo — me, representing the Allied High Command; Colonel Valerio and a hundred partisans, every one of them armed, representing the Comitati di Liberazione Nazionale.

Suppose I had tried something 007-like. In the two minutes we were alone, throw Il Duce out of the window of the hotel, jump after him, commandeer a truck, pick him up off the grass, maybe

manage to get him into the passenger seat; then drive away—
stealthily! That's right, without making any sound. In a way it
pleased me that Colby had to bring up Mussolini. Maybe he'll put
a black mark on my record for making possible Mussolini's last piss
in Italy. The hell with it. The hell with Colby. Though he is still
my boss. I have not left the premises.

It was a while before I understood profoundly the movements that
afternoon of the CLN.

The CLN had in it Italian partisans who were ideologically un-
attached. All they wanted to do was end the war and get rid of the
Fascists and the Nazis. But the high command of the CLN was
Communist, *no* doubt about it. There was a little seesawing, but
the Communists never lost control. I established this to my perfect
satisfaction before the year 1945 was out. What they wanted—Valerio and his high command—was political and historical recogni-
tion of their role in bringing Mussolini to his end. If he had let us
schedule a trial in Milan...

In the first place it would have been postponed for about a year,
crossing the judicial t's and dotting the i's. Just like Nuremberg:
convened six months after the German surrender, to hear testi-
mony for an endless eleven months of trial. And the Christian
Democrats, whom the Italian Communists would end up fighting
with for twenty years, would have had *some* role in the proceedings: clearly a dilution, as far as the CLN were concerned, of the
credit for actually capturing and bringing Mussolini to justice.

The Communists think in long sequences. The role of the Italian Communists would be decided in the years immediately
ahead. Their biggest push was toward the elections of 1948. They
could appear as the party of peace and progress, of the worker—all
of that business—but also as the party of the people who rid the
country of Il Duce.

I have been credited with perhaps the key role in preventing Italy from going to the Communists in 1948. I was the key figure in the intelligence network in Rome. And I enlisted the aid of everybody who could help, a pretty ecumenical assembly. I leaned heavily on the free labor unions in the USA to do what they could to enlighten the Communist-run labor unions in Italy (and France). Clare Boothe Luce later was made ambassador to Italy by President Eisenhower in the 1950s. She knew how close it had been, and what I accomplished. I remember on one of my visits to Rome when she was ambassador her whispering, "Jim, without you, we wouldn't be meeting in a non-Communist country."

The same problems arose in almost every theater: the ruthless opportunism of the Communists, the somnolent acquiescence of the Allies. Why did General Eisenhower and General Marshall stall the entire Allied army at the Elbe, allowing the Communists to enter Berlin ahead of us? At the time most observers dismissed this as as some kind of ceremonial wartime courtesy: *You go ahead and enter Berlin, brother; we'll wait a few days. After all, your casualties were much higher than ours.* That is how people whose vision of large political affairs is nearsighted tend to view things.

My vocation has been to penetrate apparently innocent arrangements or movements. There was a very disturbing consistency in the career of George Marshall, until he caught on with the Marshall Plan. On occasion after occasion he permitted the Soviet Union and its legions to have their way. I have mentioned the Reds reaching Berlin. Then there was the sequestering of East Berlin so that it became, really, a Soviet province. There was the loss of China—after what? After Ambassador George Marshall froze the supply line to anti-Communist Chiang Kai-shek in 1946.

My days with the Italian CLN were critical to the honing of my analytical apparatus. And then ... it is said about me, in that long brief Colby et al. prepared, that I am not always disposed to accept the word of higher authority. It happens that this is *not* (entirely) *true.* The charge grew out of a statement I made while testifying before the Church Committee, charged with investigating the practices of the CIA. That's Senator Frank Church of Idaho. Wretched man, did all but destroy the Agency. It is technically correct that I said to the senators on that occasion that it was "inconceivable" that a secret arm of the government should feel required to comply with every overt order of that government. I didn't wish to go into the matter with Senator Church — though perhaps I should have done so, and nobody said anything, the session just droned on.

It seemed a pretty routine Q&A at the time I made it, August 24, 1975. But then before the transcript was approved, Senator Richard Schweicker picked up on it. The next day he confronted me with it. What exactly did I mean, that a secret arm of the government might decide not to follow orders?

How did I *then* handle the question? I waffled. That is how one should handle such a question.

Certain things are best not elaborated upon. When you are working for the government doing secret work you simply avoid talking about it, and avoid especially any formulations that sound comprehensive, as mine had, answering Senator Church. You need to say only what is required.

— Ours is a democratic government?
Yes, sir.
— Therefore all orders from constituted authorities are without question acted on.
Er, yes, sir.

What I then said to Senator Schweicker, when my answer was brought up for reexamination, was that it had been "rather imprudent" of me to make such a statement. He sawed away at that, and I then gave him a little more catnip. "Well, if it is accurate, it should not have been said." — I remember my words exactly.

That statement got us through that part of the Church proceedings. But because of my indiscretion there were heavy footprints on the record. Of course, every sophisticated official of the Central Intelligence Agency knew exactly what I meant to say and understood what I intended to convey. But that didn't keep some of the old-timers from trotting it out when the new team decided to move against me.

I might have attempted to elaborate on the question, but what mattered during those Senate hearings was that the Communists had prevailed in Vietnam and, in the Soviet heartland, were producing SS-15s on assembly lines. The great Soviet machine was at full strength.

Chapter Seven

On May 24, 1951, three officials of MI5 in London were ready at the designated quarters in Farm Street for their interrogations of Guy Burgess and Donald Maclean, who would appear at 9:15. Two of the three examiners had reached conclusions they doubted the two skilled professionals could contravene: In their judgment Burgess and Maclean were — and had been since they were students at Cambridge — agents of the Soviet Union, whatever their long-standing roles in the British Foreign Service. The third examiner hoped that under interrogation they might be able to establish that they were in fact double agents, affecting to do work for the Soviet Union while working under deep cover for an undisclosed representative of MI6.

At 0945 they had not arrived.

At 1005 Lance Corporal Marjorie Dobson reported that attempts by telephone to reach Messrs. Burgess and Maclean had not succeeded.

At 1010 ace interrogator Colonel Skardon passed word to MI5 to look for the missing officers and, if located, to bring them discreetly to Farm Street.

At 1540 a call from Southampton reported that two men an-

swering a general description of the missing gentlemen had been
seen with ample luggage boarding the ferry to Saint-Malo.

At 1610 French Immigration officials at Saint-Malo, examining
the passenger list, reported that Burgess and Maclean would be on
the incoming ferry, scheduled to arrive in Saint-Malo at 1718.
"There is, of course, no way we can detain them," M. Dupuy of
French Immigration reported.

"They're gone," said Colonel Skardon.

It was three weeks before their arrival by train in Moscow was
made public.

That neatly ended the seemingly endless discussions in the
chanceries of loyalty/security over whether Maclean and Burgess
were loyalty risks. FBI Agent Robert Lamphere, attached to the Soviet division, had supervised the surveillance of the suspects in
Washington until they left for London in 1951. The monitoring of
suspects' activities was not the responsibility of Angleton. Suspicions of illegal activity committed inside the boundaries of the
United States are for the FBI to investigate, not the CIA, even as
crimes in Great Britain committed within the homeland are the
responsibility of MI5, while MI6 looks into British security abroad.

Now that they were documented traitors their records were vig-
orously examined. The public record was there. Who were they?
What were they like?

The reports filed in, from associates, friends, records, newspaper
archives.

On Guy Burgess—

Some casual observers of Burgess, who over several years had
followed his activity as through a silent-movie lens, would have
guessed that his true profession was the pursuit of compliant
homosexuals; his vocation, drinking anything alcoholic. He was
strikingly handsome, charming, unpredictable, disheveled, promis-
cuous, predatory. Son of a naval officer. Everybody seemed to
know him. He had powerful friends and admirers, but was thought
to be gradually incapacitated by his unruly appetites. Harold
Nicolson, the distinguished historian and diplomat, volunteered a

fragment from a letter he had sent his wife, Vita Sackville-West, as recently as in January of 1950, the preceding year: "I dined with Guy Burgess. Oh my dear, what a sad, sad thing this constant drinking is! Guy used to have one of the most rapid and acute minds I knew. Now his is just an imitation (and a pretty bad one) of what he once was. Not that he was actually drunk yesterday. He was just soaked and silly. I felt angry about it."

On Donald Maclean?

Tall, good-looking, unshakable, son of an MP who served also as Secretary of Education in the government of Prime Minister Stanley Baldwin. A prodigious worker and tense alcoholic, Maclean had homosexual flings. After a term in Cairo in the Foreign Service he was returned to London for his "nervous condition." It was after that he was given the august position of chief of the American desk of the Foreign Office.

What had they accomplished?

They forwarded documents to their Soviet handlers in huge and steady amounts. Angleton was speaking with his most intimate friend, Hugo Esterhazy. "It is almost impossible," Angleton explained to Esterhazy, "to communicate the importance of any one document outside the context of the day, the time, and the importance of that link provided by the document. The easiest way to describe the accomplishments of Donald Maclean is to say that *every wartime communication to Churchill by Roosevelt was in detail known to Stalin.* And after that, every communication from Truman to Churchill was known to Stalin. Stalin knew, for example, what he needed to know about our repository of nuclear bombs and of uranium. He knew that we would not use nuclear weapons in Korea. He knew that MacArthur would not be permitted to cross the Yalu River.

"That's a short way of putting it."

So, the defections of Maclean and Burgess closed down two players from the Cambridge set. A dozen years later Sir Anthony Blunt, royal art adviser, was caught up, and confessed his treason in return for the promise not to prosecute him. Fifteen years after that, Prime Minister Thatcher, searching out some form of punishment, removed his honorific. "A terrible sentence," Angleton mocked.

Most students of the Cambridge infestation added, in 1951, the name of Harold Adrian Russell Philby as a possible confederate of Burgess, Maclean, and Blunt. But most would concede that his was another case. He was implicated as a classmate and working friend of Burgess and Maclean. If for no other reason, the loyalty/ security officials, following the defection of B & M, removed Philby's security clearances. He had, after all, operated at very high altitudes, including as liaison in Washington between the FBI, the CIA, and MI6. Very heady stuff for someone who was suspected, by some bright security people in Washington and in London, of being, like his friend Burgess with whom he shared an apartment in Washington, a Soviet agent.

James Angleton knew Kim Philby well, going back to Angleton's days in London and later when Philby was posted to Washington. Philby's shrewd intelligence impressed Angleton. "Kim" — named, some said, after Rudyard Kipling's character — was the son of a flashy British Arabist who at various times had worked for the British government, as a spy, as a diplomat, indeed, for one spell, as a soldier. During his year in Washington, Kim Philby, up until the defection of Burgess and Maclean, often lunched with Angleton.

Philby, who stammered when relaxed, liked to talk about the "requisite sk-skills" for distinguishing between Russian information and Russian di-disinformation — stories that came out of Moscow that turned out to have reported events that never happened. He told stories of fictitious figures berated publicly by the KGB — for things they didn't do — "that, under Stalin, were hardly unusual; but also of figures who were berated, or exalted, *who didn't exist.*" The trick in that case, said Philby, was to figure out what the purpose was of the Soviet deception. "If an agent in the Ukraine reports that the grain crop last fall reached 28 million bushels, analysts in London and in New York (and indeed in other Western

capitals) have to slug their way painfully through all the possibilities. How did the agent get the information? If it was given to him
by Kiev, the Ukraine capital, was Kiev exaggerating, in order to
commend itself with the agricultural authorities in Moscow?"

But suppose the agent who was given the figures was under surveillance? The KGB could be passing on a phony figure intending
to spend the next six months watching to see whether that phony
figure cropped up in any Western document...Aha! The Kiev
man was a foreign agent!

Angleton got into the swim of it. He carried it a step farther on
his own: "On the other hand, maybe the agent was overpowered or
intimidated or seduced and was giving the 28-million-bushel figure
at the direction of the KGB—who was now using him as a double
agent. The purpose? To misinform the CIA."

"P-perfect," Philby came back. "Perhaps the idea is to suggest
that the Soviet Union's agricultural recovery is coming along at a
phenomenal speed. Perhaps to suggest that a harvest so plentiful
could only be accomplished with the use of farmhands who must
have been wrenched away from the army, suggesting that the Soviet Union was placing less emphasis than feared on the mainte-
nance of its military arm...."

Angleton and Philby loved those conjugations and explored las-
civiously all their implications.

When, with the disappearance of Burgess and Maclean, Philby
in Washington was told by MI6 first to come home to London,
then, a few months later, to find something else to do in place of
staring at government secrets all day long, the two signals were
read loud and clear by Angleton and his staff: (*a*) Philby's security
clearance had been removed, and (*b*), MI6 did not have an ac-
tionable record of treachery by Philby. If that had been the case,
he'd have been detained in London and tried for treason.

The years went by and Philby no longer communicated with Angleton. To have done so would have been professionally contemp-

tuous. He never raised the point ardently, but Angleton continued to harbor a suspicion: that Philby had been dealt with summarily; that the known crimes of Burgess and Maclean had done more merely than to invalidate Philby's security clearance. They had, in effect, attained the standing of joint crimes, committed by Burgess and Maclean *and* Philby. Whenever Angleton thought of Philby he didn't think of someone guilty of treason. Rather his memory was of a distinctively British upper-class Cambridge professional, debonair and unkempt, at times abrupt, other times ingratiatingly smooth. Above all, he remembered a man whose affinity for the brainwork of intelligence made him singularly appealing to James Jesus Angleton.

Chapter Eight

April, 1961—New Haven

Notwithstanding his exalted post as Chief of Counterintelligence, James J. Angleton made it a point, unfailingly, once every year, to interview prospective agents for the CIA. He would say defensively to his staff that he gave no preference to Yale, his own alma mater, but in fact he did. One reason was that he enjoyed revisiting New Haven; another, that Yale was where Norman Holmes Pearson taught, taught English. Pearson had been Angleton's boss in London when he was stationed there, before going on to Italy in the climactic April of 1945, and they had been in touch in the intervening sixteen years.

Professor Pearson, relying heavily on his cane, was there that April afternoon waiting for him at the railroad platform ("The train's eight minutes late," Angleton commented, after looking down at his large Omega wristwatch). He clasped the hand of his old friend. "Norman, you seem to be shrinking. Have you asked your doctor about that?" The two men were walking toward the parking lot. "I was certain you were five feet six inches tall when we last met in London. I remember looking first at you, then at the

Queen coming out of the Abbey with her freshly baptized little Andrew. I'd have sworn you were taller than she is."

Norman Holmes Pearson, eminent scholar in American studies, enjoyed the banter, which routinely punctuated their encounters over the years. On the matter of physical height, Angleton had to take the initiative quickly. Otherwise, convention had it, Pearson would have started it on his own with a deprecatory reference to Angleton's tall profile, the angularity of it, accented, this afternoon, by the black fedora and the dark blue suit and, yes, the briefcase. "What happens if you remove Angleton's briefcase?" was the wise-crack at the Agency. "Answer: The Cold War dissolves."

He got into the Pearson's car and they drove to the Fellows' suite in Davenport College. "May I suggest, Jim, that we put off a discussion of the Bay of Pigs until sometime . . . later in the evening?"

"That's fine. Sometime after midnight, I'd suggest."

But of course they did not put it off and the question immediately at hand was: Would President Kennedy fire Allen Dulles as Director of the Central Intelligence Agency?

Pearson rose to open the window wider to the spring air. "As a matter of form he has to be fired. Even if the catastrophe wasn't exactly of Dulles's own making."

It was indeed a catastrophe. The newly inaugurated president had transformed a military plan conceived by his predecessor. Eisenhower's thought was to give military training to Cuban defectors, so that when Castro appeared weak, they would be ready for a campaign of liberation. But JFK decided upon an immediate military operation. Not an invasion by Americans, but by exiled Cubans, trained in Nicaragua and Guatemala. The assumptions were that immediately on landing at the Bay of Pigs, the whole of Cuba, which had been tyrannized by Fidel Castro for two years, would rise against him. The assumptions were wrong in general (the Cubans did not revolt nor were they disposed to revolt); and in particular (the radio station that would transmit the news of the landing at the Bay of Pigs didn't fall into the hands of the anti-Castro resistance; the auxiliary bombers that were promised to expedite the invasion did not materialize). Eleven hundred prisoners were taken by Castro, triumphant.

Angleton asked Pearson if he had seen the review of the failed operation done by the CIA's Inspector General, Lyman Kirkpatrick.

Pearson nodded. "It is a royalists' summary. You need to do supplementary reading to remind yourself that the President was the Commander in Chief. Have you spoken with Allen?"

"Spoken with Dulles? I see him perhaps five times every day. Seeing him is as difficult as opening the door of my office that opens up into his."

"No, I know. I mean, have you spoken to him about the Bay of Pigs?"

"No. And I wouldn't have brought up Waterloo in a conversation with Napoleon." They had left the car and were walking into the guest Fellows' suite. "But Norman, what do you have for me on this trip?"

Pearson had two prospects. "The girl is doing a master's on the Yalta Conference. Her father was killed in Korea. Her mother remarried and lives in St. Paul. Melinda Carrothers is bright and ambitious and I know she doesn't want to do schoolteaching for the rest of her life. She doesn't want to stay in graduate school."

"Does she know what alternative we're talking about?"

"Yes. And she's coming in tomorrow at ten. She's a very independent girl, very pretty, very poised. The kid—the young man— is coming in at four."

"What about him?"

"Well, I guess his most conspicuous credential is that his father shot Mussolini."

Angleton looked up, his coffee cup still at his lips.

"Valerio's son?"

"That was his name. His adopted name is Crespi."

Angleton set down the cup.

"What's special about Crespi, other than that his father executed Mussolini? Or claims to have done." Only Allen Dulles knew at the time, and it was kept secret except to the very high command, that Angleton had been a witness to the execution.

"We got a pretty clear report" — he reached into his drawer and withdrew a folder. "Antonio Garibaldi Crespi. Born Antonio Garibaldi Valerio in Milan in 1941. His father was a schoolteacher and underground partisan with the Comitati di Liberazione Nazionale. Mussolini wasn't done in in Milan, Jim. It was a few miles away, town called Dongo. A few weeks after Mussolini was shot, hanged, whatever, Crespi's father got into a shooting match with a partisan from the other wing of the movement and got killed. General Clark got the petition from the widow's sister, who married a GI and went to live with him in Milwaukee. The general got the mother and Tony one of those compassionate postwar visas, and they went to Milwaukee. She remarried. Tony was raised by his mother and stepfather."

Angleton was curious about several matters, which he put to one side. He asked only, "Why is he interested in us?"

"He's not. But I think we should be interested in him. He still speaks to his mother in Italian, took the Foreign Service exam last month, passed like a breeze — the State Department wants him, you should know. I spotted him at a Political Union debate. The speaker was Linus Pauling."

"I'm surprised Pauling had time to speak at Yale. He's usually taken up with nuclear radiation—"

"Yes, and protesting any anti-Communist activity anywhere. He called Kennedy 'as bad as Hitler' last month, on the Bay of Pigs business. Well, last term, during the presidential campaign, Pauling was the guest speaker. The debate was on whether we should break off diplomatic relations with Castro's Cuba. Pauling was opposed. Speaking for the affirmative, the Conservative Party put up

Tony Crespi. He was very, very good. Had a fine perspective on the whole political scene. I kept my eyes on him. He writes a column once a week for the *Yale Daily News*."

"What else is interesting about him?"

"He spent last summer on a student tour of the Mideast. He spent a few days in Beirut. He came back with an interview, published in the *Yale Daily News*."

"Interview with whom?"

"With Kim Philby."

Chapter Nine

June, 1961

"Do I want to see the CIA report on the Bay of Pigs? *Should* I see it?"

"Well. You play a role in it."

The President leaned back in the rocking chair. "Very funny, Bobby. Let's put it this way — is it damaging?"

"Actually, it's too elaborate to be all that damaging. Our team — the Cuban liberators — swore up and down that the radio station at Havana would stop broadcasting the minute they hit the beach. The good guys would move in and start broadcasting the right things, *'Down with Castro!'*, *'Support the Cuban liberation!'*, the bombers would take out this and that, the Castro resistance centers. Our Cubans counted too heavily on the weather, counted on the weather being good —"

"How much space did the report give to our Zapata operation? I mean, they traced its origin, obviously, to Ike. I mean, could the reader sort of think of it as Ike's Zapata project? Ike's plan to oust Castro and get the anti-Communists into power?"

"The report says that the plan 'unfolded' during an eight-month period, which puts it back to September before our election:

Dwight Eisenhower, President; Christian Herter, Secretary of State."

"Did they rub Nixon's nose in the mess?"

"Actually, no. Tricky Dick isn't even mentioned."

"He'll probably complain to his people in the press world—the Hearst people, primarily. Speaking of unpleasant people—any word on Nixon, anything recent?"

"He's in California. Our guys say he's going to run for governor next year."

"We must remember in plenty of time to be discreetly unpleasant about him."

"I'll remind you. Right now, I remind you we have to get a new DCI."

"DCI? Speak English, Bobby."

"That's Director, Central Intelligence. Pretend you learned that in the fourth grade, if they bring it up at the press conference."

"The CIA didn't exist when I was in the fourth grade. When I was in fourth grade that would have been—"

"1925."

"Yes. I was in Brookline back then. Where were you?"

The Attorney General chuckled. "I was being born. I doubt you noticed."

"I was pretty precocious."

"Well, practice being precocious about a new DCI. We don't want to fire Allen Dulles in a gesture which turns out to be a public execution."

"Right. We'll just continue to seep it out that the whole Bay of Pigs fiasco was his fault."

"Well, sort of. Got to do that right. We don't want him fighting back."

"Allen is a good soldier. Much nicer than that prick, his brother John Foster."

"*De mortuis nil nisi bonum.*"

"Remind me—what's that?"

"That's what Dean Acheson said when he was asked to comment on Senator McCarthy's death — 'Don't say anything evil about the dead.'"

"Mr. Acheson — Dean. What was he doing, back then when Joe died?"

"He was objecting to John Foster Dulles."

"Well, that's an OK thing to do. Now, Bobby, who've we got out there for a new . . . DCI?"

"We've got John McCone high on the list. A good, tough-minded, business-background, rich westerner, shipbuilder, ran Atomic Energy under Ike. He's OK by Mac Bundy and Bob Mc-Namara. I need to spend a little time with Jim Angleton about Mc-Cone — Angleton is also key to our Castro operation. . . ."

"Yes. Just don't give me any details." The President broke out into a large smile. "Forget what I said, Bobby. Give me a lot of details. The gorier the better."

"Jack, I'll give you just the details you need not to know."

"I understand, I understand. Castro denounced me a couple of days ago as the 'leading war criminal since Adolf Hitler.' You know something, it's the goddamnedest thing. Castro's been in power since — what, the first of the year, 1959? First of all, our goodbodies refuse to say Castro's a Communist, he's just another agrarian reformer, like Mao Tse-tung. Castro goes up to Harvard — thank God I was out of town! — and he's treated like Winston Churchill. In Havana he kept telling everybody who'd listen, which is everybody in Cuba he hasn't executed or exiled, that he's a good Communist. So our gang — Norman Mailer, James Baldwin, Simone de Beauvoir, Jean-Paul Sartre — start a Fair Play for Cuba Committee. We must stop being mean to Fidel Castro. Finally — *finally* — it sinks in that Castro's just a Soviet agent with a little charisma —"

"A lot of charisma."

"OK, a lot of charisma. So President Eisenhower OKs the super-secret Operation Zapata, a CIA operation, just a little amphibious operation across the Gulf of Mexico —"

"Careful, Jack. I mean, we had a . . . hand in it."

"Yes, of course. But the point is, Castro is poison. Sitting there in Havana and sending out his people to encourage Communist revolutions everywhere else —"

"Of course. Something has to be done, right. And it wasn't done at the Bay of Pigs."

"Something has to be done about Castro, and something has to be done about the CIA. You and Ethel coming to the state dinner tonight? We got Bourguiba. Tunisia. I never know who's coming until I'm briefed on the the bore-of-the-day. At least Jackie can speak to him in French. If you need an interpreter, that nicely shrinks conversation."

The Attorney General flicked open his pocket calendar. "Yeah. We're scheduled to be with you tonight."

"Then see you later."

Chapter Ten

December, 1961

John McCone, tall, severe in expression, his graying hair neatly trimmed, was a man of some personal reserve, and although he tried, as one does, to engage convincingly the expected affabilities of his profession (McCone was an engineer by training and went on to become an industrious and successful shipbuilder), he always managed to travel on the other side of the Beltway, detached from the heavy and glamorous political traffic. But now, on his first day as Director of the Central Intelligence Agency, he was in the middle of it. He had been briefed on the centrality, in the CIA, of James Angleton. McCone had met him only twice, during the last two years of Eisenhower's presidency, when McCone was serving as Chairman of the Atomic Energy Commission.

Allen Dulles had told him matter-of-factly that harmonious relations with Angleton were quite necessary. "In the first place, he is the critical man in the organization on counterintelligence. Sure, if he were to drop dead tomorrow, most of our assets would continue to get through to us. But there is a lot — there's *always* a lot — out there that's hanging fire, and sometimes Jim does the balancing act as a one-man operation. I don't actually remember how that

arrangement ever began, but the door over there" — Dulles pointed
to one end of his office where McCone could discern a doorknob.
The door's paneling incorporated the door into the surrounding
woodwork, making it all but invisible — "that opens up into Angleton's office."

McCone looked over at it. "Does he just — come in when he
feels like it?" John McCone was a man of formal habits.

"Well, I mean, he doesn't just barge in. I don't quite know how
to put it, John. But there is a lot of... intercommunication between the Counterintelligence Chief and the DCI. I've probably
seen him ten, twelve times a week every week in my eight years
here. There are new things to discuss with him every day. When he
is routinely needed is when one of those cables comes in."

"You mean, you need Angleton to decipher a cable?"

"More often Angleton comes in with the cable to show *me* how
to read it — you'll need him to give the perspective."

They heard the knock on the door. Dulles stepped toward it.
"Come in."

It was an aide. "Sir," he addressed Dulles, "can we move out that
crate over there? It's the last one, I think."

"Yes, that's the last of it..." And to McCone: "Your office will
look a little bare right now — that's the end of my stuff going out.
But it will fill up in a hurry. OK to ask Jim Angleton to come
on in?"

Both men were standing. McCone hesitated for a moment.
Dulles spotted the cause of it and reacted instantly —

"You sit at my desk. Your desk, effective today. I'll sit over
here" — he moved toward one of the four armchairs. They had
been reupholstered since the Bay of Pigs and gave off a true, self-
confident blue.

Angleton came into the room through his special door. They
spoke of routine interoffice procedures. Dulles stayed only ten minutes, then rose. "I'm going home, John,... Jim. I can't remember
when last I left this office at noon, though I guess I did to see Presi-

dent Kennedy sworn in a few months ago." Both men got up and shook hands with the retiring ex-DCI. He stopped at the door. "John, I first laid eyes on Jim here when he was playing tennis at his father's place near Milan. At a critical moment in 1945 I remembered how well he handled Italian. I sent him off to work with the partisans. Jim — I release you from the pledge of silence. Tell the DCI sometime about your interesting encounter with Mussolini."

Angleton nodded, and gave a little smile. Their secret.

McCone sat down and swung about a few times in his chair. "Getting used to it." He made conversation. "We'll be talking a lot. I want to know what was said when the treaty was signed with North Korea last week. Khrushchev and Kim Il Sung did it, but the proceedings are a total blank. How do we find out? Talk to me about Khrushchev's Twentieth Party Congress speech."

"That was a very big event."

"The whole world knows that. To have Khrushchev get up before the Soviet Congress and denounce Stalin —"

"It was an important day. Mind if I smoke?" McCone, in fact, was troubled by smoke. But he gestured to Angleton to proceed, which he did, pulling out a pack of his regular Virginia Slims.

"I'm interested in the whole scene," McCone persisted. "A recreation of the whole scene. Khrushchev met with what, two thousand Soviet representatives?"

Angleton nodded. "Two thousand ten, actually."

"So the Soviet Congress is meeting, in February 1956, for the twentieth time since the first Congress convened in 1917 at St. Petersburg, Leon Trotsky presiding. Khrushchev proceeds to talk for seven hours. That is a very long time."

"They tend to speak at great length, sir."

McCone drew a little breath and then said, "Please call me John."

Angleton puffed lightly on his cigarette and nodded in acknowledgment of the amenity. "They go on at stomach-turning lengths.

Castro will speak for four, five, six hours, even. Tito can't order chicken soup in less than four hours."

"Tell me what you make of that. Is it a stylistic... mannerism? In what way is a long speech related to the requirements of the leader?"

"Max Weber never wrote about that aspect of it. All he said was that the leader must appear omniscient, confident, and healthy."

"Khrushchev was pretty disputatious in that speech. He was throwing over Stalinist dogma—"

"Yes, but at the time he did it, it was safe to repudiate Stalin. He had disposed of as many of the top Stalinists as was necessary."

"All right. Take me back to the scene. You are sitting—in the next room here. How do you learn that a historically momentous thing has happened? Be patient with me. I have to know something about the mechanics of this intelligence business. When Khrushchev spoke it wasn't like a shot heard round the world had gone off—"

"No, of course. There was very strict security. Obviously, no radio or television."

"So what actually happens?"

Angleton paused. He reflected. How much would he actually disclose? He had never told Allen Dulles all the details and now he was being asked by Allen Dulles's successor for a minute-by-minute account.

"Well," he began, "the daily cable traffic comes in. The speech was given on February 24, 1956. We knew, of course, that the Soviet Congress was meeting. The next day there was no reference to its proceedings in the Soviet press. Not one word. Nothing more than simple reiterations of Soviet-Marxist resolutions, and they certainly aren't newsworthy. They never change. Same thing. They just read like editorials from *Pravda*, or for that matter, our own *Daily Worker*."

"So?"

"One of our people in Belgrade sent word that Khrushchev had given a very long speech and that he had denounced Stalin. I brought the cable in here — I think my hands were probably shaking. I just showed it to the DCI. Dulles said: Do everything in the world you can to get a copy of that speech. I had already done exactly that, sent out word — *Bring us the text of the Twentieth Party Congress speech.* There was this difference in my approach after talking with your predecessor."

"What did he add to it?"

"A price tag. He said: Offer as much as $750,000 for a verified copy of it."

McCone smiled. He liked that. That was how people were: they would respond to missing speeches as they would, in a free marketplace, to a missing anything. "Did you go out with the figure, $750,000?"

"Oh no no, and I denied we ever paid anything for it."

"Just plain denied it?"

"Yes. That is how we do things here . . . , John."

"But the right people didn't need to be paid anything, did they, to give that speech circulation?"

"There were many people, some of them actually there at the Congress, who wanted very much to get the speech out. It was the most disruptive speech" — Angleton paused, to choose his words exactly — "the most disruptive single speech in human history, as far as I can see. It said to fellow travelers that they were wrong; that Stalin had in fact abused his power. It said to Communist theorists that different historical engines could contribute to the evolution of world Communism, and this put the satellite world in completely different focus. And it said that new emphasis had to be placed on agricultural and economic development."

"So." McCone rose from his chair, turned his back on Angleton, and looked out of the window at the statue of Nathan Hale. "What happened then?"

"What happened then was a big fraternal argument. Dulles Number One"—the reference was to John Foster Dulles—"was Secretary of State. Dulles Number Two was sitting where you are sitting right now. State wanted to give it to the *New York Times*."

"What did you recommend?"

"I sided with Allen. I argued that to conceal the actual text would create the kind of confusion we welcome. Twist the text one way one day and help out the loyalists, another way the next day and put the fear of God into the loyalists."

"And the other argument?"

"Give it out the way it was to blow away the myth of the great Stalin."

"How could you make sure that what you gave to the *New York Times* was the authentic thing?"

"We . . . managed to get a copy with the Kremlin frank on it."

"That was the first copy you got?"

"No. We had a draft from a friendly source in Poland. Another from Israel—I'll be going to Israel next week, by the way. Another from . . . well, no need to bury this one from you. From Palmiro Togliatti. He was eager, after heading up the Communist Party in Italy for forty years, to get it published since he had been privately critical of Stalin toward the end. You remember the . . . No, no reason you would. But Togliatti was denounced on the floor at a meeting of the Communist Party in Milan for 'revisionism.' That meant he wasn't following the Kremlin line with sufficient exactitude."

"Stalin had made the decision to oust him?"

"We think so. That Milan scene was in January, and Stalin died in March. Something was going on, and Togliatti was anxious to get word out."

"Why didn't *he* release it?"

Angleton paused.

"Strike that. Of course he couldn't release it. It was obviously privileged."

"Correct. And there was one other reason why I hesitated to encourage its publication. I wanted to take time to reflect: What was
the Kremlin up to? What other reasons did Khrushchev have for
discarding Stalin into the ash heap?"

"But didn't the speech speak for itself? I mean, it couldn't have
been Communist subterfuge. Are you saying you were wondering
whether the speech you read had actually been delivered?"

"No no no. There was no doubt about that, there was plenty of
corroboration. The big question was: What moved Khrushchev to
undermine, so organically, Soviet history? Soviet history had been
based on the infallibility of Soviet leadership as an instrument of
history. So what was it that made Khrushchev throw that useful
doctrine of infallibility away?"

"Did you answer your own question?"

Angleton lit another cigarette. "Well, actually, no, John. Before
the year was out Khrushchev ordered tanks into Hungary, to
remind a few thousand students that to interpret the Twentieth
Congress speech too liberally was to end one's life swinging on a
noose. In Poland there was rioting in Poznan. He crushed that.
Khrushchev spent several years in the late fifties ramrodding doctrine into the Soviet spine."

"But did the speech in any way weaken the West?"

"It is too early, in my judgment, to opine on that. That was only
five years ago."

McCone told his ailing wife that night that he had had a huge
whiff of Angletonism.

Chapter Eleven

June, 1961

On this trip to the Mideast, Angleton had gone first to Israel, an annual event, except that this visit had been scheduled out of sequence. Ever since his early days with the OSS in Italy, Angleton had taken creative pains to expedite Jewish refugees flooding out of tortured Europe to a homeland of their own. His attachment to Israel and his personal bonds with Israeli intelligence were ongoing. At CIA headquarters in Washington, next door to the Lincoln Memorial in the rickety World War II barracks complex, he personally manned the Israel desk.

The meeting with Prime Minister David Ben-Gurion was at four in the afternoon. In Tel Aviv, Angleton had spent a busy morning with the Mossad and inspected the new frontier maps, Egypt, Jordan, Lebanon, asking questions and answering them. His hosts knew Angleton's habits and took him to Kapot Tmarim for a vinous lunch. From there, with Major Bronstein, he walked to the office of the Prime Minister, who greeted him warmly. After a minute of greetings, Angleton motioned that he wished to be alone. Ben-Gurion dismissed the two aides. And then Angleton handed over the folder he took from his briefcase.

Ben-Gurion froze. Without expression he turned the pages and read on. Angleton smoked, while the Prime Minister read the details.

His closest aide, Israel Beer, was a Soviet agent, he read.

Finally he looked up, his face drawn. He reached for his own cigarette.

"We've been closing in on him, David" — Ben-Gurion had insisted on maintaining the old familiar forms of address they began using in 1945 — "for four years. Last week, the wiretap in Belgrade did it. I'm sorry to say, it's conclusive." By that, Angleton explained, he meant that the information he had assembled would serve to convince any military court.

Ben-Gurion spent a solemn hour with the documents and took notes on answers Angleton gave to his questions. When Angleton left the office, the tough old Prime Minister had tears in his eyes.

The next morning, Angleton was surprised to find waiting for him outside the King David Hotel the special armed car of the Prime Minister. An aide ushered him into it. Ben-Gurion was seated in the rear. "Do you know the pier number in Haifa, Jim?"

Angleton reached in his jacket and read out the ship's number.

Ben-Gurion, in Hebrew, gave the instructions to the driver, seated in front with the bodyguard. He then raised the dividing glass.

Israel Beer — Ben-Gurion spoke in low tones as the car made its way through the ancient streets of Jerusalem — confronted with Angleton's file, had confessed his guilt. During all those years at Ben-Gurion's side he had served as a Soviet agent. "He said to me, 'I think the cause of Communism is greater than our cause, Prime Minister.' He is in confinement. I will advise my cabinet at a meeting this afternoon, but I have made other security arrangements in the meantime."

Angleton mused that he thought it likely that Israel Beer had leaked to the Kremlin Israel's decision to strike against Egypt, in concert with Great Britain, protesting Nasser's takeover of the Suez Canal in 1956. "That gave Khrushchev early cover to march, that same week, on Budapest."

Ben-Gurion revealed that interim security arrangements would be implemented by Levi Eshkol, serving Ben-Gurion as finance minister, "but a very old friend of mine." He paused. "Like Israel Beer."

The Prime Minister did not get out of the car, but shook hands firmly with his old friend.

It was less than one hundred miles, Haifa to Beirut, Angleton's destination, but travel overland or by air was not permitted by either country. Angleton boarded the Greek ferryboat for the eight-hour trip.

Angleton was glad that his annual trip to the Mideast coincided with a trip to the area by Hugo Esterhazy. He had taken to sharing more and more confidences with Hugo Esterhazy of the State Department's Division of Intelligence and Research. But at dinner this night he stopped short of giving the name of the critical spy he had unearthed in the bosom of the Israeli family.

They talked about everything else. After two hours Hugo said, summoning the waiter, "Well, time to knock it off." They had eaten at Arous al-Bahr, a one-star restaurant in Beirut. ("Good research," Hugo had said as they walked in two hours earlier. "There are only three starred restaurants in the whole country of Lebanon.") Angleton rose and put on his fedora. Hugo continued his chatter. "Not all that anxious to get back home to Washington these days. We're both, so to speak, bachelors. Not much fun, is it, Jim?—as we've found out in the couple of months we've spent time together."

Jim Angleton was surprised to hear Hugo Esterhazy talk about their marital status using collective language, as if Mrs. James Angleton and Mrs. Hugo Esterhazy were in any way comparable family stories. True, Jim Angleton was resigned to being left permanently alone in Casa Nogales, that big gabled house near Arlington, and, yes, he was lonely for womanly company, any such company. But he was professionally patient and he thought in large time periods.

Yes, it was now almost two years, and his wife, Cicely, had made no serious movement toward reunification. They never spoke on the phone. Angleton had always mistrusted the telephone and Cicely, over the years, seemed to have picked up her husband's aversion. She wrote him notes. She never made any reference to Angleton's brief courtship of Anne Nickle, though of course she knew about it; and, with Cicely, there was no prospect of Angleton's affairs—that one or the previous one—simply drifting from her memory. She never gave his infidelities as a reason for her withdrawal, but he never doubted that she brooded over them. Now her occasional notes, arriving after longer and longer intervals, were briefer and briefer, until they read — as Angleton put it to Hugo — as if a timekeeper were standing over the letter writer, stopwatch in hand. James Angleton missed her greatly, and he kept her picture in the middle drawer of both his desks, at the office and at Casa Nogales. Welcome though she'd have been if she returned, he did not expect that she would do so.

Hugo Esterhazy's story was something very different from Jim Angleton's. His estrangement from his wife, Henrietta, was anything but gradual. The Angleton's separation was chronicled only by gossip in one suburban paper in Tucson, where Cicely lived. If Angleton was the supremely private man, Esterhazy was very much in view very early in life. He slid into college life as the eighteen-year-old son of a wealthy and photogenic widowed mother who lived in her schloss in Austria. He was catapulted into the limelight by his prowess in golf.

And with that, Hugo Esterhazy was a striking figure, blond hair, blue eyes, the hint of an affable smile on lips, shaped always to display just a trace of his glistening white teeth. His torso would have satisfied the most exigent model-broker, from the broad shoulders to the trim waist, the slim buttocks, the powerful legs tapering down to feet the shoe manufacturers fought over. He was a senior at Duke when he won the U.S. Amateur Championship. A week later he eloped with Henrietta Carr, the campus beauty queen. What followed was a social/academic brawl covered noisily in the tabloids. Esterhazy had been named a Rhodes Scholar one month before his elopement. And Rhodes fellows were not permitted to marry until they completed their studies. What would happen to young Hugo Esterhazy?

The *London Daily Mirror* decided to take on this conundrum with gusto and for what seemed weeks there were pictures of hallowed Oxford halls and American beauty-prize contestants and deposed dons and Rhodes alumni, all this with Hugo seemingly everywhere, swinging his wicked swings and sinking his amazing putts in Augusta, Pinehurst, and Greensboro and pledging to show up at Oxford in September ("I'll hide Henrietta in my golf bag," he told a jubilant press).

A quiet accommodation was eventually made with the trustees of the Rhodes fund. Hugo would attend classes, be assigned a tutor, and play golf for Oxford. Henrietta would live off campus, in London; which she compliantly did, but leaving Hugo altogether, at the end of the spring term, to marry an earl. At age twenty-four, Hugo Esterhazy won the Masters in Augusta and was on the cover of *Time* magazine. It greatly amused the gallery that everywhere Hugo went to compete, his mother, Lucinda, was at his side, to celebrate when he won, to explain to the press if he lost why he lost, what had been her son's special problem that day, and how confident she was that the problem would go away so that "Hugo can be the permanent champion."

"Mother says to say hello," Hugo said as he walked with Angleton from the restaurant into the taxicab.

"Give her my warm regards," Angleton returned the greeting. "And tell her to stop by, next time she's in town." He devoutly hoped this would not happen and was confident his friend Hugo would not pass on the invitation.

Lucinda Esterhazy had divorced her Austrian count soon after the world war, a mere month before his life ended in the car accident at the infamous Virage de la Rascasse turn in the Monaco Grand Prix. Lucy deeply mourned the death of Erik but was reassured, after her meeting with the lawyers a week or two later, that the large estate, which included the family villa in the Tyrolean Alps, was for all intents and purposes hers. The legacy was nowhere disfigured by dear Erik's ridiculous absorption, during that last year, with the common redhead who adorned the boards in London (Lucy had declined to attend *The Mousetrap*, in which the actress had a bit part). Although Lucinda was born in New York and raised there, she was wholly content to live in the Villa Esterhazy in the Tyrolean Alps, leaving it primarily to attend important golf matches featuring Hugo. She did spend an occasional week or two in her apartment in London, where she entertained Sir Basil Helmsley. Only Hugo knew that his mother's true interest in Sir Basil centered on his business career. He was President of International Sportsware, Ltd. This old Scottish firm was renowned for its innovative designs of tennis rackets, cricket ware, baseball gloves, footballs, and — yes — golf clubs. The romance between Lucinda Esterhazy and Sir Basil was never more intense than after he hinted that a unique new golf club was on the drawing board.

It surprised café society when, at age thirty, Hugo Esterhazy announced an end to his competitive golfing career. He accepted a job with the Kennedy Administration's State Department, in the intelligence division. Esterhazy was now in Beirut to weigh applications from regional colleges for U.S.–backed scholarships. Petitioners included Beirut University and nearby American University of Beirut.

On returning to the hotel that sultry night in June, after dinner with Angleton, Esterhazy was not entirely surprised to find ensconced in his suite an attractive woman — that kind of thing happens every now and again to celebrity sports champions, even though he hadn't competed for several years. She rose when he walked in. He said nothing, but sat down and examined her. She was young, dark-skinned, bright-eyed, and full-bodied. She wore a blue silk sleeveless dress with a collar that, faintly, brought Peter Pan to mind. "I don't think we've met," was the only thing Esterhazy thought to say.

Gabriela—as he would thereafter call her—was one part Lebanese, one part Russian. Her father, a Soviet diplomat, had been posted in Beirut to monitor the oil giants who were laying the huge pipeline from Saudi Arabia to the port cities. He had suddenly been called back to Moscow. She spoke breathlessly, but her narrative was organized. Her mother, after three weeks of waiting, had been told to rejoin her husband in Moscow. And now, a month having passed, she had a letter. She drew it out of her purse. "In this letter my mother tells me she and my father are being sent to a rehabilitation camp—just because my mother was a second cousin of Beria. She never even met Beria and anyway, he was executed back—"

"In 1953," Esterhazy helped her.

Hugo sat patiently, listening to her story, but now he interrupted her to say, "This is very interesting. Still, how is it that you are telling all this to me?"

"Because just this afternoon the woman at the desk told me you were the American consul."

"Where did you see me?"

"In the lobby, talking to a tall man in a dark blue suit."

It was Angleton, presumably, that the concierge had intended to direct her to.

"The man I was talking to downstairs is an American and he is with the government. So am I, but neither one of us is the Beirut consul and anyway, why do you need the consul?"

Gabriela raised her hand to decline a glass of wine. "I need help. I work with the library at American University and now my mother tells me I must go back—"

"How old are you?"

"Twenty-seven."

"Then you are old enough to say no."

"But my visa expires in one month and they will not renew it if my father is not here doing diplomatic work."

Hugo sighed. This was more than a diplomatic formality. This was Angleton's side of the street, obviously. He excused himself, went into the bedroom, and called the room number of his friend. Briefly, he told Angleton her story.

"Send her up to my suite," Angleton said.

The next day the two men shared the bus to the airport. "How did you get on with Gabriela?"

Angleton puffed on his cigarette and gave one of his half smiles. "She was obviously set up by the KGB. But that doesn't matter. Most of them begin that way. She is a useful contact. We'll have somebody getting to her."

Esterhazy wanted to explore the whole business. How had he questioned her? What was it she said that made him think she was on assignment as an agent? What kind of thing would he wish from her, if a liaison was effected?

But Angleton was at his most vexing, laconic worst.

"We're interested in everybody, Hugo. Remember, everybody is interested in Beirut. And Philby lives here."

Chapter Twelve

James Angleton drove his Buick Roadmaster up the curving drive to his gabled, two-storied stucco house that sat on the rise in the three acres that were once the corner of a hilly, Virginia farm. He opened the door to his garage by the electrical signal on his dashboard and drove the car in. He closed the door, walked out of the garage, and walked around the large house to the front entrance. At moments of critical national concern Angleton's house was guarded by one or more FBI agents. It had been so for several weeks after the Twentieth Party Congress speech by Khrushchev and later during the Bay of Pigs catastrophe. The alarm had been keen for a few weeks — *What was the Soviet Union up to?* Angleton never himself feared mayhem at the hands of Soviet professionals. Soviet agents don't shoot U.S. agents in U.S. territory, he knew, nor do we take them out in their own territory. There was reason for concern when a third party thought himself or his cause especially threatened: In 1940, Leon Trotsky had good reason to fear Stalin's agents, but Stalin would not have told anybody to shoot at J. Edgar Hoover.

He moved into his house, through the hall into his sacred study.

A key and a combination code were required to make this possible. He sat down, poured cognac from a bottle in his desk drawer, and allowed himself to contemplate sadly his loneliness. His mind turned to Tony.

Tony Crespi. Who would have ever predicted, a year ago, that the reclusive James Jesus Angleton would invite a mere recruit to live in Casa Nogales during the youngster's apprenticeship in Angleton's holy order, the CIA?

Angleton liked young people but never confused himself with them. Tony Crespi had come into Professor Pearson's suite in Davenport College, Yale, last spring in midafternoon wearing coat and tie, 1961 being several years before the tidal wave of student slovenliness. He was unmistakably Latin in complexion, his features slender, eyelashes pronounced, eyes brown, his hair dark and curly. What was remarkable about Antonio Garibaldi Crespi was his self-confidence. Angleton saw that he was Valerio's son, and this included the slight, suspended half smile. Young Crespi had the remarkable faculty of giving the formidable J. J. Angleton a sense that the older man was somehow being patronized. He did not take offense. He was at first quite simply curious, at age forty-three, about this exchange with a college senior, age twenty-one. He had said to him at Yale, after an hour, "I take it, then, Mr. Crespi, that you are interested in doing work for the Central Intelligence Agency."

"That's why I'm here." Crespi smiled, then added, "Sir."

"You are aware that there will be a very thorough exploration of your family background?"

"Yes. Nothing exciting there. My mother is very fine, but there's nothing... well, exciting about her. All the excitement went out with my late father. He had an exciting life and I have to guess you know all about him."

Angleton paused. The OSS secret record that documented Angleton's physical presence in Dongo during the last hours of Mussolini's life was zealously guarded. Allen Dulles had had good reason to discourage any public attention to the presence on the scene of an American intelligence agent when Mussolini was, to all extents and purposes, assassinated.

To Tony Crespi he said only, "I am aware you are the son of the late Colonel Emilio Valerio."

"Yes, and of course he was killed in a factional quarrel. Then my mother came to Milwaukee, courtesy of General Clark and an army officer to whom we are somehow related, and remarried—to my stepfather. And you know about him?"

Angleton looked down at a sheet in the folder on the desk. "We know that your stepfather, Mr. Crespi, was born and raised in Milwaukee, fought in the Philippines during the war, married, went to college on the GI Bill at the University of Wisconsin"—Angleton was now reading from the folder—"worked as a clerk for the Bradley Company, and fathered two girls—your stepsisters. Your father has been successful in the Bradley Corporation. Does your father travel?"

"He went to Chicago once, took us to a Chicago Cubs game." Tony smiled to himself, a brief sally of self-amusement at the thought of Lester Crespi, Cosmopolitan Man. "Father doesn't like to travel."

"Does he have any political interests?"

"I know what you're getting at, Mr. Angleton. No interests of that kind, none at all, though he liked Joe McCarthy, even went to Appleton for McCarthy's funeral."

"What was it he liked in Senator McCarthy?"

"To tell you the truth, Mr. Angleton—this interview is off the record, isn't it?"

Angleton was at first irritated, then amused. "Well you know, the answer to that is no. It is very much *on* the record, what you say. However"—he allowed himself to smile—"I am the only person in the United States who will ponder the answers you give, though the Federal Bureau of Investigation will be asked to verify any factual statements."

"Well, Mr. Angleton, to tell you the truth, my father thinks just about everybody in America is soft on Communism. I'm exaggerating, of course. And then the boss, Mr. Bradley, is very much that way. I mean Mr. Allen Bradley, the founder of the company. He was a great backer of Joe McCarthy."

"Your point being that your father, as the expression goes, sees Communists under the bed?"

"In a manner of speaking, yes. He's a member of the John Birch Society."

Angleton knew all about the John Birch Society, whose founder Robert Welch had written a book propounding the thesis that Dwight Eisenhower was a Communist agent. This, then, was an important question he now asked: "Do you share your father's views on the matter?"

Angleton leaned back in his chair. It was as if he was opening a seminar, anxious not to dismiss as insignificant what he had to teach, but anxious also not to lose the thoughtful attention of those he addressed.

"I think it's very complicated, Mr. Angleton. Obviously there are hidden pro-Communists. Alger Hiss was one, and there's the English team, Burgess, Maclean, Philby—"

Angleton snuffed out his cigarette impatiently. "Philby's participation in that subversive ring has not been established. A British prime minister—Harold Macmillan—spoke in the House of Commons, asserting Philby's bona fides."

"I know that's sort of open to question, his loyalty. And I have met Mr. Philby and wrote about him for the *Yale Daily News*."

"What if anything did you find memorable in Kim Philby? In Mr. Philby?"

"A very bright man. At the briefing he gave us—the traveling American Student Union group—he spoke a lot about the need to avoid ideological conflicts in the Middle East, about the excitement generated by Colonel Nasser in Egypt with the overthrow of King Farouk and the beginning of the anti-colonial period. That kind of thing."

"Did he talk about . . . U.S. policy?"

"Oh yes. He said that the anti-Castro movement was typical of the excesses of American cold warriors."

Why had Tony Crespi decided he wished to work for the Central Intelligence Agency, the head of Counterintelligence wanted to know. Crespi let it out, without any effort to conceal, or to ingratiate.

"The way I look at it, we're at war, though it's a cold war. What's going on in a big stretch of the world is what my father fought against in Italy. I figure it this way, Mr. Angleton. I have to do something after I graduate. My major is in political science. I know Italian and am pretty good in Arabic. So what is it I should spend my time doing that's more interesting and — I'd hope — productive, than taking an active part in the Cold War?

"Does your stepfather know about your application?"

Tony Crespi smiled. "No, but if he did, he'd warn me that the person interviewing me for the CIA might very well be a hidden Communist himself."

Angleton winced.

When, later, he looked at his watch he noted that two hours had gone by. He ended the meeting by telling Crespi that until a decision was made he was not to discuss his interview with anyone. And if he was accepted for duty, suitable cover would need to be arranged. In anticipation of that possibility, Crespi should inquire about the formalities of applying for work in Arab studies at Georgetown University.

Crespi left. The other applicant, Melinda Carrothers, had called in to cancel her appointment for the next day. So now Angleton walked into Norman Pearson's little library and looked through the window into the formal courtyard of the bricked college. In the library he would have the predinner cocktail earlier then usual.

"What did you think?" Pearson asked, passing over the Scotch and water.

"Very interesting," James Angleton said, giving no trace of the enthusiasm he felt for young Crespi. Never mind that Pearson had set up the interview; never mind that he and Pearson had fought side by side in intelligence during and after the war. It was none of Pearson's business what Angleton had in mind for Antonio Crespi. In these circles information was not shared, except as necessary.

James Angleton would look over his shoulder from time to time when talking about other people or groups or agencies who would need to participate in the making of a decision on the question being discussed. But most of the time—indeed involving personnel *all* the time—Angleton was absolutely in authority. On Crespi, always assuming something didn't come up conclusively negative in the FBI research, Angleton had already made up his mind.

And he burrowed out of his mind an evolving inclination to indulge himself, professionally and personally. The situation was propitious. A bright student, companionable, engaged in Arabic studies, a summer visitor to Beirut—where he had actually met, indeed interviewed, Kim Philby.

This Crespi—Tony Crespi—could serve Angleton as the instrument for getting the dispositive answer to the festering question Angleton had lived with ever since that day in 1951 when Angleton's friend Philby had been dropped from the intelligence community under a cloud, suspected of being one of the young Cambridge Apostles who had betrayed their country and the West. Crespi might be able to furnish Angleton with the knowledge he so deeply coveted, and feared. As he talked with Norman Pearson and drank the Scotch and let his mind idle on the thought of it all, he formulated the idea: To invite Crespi to come to Casa Nogales as a boarder.

Chapter Thirteen

November, 1961

DCI John McCone sat at his place, the head of the table in the conference room on the seventh floor. From his chair he could admire paintings by Thomas Downing and Jack Bush, brought in from the CIA Fine Arts Commission. On his right was his assistant, Marshall Carter. On his left, Alphonse Meadows, chief of the Soviet division. Next to him was Burl Henderson, the China expert. Opposite, Newt ("Scotty") Miler. At the far end of the table, facing the DCI, James Angleton, Chief of Counterintelligence.

The implications of a Sino-Soviet split had absorbed the CIA endlessly, ever since the first shot was fired—Mao's criticism of Khrushchev's Twentieth Party Congress speech, in 1958.

"What we have is basically a turf battle," McCone led off.

"An ideological turf battle, Mr. Director." He was interrupted by Burl Henderson—"I continue to believe."

McCone stopped. He did not encourage interruptions. Each man would have time for his full say. But one at a time. He replied with a touch of ice in his voice. "If there are deep ideological differences between the Soviet interpretation of Marxist doctrine and the Chinese interpretation, what are they, I keep asking?"

Henderson, a veteran at the Agency, bald, corpulent, and excitable, was a man of heated opinions. He was born in Shanghai, one of the multitude of sons of missionary parents. His Mandarin was fluent and he spent hours every day studying press clippings from China, speeches by the Chairman, of course, but also statements by regional Chinese Communist figures—he gobbled up press accounts of official activity.

A key to the question at hand, he said, was the effort that had been put forward by the Mao government to fire up its ideological enterprises. To this end Henderson had spent almost a full year attempting to estimate the number of human casualties of the recent period, executions by the tens of thousands, death by starvation of, he insisted, well over one million, perhaps several times that number. All of this the results of Mao's "Great Leap Forward," now abandoned, but surely the costliest social experiment in human history. "Mr. Director, the Great Leap Forward program of Mao Tse-tung of 1958 was the *equivalent* of taking Karl Marx, bending him over Mao's lap, and spanking him till he screamed—"

"Yes, but he never screamed," Miler's voice came in from across the table.

"Right, Scotty. It wasn't a congregation of Marxist scholars who have ruled: Chairman Mao has ordained that Marx had in mind a central authority organizing society into self-contained economic and agricultural units—"

"I'm not talking about the Great Leap Forward as an amendment to Marxist orthodoxy. In the first place, it's over..."

Henderson was not to be deterred. "What Mao did two years ago was to challenge Khrushchev. He said that by criticizing Stalin he ruptured the apostolic line of succession, invalidating his own credentials—"

"Gentlemen. I think we have been over this ground before," the DCI interrupted. "This morning's newspaper—not one of our reports"—he angled his head slightly, in the direction of Marshall Carter, a soft rebuke (Why should the CIA, with a budget of

millions of dollars, need updates from the *Washington Post* on critical ideological developments?)—"'Russian Advisers'"—he held
up the front page of the newspaper—"'Reported Exiting China.'
That's a pretty concrete rebuff, pulling advisers out from the Asian
capital of the worldwide Communist movement, a joint enterprise.
Last week, *Pravda* denounced Red Chinese 'dogmatism.' What's
going on? Khrushchev denounces Stalin's dogmatism in 1956, Mao
denounces Khrushchev's criticism of Stalin in 1958. A year later
Khrushchev denounces Mao's dogmatism. What have we got here?"

"Mr. Director," Carter said, "our job, as I hardly need to mention, let alone stress, is to analyze developments from a single perspective: How can we encourage what is obviously a rift between
our two superpower antagonists? How can we make it worse? More
divisive?"

"The enemy of my enemy is my friend," the Director intoned,
contributing an insight he had bumped into when in the shipping
business. It was greeted by silence. For them, that was kindergarten
talk. Carter continued: "What fronts are we looking at right now?
In Europe, Khrushchev is threatening to recognize East Germany's
authority over Berlin. In Indochina we have the beginning of a
civil war, with North Vietnam apparently determined to take over
South Vietnam. Question Number One: Does Communist China
have a stake in developments in Berlin? Question Number Two:
Does the Soviet Union have a stake in developments in Indochina? How can we accelerate, how can we deepen the polariza-
tion? Can we devise a means of making it profitable to Moscow to
discourage Peking intervention in South Vietnam? Can we see any
reason why Mao would oppose Soviet adventurism in Berlin? All
we know for certain is: There *is* a grave, profound Soviet-Chinese
split."

For the first time, Angleton spoke. A striking presence, his eyes
all but concealed by his thick-rimmed glasses, his English-cut gray
suit sharply contrasting with the sartorial informality of his col-

leagues. He spoke in his usual quiet tones; as ever, he had the effect of making all that came before sound trivial.

"I do not believe, Marshall, that we *know* any such thing, let alone 'for certain.'"

"Jim." Carter summoned the courage to interpose himself. "You are not going to tell us about the Trust, are you?"

Angleton's face was untroubled by one more reiteration of skepticism.

"The lessons of the Trust are exactly what we need to consider."

Marshall Carter thought to himself, for a horrified moment: *Maybe John McCone does not know about the Trust?* He took a precaution. "Mr. Director, Jim is talking about the—" He stopped just in time. He had been about to use "legendary" as the next word. But of course one does not suggest that one's leader is less than familiar with material that is legendary. "—the deception undertaken by Lenin after the revolution. He believes it is continuingly instructive—"

Angleton cut them short. "The Trust, so-called, operated between 1921 and 1927. Its idea—promoted by Dzerzhinsky—Dzerzhinsky was the head of Cheka... Cheka"—Angleton evidently enjoyed reeling this off—"is a Russian acronym for All-Russian Extraordinary Commission for the Suppression of Counterrevolution and Sabotage. The Lubianka prison is at Two Dzerzhinsky Square in central Moscow. It is the great Soviet torture chamber for dissidents." McCone nodded. "Its idea, the Trust's idea, was to lure into the open leading anti-Bolsheviks around the world, Russian and non-Russian. Persuade them that the Trust was organized to topple Lenin and then Stalin.

"It was a classically successful counterintelligence enterprise, luring back into Russia leading opponents who thought themselves safe under the hidden auspices of the Trust. They were one by one rounded up and executed. The principles of the Trust survive: Persuade your opponents that you are on their side, then they will

more easily fall prey to manipulation by successive Soviet feints. It
is worth considering whether the Chinese-Soviet rift is propelled
by the principles of the Trust."

"Jim, give me something to read about the Trust, will you? Now
let's tick off the other items on the agenda."

Chapter Fourteen

January, 1962

Fred Grabowski, in Angleton's inner office, actually looked as tired and harassed as he insisted he was, after seven consecutive days in the company of Anatoliy Mikhailovich Golitsyn.

"I kid you not, Mr. Angleton, he is the most imperious Russian since Peter the Great." Fred paused. "I can't remember. Peter was very imperious, wasn't he? Or do I have him confused?"

Angleton nodded, suppressing a smile. Fred Grabowski, CIA chief of station in Finland, had a reputation even at his young age (he was just thirty) as a deeply informed student of Russian history and Soviet practice.

"I know you know the basic story, Mr. Angleton, but anyhow... Golitsyn—a middle-aged stranger—arrives in my house in Helsinki—not my office, my *house*—walks into my bathroom *while I am shaving*. I sort of have the sensation that up until now—eight days later, because I'm booked back to Helsinki on the flight tomorrow—I am still working on the same shave, like as if Anatoliy Golitsyn has been with me inside my own bathroom ever since that day. He wanted—you *know* this, I'm sure—to be taken—him, his wife, his seven-year-old girl—to the States, because he was, I quote his language exactly, 'The most important defector in history.' He wanted a private jet plane to pick him up before eight o'clock. Eight o'clock *that night*. He wanted—I'm compressing this—he wanted to fly nonstop to Washington. When he was told we'd have to go first to Stockholm and then to Frankfurt, he said maybe he should make 'other' arrangements! *'Other arrangements!'* Scared the *govno*—that's Russian for *f-u-c-k*—out of us. After the third day, I had the feeling I was arranging a state visit, not just a visit of a low-level, would-be Soviet defector.

"Oh yes. He wanted to talk with the President. After a couple of days he said he'd settle for the President's brother, the Attorney General. He wants to start his own counterintelligence Soviet division and wants fifteen million dollars to bankroll it. He'll agree to tell us where to deposit the money, he's very obliging on that score. He consents to being debriefed but wants no session to last for more than two hours. He wants the debriefings to be recorded, but only he—Golytsin—is to get the transcript. Oh, maybe you didn't hear this yet: He will not consent to speak with anybody in the Russian language. Anybody who knows Russian, he told me, is probably a KGB agent."

Fred Grabowski put down his notes. "Well, he's all yours, sir, and I hope you find out from him what Khrushchev intends to do next week, next month, and next year, because unless you do, you're going to say: Life isn't worth it, life with Golitsyn under your bed just isn't worth it."

But Jim Angleton was not put off by Golitsyn's importunate ways. On the contrary, three months later he was convinced that the defection of Golitsyn was the single most fortunate personnel development in the postwar history of U.S.–Soviet relations.

On a summer evening he dined with Hugo Esterhazy at the Chevy Chase Country Club. The dinner meetings at the club had become a habit. The two men, one of them professionally reclusive, the other a sports-page celebrity since the age of eighteen, enjoyed a long evening together once every month or so. Angleton was frequently at the club. He did not play golf or tennis, and there were no facilities at the Chevy Chase Club for fly-fishing. To engage in his one sport, Angleton had to leave Washington. If he had only a day to spare he would go to the Blue Ridge fishing club in Virginia. When he had an entire weekend—and once or twice he took an entire week—he would go to the Brule river area in Wisconsin. Jed Jasper, a classmate, class of 1941, kept a private fishing lodge there and his guests were well treated.

Angleton's contribution to the Chevy Chase Club had been carefully negotiated in 1952, when Allen Dulles persuaded him to accept membership. "It has a great bar, Jim, and they leave you absolutely alone. You can bring whoever you want and just take your own table, order what you want. And they're looking for younger members."

"What do I contribute to Chevy Chase?" Angleton had asked.

"Well, you contribute your annual dues."

Angleton had formal ways of arranging his life and acknowledging what he thought collegial obligations. "I think I should do something more," he said.

"Like what?"

"They have a very substantial greenhouse, I noticed on the tour you did for me."

"Yes, they do. Alistair Forbes—he's the head groundskeeper—is very proud of it. All the flowers we display, twelve months of the year, are grown there."

"Do they grow any orchids?"

"Orchids?"

"Yes."

"I shouldn't think so." Dulles laughed. "Oh. I forgot. You... know a lot about—you actually *grow* orchids?"

"Yes," Angleton said. "I will supervise a modest orchid garden, if you like. If the Chevy Chase governors would like."

Dulles replied that he thought this a capital idea. About six months later the ladies who went to the Chevy Chase Club had an orchid to take home, provided—they were on the honor system— that month was the month in which they were born.

"I looked in on your orchid spread this afternoon, after golf. Very impressive."

"Was your golf game impressive, Hugo?"

"I had a seventy-one. Not impressive."

"What did you shoot when you were world champion?"

"Around here?—maybe two, three strokes under. I got to say, it's great to get out here on the Chevy Chase course. Ike was playing in a foursome just behind me. Big deal, because usually he plays at Burning Bush." Hugo drew a breath. "Jim. You have something on your mind. I can always tell."

"Yes, I do."

"I'll order another mint julep. Tell me about it."

Chapter Fifteen

Whenever Angleton violated a rule, whether somebody else's rule or his own, he didn't do so inadvertently. He actually remembered when it was that he decided to speak to Hugo Esterhazy about matters Esterhazy had absolutely no need to know about. It was simple and basic: He wanted a confidant. And he was certain, after an informal friendship that had lasted over a year, that he could safely break his rule — with Hugo. Angleton tended to look for theoretical formulations to frame his thoughts. So why Hugo? He asked himself that question several times, and taxed himself that he hadn't got an answer to the question Why Hugo? that rested on theoretical legs. He had simply decided — early in 1961 — that he felt a total confidence in Esterhazy and that he was dealing with a man of genial intelligence and absolute reliability.

Esterhazy had done some academic work, but didn't fancy himself especially equipped in any one discipline. Angleton could not use him as a disciplined researcher.

On the question of character, Angleton had no misgivings: Esterhazy was genuine stuff, self-propelled stuff. He made his own decisions from a young age, tolerating and, indeed, maintaining affectionate relations with his idiosyncratic mother, but keeping her out of the way. His dramatic decision suddenly to leave professional golf within a matter of months after achieving world championship status told a story of maturing perspectives. Angleton didn't know whether Esterhazy had benefited independently from the will of the Austrian count who had begot him. But whether the patrimony flowed in directly to Esterhazy from a trust or indirectly from his now affluent mother, or whether he lived as well as he did by tapping six years' earnings from professional golf, Angleton didn't know, and it didn't really matter. Esterhazy, Angleton deduced, had joined the Foreign Service because he wanted to move away from sports, as also from academic work. That, a few years having gone by, he was still in Foreign Service, in intelligence, meant simply that he enjoyed the life and the duties at which, Angleton easily established, he was proficient.

Those were the objective indices of his stability. What moved Angleton was the spontaneity of Hugo's references to his own work and the frankness of his discussions of foreign policy. After the long evening spent together in Beirut they took to meeting for lunch every week or ten days, where the rhythm was very different from that of the Chevy Chase Club. Here at the club the inclination was to fuller personal discussion. It was at the Chevy Chase that Hugo told Angleton why he had married Henrietta Carr ("she was pregnant") and why he was not really made jealous when she left him after a year for the British earl ("I never met him, but on a visit to the House of Lords I spotted him. Nice guy, they say. No prospect of Henrietta getting pregnant again").

Tonight Angleton did indeed have the agenda that Hugo anticipated. They were comfortably seated at the corner of the large oak barroom reserved for male members and the light was falling on the first tee, a few yards on the other side of the large mullioned window. James Angleton wanted to talk about the theory of intelligence activity.

"My theoretical training in the discipline came from my days with Ultra, before I went to Italy. Ultra, you may not know, was almost certainly responsible for shortening the war in Europe. May even have been responsible for our winning the war."

Esterhazy knew about Ultra only that it was a sacred subject in the intelligence community. Angleton explained that by extraordinary good fortune, the British had got, through espionage, a model of the machine that the German High Command used to encipher all their signals sent out over the airwaves to military units and intelligence agents. "It was called Enigma," Angleton said. "We also got hold of the manual for this machine and its code settings. By 1941, a team of mathematicians developed the means to read those coded messages. That's the information code-named Ultra. We—the Brits—could then figure out how each of the clues we planted in German channels was being received, and therefore how to modify them to make them more credible. Doing that completed the deception loop."

Angleton found himself whispering, though there was no need to do so where they sat.

"The key to our continuing use of Ultra was a consistent policy of being enlightened by what we knew from cracking the code— but not taking interpretive action on it."

"What does that mean, exactly?"

"Espionage, at heart, is the effort to compromise the enemy's security of communications—"

"So counterintelligence is—the counterpart? Protecting one's own security of communications?"

"Yes, but any success in that exercise requires us to estimate and act on our knowledge of the enemy's skills and techniques of penetration. And this is where Golitsyn is so revealing."

"I know you've been spending a hell of a lot of time with a Soviet defector. Is that who you are talking about?"

"Yes, and you now know that name—in violation of all the rules."

"I understand. *Never tell anybody anything that person doesn't need to know.* On the other hand we've got to assume, don't we, Jim, that the KGB knows about your Mr. Golitsy?"

"Golitsyn."

"And if they know that a defector has come to Washington, they know Angleton at some point is going to weigh in. I guess I'm asking—not in the spirit of a *Meet the Press* interviewer—wouldn't the KGB know that you and Golitsyn were spending a lot of time together?"

"Yes, but go beyond that deduction. When a defector comes over, my rule is: Let's *assume* he's a phony. A very good rule, in my experience. When a 'defector' comes over, he pays what I like to call earnest money. He says to you—for instance: 'I have reason to believe that a clerk in the NATO high command in Paris is working for the KGB.'"

"So you start to work? Try to find the guy—if there's a guy?"

"Yes. We try to find him/her. But after we find him/her/it then we need to ask: Did A betray B because Moscow wanted to convince C that A was on the level? Is B just a sacrificial lamb, used for the purpose of giving credibility to A? And on and on it goes . . . For instance, is Moscow maybe intending to throw up B in order to create a vacancy for the purpose of advancing policies apparently unrelated to B's activity?"

"You can get lost, I should think, following those circles around."

"Yes. You begin by asking yourself, What kind of effort is the enemy willing to put in, in order to advance another strategy? The great model is the so-called Trust. I told McCone about this just last week. That was the master device of Lenin. Get the White Russian exile community to concert on a plan—or ten plans, for that matter—to overthrow Lenin. Or Stalin. Let them raise money *for that purpose.* If necessary, contribute your own money for that purpose. Two, three, five years go by—as happened between 1920 and 1923—and Lenin doesn't get killed, but Mr. Dzherzinsky, the estimable founder of the Cheka, which became the GPU, gets to know who, where, what, when, about every White Russian enemy of the Soviet Union. It's no wonder they placed that statue of him in front of the Lubianka."

"But what does it add up to? That you can't believe *anything*?"

"Not quite. But it does add up to this: If you look at a point—a datum of information—you train yourself to visualize a circle around it. What, along that perimeter of knowledge or assumption, is affected by accepting that datum as genuine? Having done that, visualize a second circle, surrounding the first, with respect to which the datum continues to be a common center. How do different estimates of characteristics touching on the first circle affect the second circle?"

Esterhazy laughed, and waved at the waiter. "Stop! Jim, stop! Or you'll persuade me that you are a Soviet agent."

Angleton was not surprised. Esterhazy could be counted on to react wholesomely. React as a good healthy reasonable Westerner would be expected to react.

"That I am actually a Soviet agent is a proposition which, under the rules—my rules—can't be excluded other than as a hypothesis."

Esterhazy gave the drink order, exchanging a word with the excited waiter about the prospects at the U.S. Amateur Championship. "Keep your eyes on Jack Nicklaus," the waiter counseled. Jack was the local favorite. For four years, beginning when he was eight, Nicklaus had played golf with his father at the club—"right out there, Mr. Esterhazy, you could see him driving off."

Hugo knew that if Jim Angleton wanted to get back to his theoretical talk he'd do so. On the other hand, if he wanted a breather, now he had it.

Chapter Sixteen

It was at a debriefing session several months after Golitsyn's arrival that something he said especially interested James Angleton.

In that year, 1962, and the five preceding years, the battle for satellite supremacy raged. The Soviet Union had won the psychological war in October 1957 by launching the first *Sputnik* satellite, causing consternation in the West and a mobilization, under President Eisenhower, to catch up and to exceed the Soviet Union. The implications of satellite technology for war-making missiles with nuclear warheads was keenly understood, and U.S. intelligence agencies concentrated on ascertaining the developing resources of the USSR, information vital for counterplanning and for directing our own scientific enterprises.

Fort Meade in Maryland is where the total product of U.S. electronic interceptions is processed and analyzed, the data on Soviet satellites "vacuum-cleaned from antennae in space satellites," to use the graphic metaphor of historian Joseph Epstein. We use those vacuum cleaners, Angleton explained to DCI McCone, in addition to naval spy ships and planted listening devices in hostile countries.

Golitsyn, in conversation, talked about continuing Soviet efforts in space. "And, of course, they review at a meeting every month in Tyuratam what they find out that you, that we" — Golitsyn was becoming accustomed to his expatriation — "had learned about Soviet prowess."

"*Review every month,* did you say, Anatoliy? How can they get monthly updates?"

Golitsyn shrugged his shoulders.

Angleton turned the hounds loose.

He called Colonel Hal Knoblock, Fort Meade security. How could our superconfidential stuff be getting out of Fort Meade? He put the question obliquely: "Assuming something was getting out, where would we catch it?" What exactly *were* the security arrangements at Fort Meade?

"Simple," Knoblock said. "We do it the basic way, the elementary way — which happens also to be the most sophisticated way."

Colonel Knoblock informed Angleton that "not one human being, not even General Coverdale" — Chief of Staff of the National Security Agency — "is allowed to leave Fort Meade without being personally searched. Remember, Jim, the kind of information generated by the NSA at Fort Meade isn't the kind you can spirit away under a postage stamp. There's a certain... bulk in intelligence technology. The Enigma model we got in 1941 had the weight and size of three automobile tires."

So here we are, Angleton thought, with our own... enigma. On the one hand, "Nothing can get out of Fort Meade." On the other hand, things *must be* coming out of Fort Meade, if Golitsyn is correctly reporting on the scene there.

Angleton conferred with his aides Raymond Rocca and Scotty Miler late into the evening. They forced themselves to think through explanations that soon came close to being ludicrous. "Hey," said Raymond Rocca at one point, "maybe they have a trained eagle that darts in every night and scoops the stuff up?"

Scotty Miler got into the spirit of their desperation. "But do they have eagles big enough to lift our material?"

Angleton went back to Colonel Knoblock. Was there *any* exception to the rule — the body-search rule on personnel leaving the fort?

Under hard pressure, leafing through the bound security regulations, the Colonel said, "Well. Yes. We don't search General Coverdale's chauffeur."

"You search the general, but not his chauffeur?" Angleton pressed.

"Well, yes, if that's the way you want to put it, Jim."

"How often does the chauffeur, as you call him — what is he? A corporal? Warrant officer?"

Knoblock looked down at his documents. "He's a staff sergeant. The records show that he brings the car in and out three, four times a day. Guess he runs a lot of errands for General Coverdale."

The FBI was given search orders, highest priority.

Angleton recounted the story to Esterhazy.

"Well, Jack Dunlap, the chauffeur — the driver — a plain old sergeant — it turned out, after I can't say how many hundreds of hours of investigation had been recruited as a Soviet agent in Turkey in 1957."

"How did he escape notice, if he was coming out with tire-sized material?"

"Dunlap was a shrewd fellow. There is a lot of enticing stuff at Fort Meade that doesn't have anything to do with national security. Like cartons of cigarettes and booze and typewriters and chairs and desks. All available from the PX at huge discounts. The word got around: If a senior-grade officer wanted anything from the Fort Meade PX to take home — a violation of the rules, though petty larceny doesn't affect national security — just get Dunlap to stick it in the trunk of the general's car. Tell him what you want and give him the key to your office at home, so he can deliver it. After he extracts our top-secret material."

"Had he got careless?"

"No, not in the sense of sticking anything into a briefcase. But he was very thorough. He was now delivering to Soviet contacts microfilmed copies of all the instruction books, repair manuals, mathematical models, and design plans for the machinery used to encrypt American data. Dunlap didn't have to stow all the secrets in the trunk. He was given responsibility by the Chief of Staff for shuttling secret data back and forth between Fort Meade and CIA Counterintelligence officers on *my* staff, all six of them cleared on a 'need to know' basis to see the interceptions. This gave Dunlap the opportunity to ascertain—and feed back to his Soviet case officers—the questions that CIA Counterintelligence was asking about data intercepted from the Soviet Union.

"Knoblock put that neatly: 'Dunlap was in a position to deliver the *methodology* for our intelligence protocols.'" Angleton lit up another cigarette and spoke now with visible pride. "I fought hard, Hugo, to let Dunlap continue doing exactly what the traitor was doing. My—self-assigned—challenge was to conceive the most massive disinformation campaign in the Cold War. I worked on it, with the help of Rocca and Miler, around the clock. When I think of the complexity! Keeping that whole wind tunnel of top-secret information flowing into Moscow and just gently tilting it in one direction or the other! It required, of course, that Dunlap should remain absolutely unmolested.

"We did it! And we persuaded the FBI, the NSA, the White House to play along."

The pause was dramatic. Angleton took a slug from his drink. "And then on October 10, 1961, Dunlap died of asphyxiation in his own garage . . . Son of a bitch. Finally caught on we had his number and committed suicide. I agreed: the thing to do was just pass it off as a routine suicide."

A gritty smile broke through the smoke. "I hoped one day we'd come up with a Suicide Facilitator. If I had, I'd have used it on Colonel Knoblock."

Chapter Seventeen

August, 1961

Sometimes Angleton would call Tony Crespi on the house intercom. There was in place, at Casa Nogales, an intercom installation with extensions for his wife's separate suite of rooms, one for the guest room, another for the kitchen, a fourth for his study. Jim Angleton kept late hours, as did his young boarder. Sometimes Angleton would ring the number impulsively, at ten or even as late as midnight, and ask Tony if he would like (the answer was always affirmative) a nightcap.

Their conversation would last an hour or more. Angleton was intensely curious about Tony's evaluation of his training as a covert agent. Angleton knew that half of his time was spent at the university on Arab studies. Angleton had been advised, from Agency reports, that Crespi was receiving high grades from his instructors. This didn't surprise; what did surprise him was Tony's uneasy reactions to challenges he routinely faced in his training as a covert agent for the CIA.

"There was this . . . colored gentleman, Mr. Angleton, and I had never seen him before. We were in the bus, my trainer and I — this is my ninth trainer, Mr. Angleton, I don't know how you people can support such an extensive team of CIA agent trainers. This one—his name is "Bob"—specializes in surveillance—tailing—and today was my first live tryout. All he said was, 'When we're in the bus, I'll point to someone just when the bus door is about to close. Your assignment is to follow him for four hours. I'll step out of the bus right after pointing him out to you. At 7:13 tonight, call me at—ready to memorize the number?—DUpont 8-3774. I'll be waiting to know exactly what the mark did, everywhere he went during the afternoon' ..."

Angleton knew Tony's social habits well, after observing him for nearly three months as his tenant. He knew that with the slightest lilt of impatience he could abort what he was now listening to, an autobiographical account of Tony Crespi and his mark. But he wasn't disposed to make any such movement. He liked what he heard, both as a reminder of the gymnastics of the covert trade and as a happy listener to Tony's way of recounting his adventures.

"I did all the right things, all the things I was trained to do. Never looked the mark in the face; left the bus after he got out; walked at a pretty good pace in a different direction from where I figured he was going—but this part was hard, because he just stalled *right outside the bus*. I mean, Mr. Angleton, for no reason at all. It isn't as though he was waiting to use a public phone. He just stood there. Great big tall black brooding gentleman.

"And you know, I never thought to ask, and tomorrow when I talk to Bob I *will* ask: Is the mark a CIA employee?"

So went one such conversation about a few hours of training. But Tony Crespi was interested—very much so—in the wider picture. He was especially stirred by Khrushchev's most recent threat to Berlin. Angleton thought it refreshing that Tony's answer on how to cope with Khrushchev's threat, if it materialized into a divided Berlin, wasn't the predictably simpleminded answer of a young man who thought in straight lines. Angleton knew that exactly that recommendation had been made by Dean Acheson to Kennedy: just order an army division to go down the autobahn *right to Berlin.* Tony weighed a number of possible responses of Khrushchev, in the manner of a seminar master canvassing alternatives.

Tony never initiated a social call to his landlord. Whenever there was a practical need for a meeting—concerning a rental payment, a phone bill, whatever—Tony would leave a note on Angleton's engraved silver tray on the hall table. On that tabletop, polished occasionally by the cleaning woman who came in three times a week, there rested, always, a package of Virginia Slims cigarettes, a key chain to which a single brass key was attached, three—sometimes four—Vicks cough drops, and, from time to time, a scrawled-out message for Thelma, who by that means would learn of any special requirements of Mr. Angleton when she came in, cleaned, and replenished the refrigerator. Tony would leave a note on that tabletop and did so this morning: "Mr. A., could I see you for a minute or two? Tonight, or if that isn't convenient, tomorrow?"

Angleton saw the note when he came in from dinner. He picked it up and moved to his leather armchair, next to the telephone. He was within arm's reach of his poetry books. He lit a cigarette and reached down to the telephone, depressing the button for the guest room.

"Tony here."

". . . It's me. You want to see me?"

"If convenient, yes, sir."

"Come on down."

When Tony came in, Angleton handed him a beer, which, in anticipation of Tony's arrival he had taken from the kitchen refrigerator. He detested beer but Tony did not.

"What's up?"

"Well, Mr. Angleton, you remember you were scheduled to interview a girl at Yale who canceled before the meeting? It was the day you came up to Yale and interviewed me."

"Yes. I remember." Angleton displayed his memory. "Her name was Melinda Carrothers."

"Well, I know she didn't get... picked, didn't get invited to try out for the Agency. But she is coming down to Washington—she's still at school, doing another graduate year—she's coming down for a few days to do Foreign Service interviews. And what I was wondering is..." Tony stopped speaking. Angleton said nothing. "What I was wondering is, could she bunk in with us. With me?"

Angleton had once, in a clinical frame of mind, asked himself whether any man alive could be found worldlier than he. James Jesus Angleton had seen everything; participated in practically everything; read the most intimate reports on everybody; rifled through psychiatric reports on world figures; supervised the bugging of bordellos in four countries and of individual women in twice as many. For reasons he could not explain to himself he was taken aback by Tony Crespi's question and found himself saying words so awesomely clumsy he could not a second later believe he had spoken them.

"You mean, sleep with you in the same bed?"

Tony wondered if he was actually blushing. He felt the heat in his face. He thought briefly to make a sarcastic rejoinder. He stopped himself. He thought instead to tiptoe in the direction of convention.

"Well, uh, I would sleep on the couch on the parlor there, and she could have my bed." He paused. "I mean, only if it's OK. She doesn't have much spending money."

Angleton had composed himself.

"What you do in your quarters is your business. Yes, she may stay there. But I will wish to meet her. I am not about to countenance a situation in which I am not even introduced to someone boarding in my house."

Tony Crespi had got his wind back. "I would *love* it if you would speak to her. You never met her because she withdrew her application. Melinda is very nice, very—attractive. She's doing a master's on the Yalta Conference. Her dad was killed in Korea. She lives in St. Paul, in Minnesota."

Tony's equilibrium was completely recaptured now. He thought it safe to change the subject. "Mr. A., did you by any chance know any of the people at Yalta? Like Alger Hiss?"

Angleton smiled, filled his cognac glass, and nodded toward the kitchen. "Get another beer, Tony."

"Yes sir, I think I will. Thanks."

Chapter Eighteen

It was—for Angleton—a relaxed time. Golitsyn was in England, exchanging deep-cover talks with "Bleake." The summer heat was substantially vitiated by the new air-conditioning system. He had ordered a unit at first only for his own bedroom, a second unit for his study. He saw no point in installing one in Cicely's bedroom, unused for so long. He did hesitate, but only for a little bit, about installing one in the guest quarters. But yes, he'd do it. Even though it cost $125.

Tony Crespi was young and could live anywhere without air conditioning, and for that matter without central heating. He hoped Tony would never be as cold as Nicola Paone had been during that month in north Italy, "waiting to kill Mussolini," as he permitted himself, in his ruminations, to put it, having done so aloud only once, in a nostalgic conversation with Hugo Esterhazy. But Tony would not be occupying those quarters forever; older people, more exacting, could reasonably be expected, occasional guests, mostly professional, and in the summer of 1961, it was simply inhospitable not to have air conditioning in Washington, D.C. Certainly he could never invite an older person, in the hot months, to stay overnight, let alone stay a weekend or a week, without such relief.

And Melinda! When she came in she wore a striped knitted dress with short sleeves and a flared mini-length skirt. That was how the *Washington Post's* style section would describe it, he guessed. Tony had met her at the railroad station and brought her to the house. They used the same back entrance Tony always used. And then Angleton's own intercom rang. This startled him momentarily. When last had anyone rung his number? He had been used to thinking of his system as one-way, outbound.

But of course he had instructed Tony to call and tell him when he would be presenting his guest, Melinda. He had thought about what exactly to say, and how to say it. "I am very happy, Miss Carrothers, that you have come to my house to cohabit with your boyfriend?"

No. Obviously, no. But he had to say *something*, surely, about his knowledge that she would be sleeping in his own house. He didn't want to say he hoped she would be comfortable. "Comfortable" is not the right word to describe quarters primarily coveted for sheltered copulation.

He would not prolong the meeting. *He would completely ignore that she would be spending nights there!* Just say nothing about that aspect of affairs. He hoped Tony would be intensive in his focus on other matters. There was always the pending German crisis.

He had not anticipated a young woman so outstandingly ... mature, at ease. There was a lightness about her. She wore her lipstick lightly, her light brown hair—yes, light brown hair—rested so casually and artfully over her animated face, falling lightly over turquoise earrings, with the little pearls. She made no excuse for canceling the interview that had been scheduled at Yale, nor had he expected that she would. She sat confidently at the end of the couch to which she was motioned, smiled, and when she saw Angleton open the door into the kitchen, sprang up and in a voice calm but concerned simply informed him that she would help with the drinks. She opened the nearest cupboard before James J. could protest.

"Shall I bring out wineglasses? I see you have the regular glasses out in the study." All that Angleton could do was to say yes. As he broke open the ice tray he added, "Thank you." Tony Crespi knew nothing more about Mr. Angleton's kitchen than that its refrigerator kept chilled a half-dozen bottles of beer. Angleton pulled out a box of saltines and simply handed it to Tony, who looked about and found a plate to put them on. Meanwhile Melinda was talking about the railroad ride and gave with controlled delight an account of the conductor who had threatened to stop the train if the quarreling couple did not quiet down. "They were arguing about whose fault it was that their daughter Susan wasn't learning how to read."

She accepted the glass of wine from Angleton, returned to the sofa, and said with just a trace of challenge in her voice, "I think it was *her* fault." She turned to Tony and laughed engagingly. "It's *always* the mother's fault." And then facing her host, "One day it will be *my* fault if it happens, but it won't." She tipped her glass ever so lightly toward Angleton, and said, "Thank you." Angleton nodded and looked over at Tony. Tony was beaming with pride and pleasure.

After fifteen minutes Tony said he didn't want to interfere with their host's "evening plans." Angleton said he would be going out, but why didn't they stay another fifteen minutes as he was in plenty of time. They stayed gladly, and Angleton listened with quiet pleasure and fascination as Melinda gave Tony bulletins on academic figures in New Haven, but this was done without any hint of excluding the interests of their host, who had graduated from Yale twenty years earlier. They had a second drink and it occurred to Angleton that it would be more discreet for him to leave the house alone than for them to leave together to go not out of the house but into it, to the secluded second floor. He rose, motioned to them to stay seated — "Finish your drinks" — smiled, and walked quickly to the front door.

Dinner that night was with Allen Dulles, at Dulles's grandly comfortable house in Spring Valley. The butler took Angleton's hat and Angleton was ushered into the walnut study by his old friend and senior.

"Well, Allen, it is a good thing that you were a prosperous lawyer before you submitted to the indigence of life as a public servant."

Dulles smiled. He rather enjoyed references to Dulles the Wall Street lawyer-tycoon. They were very few, after so many years with government. But he would not let Angleton off scot-free. "Yes, Jim, and it is a good thing you took the precaution of being born to an affluent father."

They sat down then and for two hours dined and talked shop.

Angleton was back home at eleven and not in the least disposed to go to bed. He did not need many hours of sleep, never thought of sleep until well after midnight.

Tonight his thoughts turned to Tony and Tony's overnight guest. Angleton was aroused. He reached out and turned the covers of a book of poetry, flipping to pages by Keats. His eyes traveled over the poem titles. He closed his eyes when he came to *"La Belle Dame sans Merci."* He was able to recite those lubricious stanzas from memory. After a time, Jim Angleton began to ache with longing.

He closed the book suddenly. The thought was electric: *The system was presumably still working!*

It had been installed for a single use, to record a conversation by a suspect British diplomat. But it had never been removed. The system was an installation by Guido Andreotti, who still worked for the

Agency. The most skillful of those specially skilled technicians, it was Guido who had designed his personal vault and who had been given the assignment to bug the limousine Khrushchev would ride in on his visit to President Eisenhower at Camp David in 1959. Angleton had told him to abandon any attempt at the installation if there was any possibility the KGB would dig it out.

"Don't worry, Jimmee. They'll never have-a a hint of what I'm-a going to do."

Angleton found himself standing up and walking softly, as if on tiptoe, to the section of his study where the record player and radio were kept. He opened the door of the cabinet underneath, took out the headphones, and secured them over his ears. He moved the set slightly to the left, exposing the tiny plug.

He paused. Could he bring himself to do this?

He reached with one hand to the bar at the side and poured himself a deep glass of cognac.

Yes, he would do it.

He had to do it.

He inserted the plug and then, with quivering fingers, adjusted the volume.

He heard the words as if they were being spoken at arm's length. He closed his eyes. In moments he was startled and overwhelmed by Melinda's total voluptuarian dominance of the scene. Her voice, husky now, dictated the man's every movement, set the rhythms of sound and motion. Tony hardly slept through it all, but she was the succubus. Angleton needed to imagine the moves that accompanied the words. He pictured her on the bed. She was now teasing him about where she desired his legs, exactly. Tony's replies were sounds between words of ecstatic compliance. She joined in making her own sounds and it was now as if they came from a single person, then, silence. Angleton was frozen in place, in high delirium, the high heights of empathy. He stayed standing for long minutes, wishing for a revival. But suddenly he opened his eyes.

He was for a few moments immobile. Then he wrenched the plug out from its womb. He grabbed an ice pick from the bar and plunged it into the socket, twisting it fiercely right left, up down, out in.

He knew he had destroyed the wiring. But he wondered whether, ever, he would destroy the memory, the memory of his terrible, indefensible conduct, and the memory of those exhilarating few minutes.

Chapter Nineteen

What would be called the Berlin Wall crisis was mounting. Khrushchev reiterated his position. It was that, fifteen and more years having gone by since the end of the war, the Soviet Union would sign a peace treaty with the Democratic Republic of Germany. That treaty would, of course, cover Berlin, which was there, embedded deep in East German territory.

The West responded with the argument that the subdivision of Berlin at war's end had not signified the relinquishment by the four allies of their authority over conquered enemy territory. The administrative subdivision of Berlin, Kennedy's Secretary of State Dean Rusk explained to the Security Council of the United Nations, was simply a convenience, one section governed by the Soviet Union, one each by Britain, France, and the United States. Any peace treaty with East Germany to which all the allies didn't subscribe was illicit. And especially illicit any attempt at incorporating Berlin into East Germany.

Angleton bore down hard on all the Agency's assets. One thing was plain. If the Soviet Union imperiled the freedom of West

Berlin or interfered with the right of access to West Berlin by the
NATO powers, force would be used. How much force, in what
way, was a tactical decision—Angleton did not concern himself
with this aspect of the question and didn't even speculate very
much about it. *His* job was counterintelligence, and he accepted
his mandate with enthusiasm for its relatively narrow scope.

What was wanted by the President and his national security
counselors were the estimates Counterintelligence could make on
the questions: What was Khrushchev's intention? How far was he
willing to go? What and when would he move, and what would be
that move? What would deter Khrushchev? A show of force? If so,
what kind of force? A countersalient perhaps? A renewed and credible threat against Cuba? If the Soviets attempted to restrict traffic
within Berlin, for instance—blocking traffic east-west, stopping the
subways and buses—how much resistance would be needed to
make Khrushchev back off?

And although it was never in doubt that critical decisions would
be made only by the Kremlin, how much of the operational enterprise would be turned over to Walter Ulbricht, boss of the East
German Democratic Republic, as they playfully called non-
democratic, non-republican East Germany? Angleton spent long
deliberative hours on these questions, digesting tens of thousands
of words sent in from agents and assets everywhere and closely
studying the huge rations of telemetry from satellites and submarines. The White House and the Pentagon had their own resources, of course. But there was one common and burning
question, each every day asking the others: When would the Communists move?

Angleton worked late hours and even forfeited, several times, his
beloved lunch at La Niçoise. He greatly missed any lunch taken
from him. At such lunches he would converse with friends and associates. Jim Angleton was renowned for his willingness to listen, to
discuss, and to devote what seemed all the time in the world to the

restaurant's repast. Ray Rocca, his closest associate within the Agency, one day broke silence on the forbidden question and said, "Jim, you got to be crazy, you think you can order a cognac at this point? I mean, I know your insides are going to the Smithsonian someday, but you've had *three* martinis, we shared a bottle of wine, you had a Kir with the coffee, and now you're talking about a cognac?"

"Raymond, there is no reason to disdain whatever biological attributes you are born with. If my eyes permitted me to make out" — he pointed in the direction of the restaurant's discreet little window, with LA NIÇOISE, to be read from outside, sketched over it in gold leaf — "if my eyes permitted me to discern the license plate of that car going by at this distance, would there be a reason *not* to use my eyes if I were curious about that car?"

Raymond Rocca laughed. "What really gets me is that you can go back to work after this."

Which Angleton did, and no one ever caught him napping, or slurring his speech, or forgetting a detail. His judgments were always his own, but for all that they were sometimes idiosyncratic, it was never suggested that they were the fruit of the grape.

But he did come home tired, if not sleepy. Still the presence of Melinda in his house was an undiminishing source of desire and frustration. He did not lay eyes on her on Day Two but on Day Three he heard her laughter and was inflamed by it when she and Tony left their car to come into the house from the back. He thought to ask them in for cocktails, but concluded that that would sound intrusive. After dinner he toyed with the idea of asking them if they wanted a nightcap. His mind permitted itself to repose on the scene upstairs. It was just after eleven. They were home — he knew that because Tony's old Ford was parked in its place in the garage.

He wondered: What were they doing? Were they perhaps watching television? He discarded that detumescent thought. Were they clothed? Were they examining each other's bodies? Were their bodies united? His heart was soon racing again and he forced himself to the television set, turned it on, and watched absentmindedly what was left of the late-night news program.

Maybe tomorrow. Maybe tomorrow he would ask them in.

The next day there was one of those notes from Tony dropped on his silver tray. Might he talk to Mr. A. later in the day, or if not, the following day, Wednesday? Angleton made a note to call Tony on the intercom and did so sometime after six. Yes, he could come down. He did not ask whether he would come down with Melinda. Presumably not. But Angleton would look for an opening.

"Mr. A., there's some good news on my front, but a little complicated. The good news is that Melinda struck oil! There is an opening for her in Foreign Service, like right now. She'd have to pull out of the summer session at Yale and be ready to start in two weeks. She has some more testing to do, three or four days of it. My problem is I'm being sent out of town . . ." He paused and allowed himself a genuine peal of laughter. "Of course, I'm not allowed to tell *anybody* where I'm going or what I'm supposed to do. But I'll be gone forty-eight hours beginning tonight. Mr. A., can you guess what I'm going to ask you?"

"If Melinda can stay for the two days you're gone? The answer is yes."

Tony reacted with his usual comprehensive smile-of-delight on hearing news he wanted very much to hear. Angleton was breathing deeply, his lips slightly parted to guard against the sound of palpitated air escaping.

"Of course, she will be getting her own apartment when she goes to work for the State Department . . ." Tony hesitated for a moment, and then, "Of course, Mr. A., I'm sure she will, of course. Is there . . . a deadline on that matter?"

"No no. I mean, I assume she'll have got something by, oh,

Labor Day?" He was terribly saddened at the thought that, almost surely, Tony would then leave, to share her apartment.

Well, if that was going to happen, there was nothing he could do about it, even as there was nothing he could do about the Soviet determination to sequester East Berlin.

Chapter Twenty

Tony Crespi didn't in fact let his landlord know ahead of time exactly when he would be leaving for his training exercise. What he did was leave a note saying that he had gone. Angleton found it on his tray when he got back from his dinner with Esterhazy at the club, just after ten o'clock. "Mr. A.: Have left on highly s-cr-t mission. Will be back Friday night. Hope all goes well with you. Respectfully, Tony."

There was no mention of Melinda. But there was no reason to suppose that, Angleton having OKed the request that she be permitted to stay, Melinda would not be acting on it.

He began to think it through piecemeal.

Was she there now? Upstairs? He would look to see if the light was on.

He stepped outside. No light.

The car! Tony's car. He walked to the rear of the house. Tony's car wasn't there.

Angleton was an old hand at working out possible alternatives.

(1) Tony drove his car to whatever rendezvous he had been assigned by his training agent and left it there. In that case, Melinda

(*a*) was upstairs, asleep; or (*b*) hadn't come back from wherever she was having dinner. That meant she'd get back, whenever — by taxi; or else she'd be brought home by a friend in his/her own car.

Or, (2) Tony might simply have turned over his car to her to use in his absence; in which case she would be driving herself back to Casa Nogales at some point.

He found himself engrossed in the question, *Where* was Melinda? Or better, where *might* she be?

After so many years, he had accustomed himself to pulling information from the extraordinary resources of his office, at any time of the day or night.

He called the aide on duty. "Angleton here."

"Yes sir."

"I want to know who is in immediate charge of the training program of" — he searched his memory for the code name assigned to Tony Crespi — "Harry Bolgiano."

"That will require a phone call or two, Mr. Angleton."

"Find out who it is and get back to me — you have the number here, CApitol 2-6657 — with the phone number of the training officer."

It didn't take long. "Sir, the training officer of Mr. Bolgiano is Henry Pizzero — P-i-z-z-e-r-o. I've established that he is at home, and his number is SHenandoah 4-4144."

"Thank you."

He rang the number. "Mr. Pizzero? This is James Angleton. I think my office told you I'd be calling."

"Yes sir."

"I need to know something. Where was the trainee Harry Bolgiano sent today?"

"He went to Columbia, South Carolina. Training mission . . ." Pizzero wondered whether the boss would ask exactly what the training mission was. He didn't.

"I assume he traveled by train?"

"Yes sir, Silver Meteor line. He left before noon. Do you need me to be in touch with him?"

"I don't think so. If I do, I'll call. Thank you and good night."

Casa Nogales was fifteen minutes from Union Station. It wasn't inconceivable that Tony had parked his car in the lot near that station. On the other hand, public lots were charging three dollars a day. Tony would probably not stake out nine dollars in parking fees to save himself thirty cents in bus fare or two dollars in taxi fares. He was pondering the question when he caught the passing glare of headlights in the corner window.

Melinda was back!

Was she alone? Driving Tony's car?

Whichever, she would be using the usual door from the garage that led to the back staircase. The route Tony took.

If he happened to have been outdoors at the moment when she drove in, he could discreetly have established whether she was alone at the wheel. But he could not now leave the study, step outside, and get around to the garage in time to see anything. So he waited a few moments then stepped outside and looked up at the guest quarters.

The light flashed on.

She was home. Alone.

He could see her.

It was past eleven before he wrestled his way through to a decision. He would call her.

The intercom rang three times.

"Hello." He heard her voice, finally; so poised, so fragrant with self-control. He cleared his throat.

"Jim Angleton here, Melinda. Just wondering whether everything was all right. Saw the car coming up, I know Tony is away."

She answered with an ebullient, "Mr. Angleton? That's so nice of you—no—"

"It's not too late and I thought you might want to come down and have a nightcap. I'd be very interested in how the Foreign Service people are treating you."

"Oh, I would just love that. I really would. And maybe I could ask you a couple of questions about government work?"

"Of course. Come on down. I'm going to have a gin and tonic. What can I be fixing for you?"

"I'd like a vodka and tonic, if that's all right."

She knocked on the door five minutes later. He rose to open it for her. She wore an orange linen beach dress with a wide slashed neckline and a short flared skirt. "It's hot out there tonight, Mr. Angleton."

"Yes, indeed." He pointed to the sofa and got her the drink and handed it to her, sitting down in the armchair opposite.

Melinda accepted the drink and began instantly to talk in her self-possessed, melodic voice.

"It has been a really wonderful couple of days. And I guess Tony told you they've offered me a job; I have to begin very soon — "

"Yes, Tony told me about it. What do you hope to do in the years ahead?"

She talked with enthusiasm. About her studies, her travels, her interest in the diplomacy of the postwar years. She asked him about the forces that met at Yalta, the special pressures felt by Winston Churchill. In a very few minutes, she had become the protagonist of the evening, and Jim Angleton found himself transported with the delight of it. He brought himself, and her, another drink, explained about the protocols of Yalta, listening to her complaints about the biases of her professors. She wondered at some length how the same people who met at Yalta would have handled the crisis in Berlin today, sixteen years later.

Angleton spotted the clock on the bookcase. Would she like to look in on the midnight news? There might be something there on Berlin. She would *love* to get an update on Berlin. In order for Angleton also to see the screen he needed to sit down on the sofa next to her.

The announcer brought the news. *At dawn, Berlin time, the East Germans halted all traffic across the Berlin boundary.*

They had constructed barbed wire and cement blocks at intersections. Melinda clutched Angleton's left hand. "Oh my god!"

Angleton returned her grip, which soon was a caress. They sat wordless opposite the screen listening to the bulletins. Melinda put her head on Angleton's shoulder. He reached over and turned down the sound, then put his arm around her. She drew her head up and kissed the side of his face. Now Angleton turned off the screen. The only light in the room was what drifted in from the two sconces by the main door. The only sound was the purr of the air conditioner. She whispered to him, "Will you love me here? Right here? Right now?"

Slowly he removed his jacket, and at his quiet direction, she composed her legs on the long couch.

Chapter Twenty-One

January, 1975

CASA NOGALES

They never spoke of the Philby business but of course I have ears everywhere, and Raymond Rocca—he was very proper, he didn't give me any details—but he did say that that was a chapter in the final assessment of my work. Philby. Esterhazy said to me once—it was during the missile crisis, October 1962—he said, "Jim, are you maybe a little obsessed by Kim Philby?"

I got to be breezily familiar with that word "obsessed," after Golitsyn came into my life. I almost called in for a consultation with the office psychologist. I thought to say to him, "Doc, tell me about obsession. I have been accused—to my face—of being obsessed with the Soviet intelligence offensive. Now what I have done is to apply twenty-five years of experience and my own highly informed intelligence to pointing out what the Soviets are up to and how we get fooled by them, time after time. Is that obsessive?"

I didn't do it, of course. For one thing, Dr. Ekaterinburg—I probably have his name wrong, but I'm not going to stop to look it up. Anyway, who cares? Come to think of it, I could have asked Dr. Ekaterinburg if he has a psychological explanation for why I'm putting these words to paper. But I know what his answer would be.

He would say I am letting off steam. Could be right. Although if he knew me better he'd say it better, he'd say I wished to record, for my own sake only, in *exactly* the language I choose, my thoughts on some of these controversies involving me. God knows doing *that* isn't obsessive.

Or is it?

I constantly surprise myself by how open my mind *really* is. Golitsyn once remarked on this, when we were discussing the absence of a Soviet envoy at the Red China anniversary and I said maybe it was a mere matter of a diplomatic screwup in Moscow. That's when he told me I had a truly open mind.

But on the matter of Philby. Is it unnatural to have had a highly developed curiosity about a man I fought shoulder to shoulder with who all of a sudden—it's said—was actually a Soviet agent? Someone I had lunched with maybe thirty times? Discussed every aspect of the Soviet question with?

Burgess and Maclean pulled away in May. May 1951. After that, Philby was called back to London. There was the usual tabloid stuff, though it concentrated on Maclean and Burgess.

Sometimes we all have to be grateful for the British libel laws. At this end of the world not even Joe McCarthy came out blasting Kim Philby. The official verdict of MI6 was: We have no reason to believe Philby betrayed his country, but because of the closeness of his contacts with—with those wretched fag traitors—we can't run any risks. So they let him go.

Philby wrote to me only once. He enclosed a clipping from the *Daily Mail*, which spoke of the two traitors. He circled one sentence in the story. It was one more report on how wanton Burgess was in looking out for boys/men to sleep with. Something like, "Guy Burgess, known since his days at Trinity College, Cambridge, for his homosexual activities, some of them, it is now surmised, shared with Donald Maclean..." Philby circled that sentence in blue crayon and wrote, "Jim, I've been married three times and I'm not through. So don't believe it if ever they said that kind of thing about me! Fondly, Kim."

Fondly, Kim.

That clipping and the note on it burrowed very deep in my mind. For one thing, and Philby is a very cool customer, it *seemed* to be saying that he absolutely was not homosexual—while not quite saying that he absolutely was not a Communist agent! If he hadn't meant for me to concentrate on the sexual charge, why would he have circled that passage, instead of one of the others, the half-dozen others, that spoke of the espionage?

That was arresting. But then there was the fillip, *"Fondly,* Kim." Now Philby and I had a good and full professional relationship, and he did spend Thanksgiving with the family, in 1950, but we were never "close," in the way, for instance, that I have been close to Hugo Esterhazy or even Tony Crespi. In not closing his note with, say, *"Ever"* or—very British—*"Cheers,"* he was surely saying something, I thought. He was taunting me. He was, I'd swear by it, saying, "I have a warm feeling for you" which, in the context of this note and this clipping and this episode, is more than merely fraternal in nature.

Then I thought—Why did he tell me he had been married three times? The conventional understanding, if you say something of that kind, is, "How could I be homosexual? I am quite the opposite. I am a satyr, witness that I have been three times married."

But was he really saying something else? Did he discard his wives because he wanted fresh sexual experiences with other women, with *more wives*? Or was he asking me to understand that his experiences with women are not fulfilling because he is really a homosexual?

Hardly obsessive, to wonder about that.

But it is true that I planned very hard, very extensively, on how to close out the affair of Kim Philby. I *had* to know. There wasn't any point in asking more of his colleagues or getting somebody to scare up more of his classmates. Everybody had reached a conclusion and let it drop. There was always the possibility that a Soviet defector with a direct experience, during the Philby years, 1949–1951, would come in and provide *absolutely positive* evidence that Philby was a traitor. Or . . . he might have come through with something convincing that was exculpatory. For instance, suppose this defector had been in close touch with Maclean and Burgess in Moscow. Suppose they had revealed that Philby never coordinated with them in any act of espionage? What if Philby had gone farther and told them to be more careful to advance our interests and frustrate the enemy's? Would that have been inconceivable?

Very little is inconceivable, but if thinking about Philby for year after year, wrestling with the question — *Did he deceive me?* — is obsessed, then go ahead, say that about me.

But it's true that I thought a lot about it, wondering in what way I could get at the truth.

And the idea came to me. Came to me like a flash, that day at Yale, using Norman Pearson's little study to interview a prospective agent.

I got then, there and then, the idea of using Tony Crespi.

Chapter Twenty-Two

It was getting to the end of the protracted period of Tony Crespi's training. All the material discussing him and his work and the training he had received lay in a single folder. It was labeled "Harry Bolgiano." The chief of the training division did not know the real name of Harry Bolgiano. That is how deep-cover people were handled. As Tony passed from trainer to trainer, remarks about his work were passed into his file. No copies were made. The trainee had been instructed not to engage in any conversation with his tutors that might serve to identify Crespi. "Some of the exercises and training you are made to go through, Harry, will prove unnecessary, given that you are training here in Washington. When it is decided which will be your station, you'll get more specific information and, perhaps, training especially tailored to that mission."

Tony was curious about it all, of course, and thought to probe odd aspects of his imposture under another name. "What about my driving license?" he asked Jerry. "I mean, I drive around in my own car. If a policeman stops me, I can't very well tell him I'm Harry Bolgiano, right?"

"Of course not. If a policeman stops you and demands to see your driving license, you will show it and it will reveal to him your real name, whatever it is. The rule here is that no one who handles you officially, from within the Agency, may know who you are. As long as you remain in the covert system, only a single official will know who you really are. You must understand the purpose of this —"

"No, Jerry, I get it. Not so hard to understand. It's the old business. They trip me up, they torture me, but I can't do much damage because all I can tell them is the name of one person in the trade, not a dozen people —"

"That exactly is the idea. You have come up with a melodramatic example but it helps in understanding the whole trade, as you call it. So now, Harry, I'll give you a slip of paper, as my predecessors did, leading you down the line from instructor to instructor. It has the address to which you are to report. Your appointment is for 10:13 tomorrow morning. You are to decrypt my note by using the code for tomorrow's date, May 2, 1962. That decryption will disclose the address you're to go to. As you know, that code has been individually devised — no one but you has it. Your training is completed, and tomorrow the agent finally in charge will tell you what your mission will be." Jerry stood up. "Good luck to you, Harry. It isn't a security violation to tell you your work with me was first-rate."

"Thanks, Jerry." Tony really liked Jerry. He calculated offhand that he had spent more hours alone with Jerry than with any single other person since leaving home, not counting roommates. It was appropriately spooky, he thought, that he, Tony Crespi, knew nothing about him, Jerry Whoever, and that he would never see him again.

He had already arranged to celebrate his graduation, as he called the end of his training in conversations with himself. Melinda would meet him outside the movie house at 6:15 for the early showing of the hot new movie. Then they would drive to Harvey's restaurant. Then?

In the months since Melinda began her Foreign Service training she wasn't always predictable. She had gone one entire month, the first month, resisting any amorous overture, so much so that Tony thought her affections vagrant. He knew only one thing, that Melinda would not have slept alone. Not Melinda.

It was better now, but not quite as it used to be. It did not help that for several weeks Melinda was saddled with a roommate — a remote cousin from Minnesota, in Washington to work as a volunteer (her father was well-off) at the Democratic Party Congressional Election Office gearing up for the congressional elections in November. Sometimes Cousin Ella would get the hint, yawn ostentatiously, and say she was going to bed early, shutting the door loudly and leaving Melinda and Tony the living room. They made voluptuous use of it, but it wasn't quite like their old, roomy, secluded quarters at Casa Nogales.

At the restaurant, nervously exhausted from seeing the screening of *Sweet Bird of Youth*, Melinda said, "Imagine, living in Tennessee Williams's cozy southern town. My guess is Williams is a nervous wreck himself, or he couldn't have portrayed that household."

"What we both need is a drink. I bet the actors had plenty of drinks making *that* movie."

Melinda had gone to the movie house from work and had warned Tony on the telephone that she would look "all but undressed." In fact, Tony mused, she always appeared undressed to him, thanks to his imaginative initiatives. Tonight she appeared, thought Tony, her usual stunning self, dressed in a plain wool-tweed collarless dress with suede buttons neck to hem. Tony hailed the arrival of the daiquiris, simultaneously downing half of his and ordering the waiter to bring on another round.

"What makes you so giddy tonight?" she asked. "Another exam?"

"No, but I finished and sent in my paper, and now all I have left is the orals and off I go."

That put her in a bad mood. She didn't like to be reminded that Tony was going off to Beirut for ARAMCO, the Arabian American oil company. But they had talked about that before and she didn't think it worthwhile to try again at this point to persuade him to forsake Arab studies. "If it's of any interest, we Foreign Service students are scheduled to spend all of next month on the Near East, and three of us"—there were twenty in her Foreign Service training class—"will be traveling to the Near East. Three Europe, three Latin America, three Japan, three Southeast Asia, if anybody is left alive in Indonesia after the purge."

"Three times... five makes fifteen. What happens to the other five?"

"They flunk out."

"I know you won't flunk out."

"Not a chance Melinda Carrothers would flunk out"—she raised her glass coquettishly—"in anything I take up."

They talked into the night. Nearing midnight the thought flashed across his mind. "Hey! Melinda! Listen," he whispered, "... why don't you come to my place tonight? No chance *he'd* know. I can tell before we turn into the driveway whether Mr. A.'s even at home."

She answered him sharply. "No." And repeated, "No no no." And then, with some impatience, "Why don't you start your overseas training tonight by... practicing celibacy?"

"You don't mean that, do you, sweetheart?"

She paused. Her eyelids moved down. "No, actually, I don't.... Let's go home to my place. Cousin Ella is probably asleep. If not, I'll just—"

"If not, we can do it in front of her. She has to practice for all those voters she has to seduce."

It was very late by the time Tony got home. Ten-thirteen struck him as terribly early for his appointment with Mr. Spook, who would tell him what, after all these weeks and months, he was supposed to do for the good old USA.

He dressed carefully. "Nothing conspicuous," had been the rule, from Day One. "Practice blending into the background."

He left Casa Nogales wearing a blue shirt and tie, light khaki pants, and a blazer.

As trained to do now for all those months, he gauged his stride to arrive exactly on time. He walked down P Street to number 1114, the deciphered number, ringing the bell at exactly 10:13.

The door opened.

"Come in," said James Angleton.

The Chief of Counterintelligence would be twenty-two-year-old Tony Crespi's own case officer.

Chapter Twenty-Three

May, 1962

Esterhazy had returned from one of his regular inspection trips to the Mideast and spoke to Angleton of the political climate there. The impunity with which the East Germans, at the prodding of Moscow, had proceeded to build a wall right through Berlin was very much on everybody's mind. They were seated at their regular corner table at La Niçoise.

"There's one sense in which Beirut is a beneficiary of the Berlin business," Esterhazy said. "Berlin, as God knows you're aware, has been the headquarters of European intrigue, just like back in the 1920s. But it isn't quite as easy anymore, now that the wall cuts the city in half. I was in West Berlin on the first leg of my trip last month. Getting around in East Berlin—I found out—is a perilous business, and you'd better explain who you are, how you got there, and where you're going. In Beirut anybody can go anywhere, and if they're not eating or seducing somebody or arranging to bribe or kill somebody, they settle down to routine, meat-and-potatoes conspiracy. All you have to contend with in Beirut is Muslim fundamentalists, Christian Arabs, last-ditch anti-Zionists, Zionists, Saudi protectionists, Egyptian revanchists, and Communist agents aching to get into the oil play."

"Sounds like *Casablanca*," Angleton suggested, taking the cigarette from his mouth to free his hand for the wine.

He invoked the movie best known to the American public as the quintessential documentary of romantic intrigue in wartime, portraying the forces of Vichy contending with those of Free France in a maelstrom of mystery, tobacco smoke, and café-style piano tinkling. Esterhazy liked the metaphor. *Casablanca* was a nice romantic bowdlerization of the world of espionage and counterespionage. "At the American University in Beirut, Hugh Auchincloss—he's the rector—is pretty apprehensive. The Israeli military under Ben-Gurion are getting restless and the PPS—that's the Parti Populaire Syrien—are logging a hit practically every week. The social life is jumpy and round-the-clock, and there's the huge entrepreneurial class coming in from everywhere, hungry, as I said, to get in on the oil boom, happy with the high wage rate, fat with the professional resources from four different college campuses—88 percent of Lebanon is literate—did you know that? It's a Middle Eastern Hong Kong, and my guess is there's an explosion building up and I'd guess the Soviet machinery is in high gear to take advantage where they can."

"Did you talk to the newspaper people? Do they still have that Société Libanaise bar on the Place de L'Étoile?"

"It's thriving. There are now 125 full-time newsmen and stringers working out of Beirut."

"Did you run into Philby?"

"I was having a drink at the Normandy bar with Auchincloss and he pointed him out at the other end of the room. He was with a Russian radio journalist, somebody Auchincloss knew. Philby's a common sight, apparently. Nobody pays special attention to him but he always appears busy."

Angleton asked whether Hugo had felt he was under surveillance while there.

"I didn't *feel* they were following me, but my phone was tapped."

"Probably all the phones at the Phoenicia Hotel are tapped."

"Exactly. Except that I was tired—both nights were late nights—I might have played some games with the tapmeisters. I just didn't have the energy. I'm sure I pleased the people in the cellar or wherever, who were listening in. They must have been glad I was speaking in English rather than Kurdish, Hebrew, Coptic, or . . . or what? . . . or Cushitic."

"Where did you come across Cushitic?"

"American University. They want us to underwrite a few more foreign-language courses. I remember the language, Cushitic. I don't remember where they speak Cushitic."

Angleton furrowed his brow. Hugo thought he was going to come up with a discourse on the Cushitic tongue. What he said was, "I wonder what Philby is up to?"

"Why don't you have one of your people find out?"

Angleton didn't reply. He turned on his enigmatic look.

"Got to go to work, Jim."

As usual, they split the bill.

In the two weeks before leaving Washington, Tony had a session with his tutor, packaged the special reading recommended, and boarded a flight to Milwaukee.

Maria Crespi was at the airport. He looked at her. He had seen pictures of his mother taken when he was a boy. The wedding picture of Maria and Tony's father he had found accidentally, when packing to go off to college in 1957. It lay with discarded books in Italian in a suitcase, left in the cellar and disregarded. She was slim, twenty-two years ago, and the sepia photograph showed that her eyes were closed. In her hands she was clutching what seemed a Catholic missal (the gold cross on the cover was discernible)— his father would not permit a priest to officiate. Tony had never before seen a picture of his father. His new father, his stepfather, didn't want photographs in the house recording the other marriage, to the other man, who may have been a resistance hero, but who was also a Communist.

Tony had gazed on his father's face with intense interest. He wore a tie at his wedding, appeared calm and domineering. Tony thought back on the day of the marriage, in 1941. He wondered how many people his father had killed—that day? Perhaps he had been inactive on December 28, 1941. Lucky day for the Fascists. Tony sneaked the picture off to a film and photo shop, had it copied, and posted it above his chest of drawers at Yale.

Twenty-two years later, Maria Valerio Crespi seemed an old lady. Her frame was still spare and there was a touch of lipstick and makeup, and when she kissed him, he could detect the perfume. They spoke in Italian, and lapsed unselfconsciously into English when they left the garage and found Lester in the kitchen, waiting for his wife and stepson. The television set was on.

The Crespis had indeed baked a cake. The guest for dinner that night was the headmistress of Nicolet High School. Tony had served his high school as valedictorian, and Miss Hemphill reminded him that—it was only five years ago—Tony had predicted that a world government would stabilize the entire world by the time he, Tony, came back for his tenth reunion at Nicolet. Lester Crespi chortled.

"Actually, I shouldn't laugh. Five years from now there may very well be a world government. And we know—*I* know—who will be running that government. The Communists. We can't keep them away even in Cuba. That slick Harvard Irishman who bought his way into the White House—what does he know about handling the Communists? If Churchill couldn't handle them, you can hardly expect Kennedy—"

"Lester, we must not spend the entire evening on politics. There is so much to talk about, especially with the exciting times Tony will have. In the Near East."

Miss Hemphill asked him where exactly he was going, and Tony answered. Miss Hemphill dreamed of making a trip to the Holy Land, she said, and if ever she could manage to make that trip she thought she would also visit Beirut and Cairo, but she knew how troublesome it was to travel from Israel to adjacent Arab countries.

Lester cautioned his son to look out for "enemy activity" — he meant by that Communist initiatives anywhere. "The Israelis! Smartest people in the world. But they find this Israel Beer man, right in the top echelon of Ben-Gurion's government, and he's a spy. And now they're breaking the rule, the rule against capital punishment, and they're about to hang Adolf Eichmann, blast his soul. They ought to hang Beer."

They had eaten well and Maria served a Chianti. But soon after, the headmistress said she would have to leave because she had a violin lesson appointment at nine.

"You're still teaching violin, Miss Hemphill?"

"Why not, Tony?" She smiled. "Violins aren't wearing out just because Elvis Presley has taken over modern music."

Tony grinned. His courtship of the violin had lasted only one semester, yielding to baseball and football. "Elvis is OK, Miss Hemphill. Actually."

They got up and walked the headmistress to the door and saw her into her car. Then Lester Crespi turned and said he wanted to drive Tony by to see the new factory building brought up by the Allen Bradley Company. "It cost eighteen million dollars, Tony. That's eighteen followed by six zeroes. Wait till you see it!"

They drove in that soft May evening down to central Milwaukee, and Lester, running the car at low speed, showed off special features of the building ("Behind there is a gymnasium and swimming pool"), pointed to the entrance door to his own office, and jutted his jaw with pride at the three surrounding acres of park. They were headed back home when Tony turned from his seat next to his father and addressed Maria. "Mum, does the Beaver nightclub still operate?"

"Yes," she said. "I'm quite sure it does."

"Well, I want to take you both there and to order champagne."

There was a half-second's silence. But not more. Lester Crespi said, "Anything our Tony wants, right Mother?" He turned at the next corner.

It was a Saturday night and the club was active but the maître d' found them a table far enough away from the piano and drums and double bass to let them hear. Lester ordered a Budweiser. "It's unpatriotic to order anything but beer in Milwaukee, you may remember, Tony."

Tony ordered a bottle of champagne.

"Where you're going they don't let you drink, the Arabs don't, I think I've read. They cut off your hands if you drink, don't they?"

Tony was reassuring. "Not in Beirut, Dad. It's pretty modern. You can get pretty much what you want."

Lester acknowledged the observation with an exaggerated wink. "Anything you want? That sounds like Manila. In 1945 they certainly offered anything the GIs wanted. Or"—he smiled coquettishly at Maria—"*shouldn't want.* But I've told you about Manila. Biggest mistake America ever made, not making MacArthur president in 1952. He won the Pacific war and would have won the Korean War if Truman had let him."

Tony drank lustily. His father spoke of the U.S. nuclear test missile that had failed over the Atlantic, and of the anti–U.S. riots in Korea the week before. "We go over there and lose forty thousand soldiers dead to keep South Korea free. And now the students are rioting at who? At the Communists? Oh no. At Uncle Sam."

An hour later his father leaned over toward his son. "Do you mind telling us, how much are they going to pay you in Beirut, while you're studying Arabic before going over with ARAMCO?"

"They'll pay my tuition and board, and two hundred dollars a month."

"Not bad, not bad. That's fifty dollars more per month than I was paid when I got back from the Philippines. Of course, I didn't have a college education."

Maria was enjoying her champagne and didn't protest when Tony ordered the second bottle. "Your father has done very well without a college education, Tony." But then she paused. "But we're very proud of your education. Have you, Tony, met any nice young ladies in Washington?"

Tony said there were a lot of nice young ladies in Washington, "and several also in the graduate school at Georgetown."

"Well," Lester opined, "there's hardly any hurry, for somebody twenty-two years old." He leaned over and put an arm around Tony. "You're my own son, as far as I'm concerned, Tony. And it's because of you—of your generation—that we have to keep our minds on what the Communists are up to."

Tony returned the hug and said, Yes, we had to keep our eyes very wide open, and he had done a lot of reading lately to update him on the situation in the Near East.

Driving home, Lester addressed Tony in a muted voice, as if he hadn't wanted his wife to hear what he said. "I've put by your bed, on the table there, a book. It is a very confidential book. It is called *The Black Book*. It is written by Robert Welch. He's the founder, I think you know, of the John Birch Society. The most important anti-Communist movement in America. *The Black Book* tells what looks to me like the inside story. You know who gave me a copy? Mr. Allen Bradley himself! He is a director of the John Birch Society. In that book Welch gets to what he thinks has been the nub of the matter. He thinks..."—he lowered his voice even further— "he thinks that... President Eisenhower was on the other side! That would explain a lot of things."

Tony promised to read the book before returning to Washington on Monday.

Two weeks had gone by since Tony Crespi's formal meeting at P Street with the Counterintelligence Chief of the CIA. Now Tony was spending his final night at Casa Nogales before shipping out. He didn't know whether his invisible colleagues—other trainees going out to ply the Agency's wares—used that military expression, "shipping out." But the words seemed right for him, in these circumstances. He wasn't going to Beirut for academic purposes, though he welcomed the ancillary benefits of the academic experience he would be having.

There was no one to talk to about such thoughts, not for a covert agent. He had no one to try them out on—except Mr. Angleton. He was surprised, but pleased, when the intercom rang that morning. For the first time, in all the months Tony Crespi had lived in Angleton's house, Tony was invited to dinner. "I've given you your formal instructions, Tony, but there are one or two personal matters we might go over."

"Where'll we be eating, Mr. A.?"

"At home. Seven o'clock."

Tony Crespi didn't say anything. He didn't know that Angleton *never* ate at home. At seven promptly, Tony, dressed with shirt and tie and a seersucker jacket, walked down the back staircase into the hall and knocked at the study door. He heard the voice from the kitchen.

"Come in, Tony. Come right into the kitchen. Grab a beer and"—Angleton turned to the kitchen table—"have a go with that corn. Do something with it. Either shuck it and fry it, or bake it or roast it or anything else you want. I am working on a pasta dish I was taught in Italy a hundred years ago. And I have steaks on the grill. If the consumption of beer hasn't ruined your palate, you may want to share with me that bottle"—he pointed and proceeded with a hint of reverence: "a 1949 Clos de Vougeot."

Tony accosted the corn. Then, "Shall I fix a bread plate?" Angleton stopped. As if a bullet had hit him in the back. He had forgotten to buy bread! "One must have bread," he said slowly.

"On the other hand"—Tony had brought hope!—"since you're serving pasta, maybe we can do without bread?"

Angleton hooted with relief. "Of course. You are correct." He reached into the cupboard and brought out a cardboard carton. "These are Triscuits. They can be used for this and that, to eat, to push the peas about—if we were having peas. Now, Tony, open the wine and go into the study with one of the trays. I will serve the supper."

It was good. The meat had a western flavor, prickly, spiced. "My mother taught me this sauce. She was from Nogales. Do you happen to know where Nogales is, Tony?"

"Border town in Arizona," he managed to say, though his mouth was nearly full.

"You need—most important—some chile jalapeño. Mother then used some soy sauce and salted tomato with the chile.

"You will need to develop a personality and to try to live that personality. You are a dedicated student of Arab culture and history. You gave an early indication of your desire to learn more about the Arab world by taking that summer off from Yale and going to Beirut—"

"But that summer, two summers ago, I was as much a kid journalist as I was a scholar—"

"So. You were twenty. Now you are twenty-two . . . You have thoroughly practiced, in your training sessions, your personal history. We've kept it pretty close to the truth, omitting the special historical act done by your father in 1945. You are better off toning down, or indeed eliminating, your stepfather's passionate anti-Communist prejudices. On the matter of the Cold War—why, it is, as far as you are concerned, something you read about, live through, but are hardly obsessed by. You are, of course, if only inertially, pro-American. Your interest is in your career, as a future employee of ARAMCO, the imposing Arabian American Oil Company, a glamorous ambitious company investing two billion dollars in a critical oil pipeline. You've made a deal with them. You study Arabic and Arab culture, they pay your way; a year or so from now, you begin as a full-time employee."

"I wasn't told one thing. How much do I get in spending money? I made up a figure talking to my family in Milwaukee over the weekend. I didn't want to say I didn't know how much I'd be paid."

"Here is your full correspondence with ARAMCO." Angleton brought a folder over from the sideboard. "Your application to them, their reply, the arrangements you both made, and their agreement to pay tuition, room and board, and $150 per month in what you'd call spending money. The balance of your salary from the Agency will be made available to you by your controller in whatever way you designate. You are on the honor system with respect to Internal Revenue — calculate what you owe and send in your check. When you write out your tax return next year you will record what we pay you as 'incidental income.' You have your own room at the college. It is entirely possible it will be bugged. Try to establish whether it is. Most students get about on bicycles; some have motor bicycles. If you end up using one of these, be careful to get a modest one. A utilitarian bike, not a racing machine."

Angleton poured the wine.

"Now you have been told about Gabriela Semenenko. My chance meeting with her was almost a year ago. As you know, she works at the American University library and her parents are in a Soviet rehabilitation center. There is no question that she was directed to attempt penetration of our operations in Beirut. The KGB just doesn't ignore a daughter of diplomats, in a foreign country, whose parents have been brought back as suspects. But we are pretty confident she has been turned around. Our man has had dealings with her. We have leverage because she needs Beirut approval of her staying on in Lebanon, and we can handle that end. But to keep her parents out of trouble she has to play along with whatever her handler asks of her. We can't establish that they've asked her much of anything — they have full-timers in Lebanon. She is a double agent, in our books. We've used her, successfully, twice, when we wanted to know something about the politics of AUB, the university. She will never know, of course, about your background, but you must find a reason to cultivate her, as a friend or even simply as someone useful to your academic work and contingently useful to your assignment."

Angleton finished his meat and moved his plate to a table end. "Now I will tell you the name of your controller."

It was a grave moment, but Tony Crespi thought to interrupt the great man—half in fun, half with genuine curiosity. "Is there any chance that we are bugged here, in your study?"

Angleton raised his head. He was surprised. And he was intrigued. And he felt himself challenged.

"You are quite correct to ask that question," he remarked in professorial tones. "My study is swept once every month. But for reasons of occasional convenience or of opportunity, every room in this house is bugged." He paused. "I can, if I wish to do so—and I have in recent months wished to do so—hear in this room activity going on in any other room in the house."

He didn't look directly at Tony's face. But he knew that providence had manipulated him into doing the right thing, however mortifying. Tony would not have missed the meaning of what he had been told. James Angleton was left humiliated, but relieved.

Quickly he went on. "Your controller is not a deep-cover agent. He has the most conventional cover we provide almost everywhere. He is the cultural attaché at our embassy.

"His name is Robert Matti. He is forty-two years old and has been with us—he began with OSS—since leaving Yale, as it happens, in 1942. He reports to us through his own channels. What material you wish to get through to me, will be through Matti."

"Does Matti know about your... personal interest in Philby?"

"Not in the detail you have been given. Philby is a professional object of continuing concern for us. He was fired by the Brits as a security risk, and the operative opinion is that he did, in fact, work for the Soviet Union, in which case, I've been told, he is probably still working for the Soviet Union. As you've been told, we want to know what he is doing. My private interest is generated by the long hours I invested with him as collaborators in the anti-Soviet enterprise. In the best of all possible worlds, you would discover that he was in fact... on our side. If he were disposed, after all these years, to come back into active service, that would be a great, great event. And, as you would guess, would give me very special personal satisfaction."

"I got it. I think I do understand, Mr. A. What about the mechanics of my first contact with Mr. Matti?"

"That has been anticipated. Matti gives a half hour to every American student coming to Beirut to study. This is a quite conventional arrangement. There are twenty-six American students in Beirut so that his load—a little light indoctrination for them about life and conditions in Beirut—is not heavy. It is in your case a very useful procedure. The KGB of course know that Matti is one of our operatives, they know also that it is entirely routine for an American student in Beirut to seek out his help or his advice. He makes it a point to spend considerable time on campus and in activity related to the American University."

"Has he developed lines to Philby? I mean, is Philby being surveilled under Matti's direction?"

"Details of that kind, my dear Tony, you will have to discover for yourself. Now, it is"—he looked over at the clock on the bookshelf—"just after ten. You will want an early night. I hope you have already said good-bye to Melinda Carrothers. And that you will consider making that separation—permanent. As for me, I have reading to do. What time is your flight? What is your route?"

Tony struggled to ignore the provocative reference to Melinda; he simply answered, with some eagerness, anticipating his second visit to Beirut, "I go to London. Then to Cairo. Then Middle Eastern Airlines, Cairo to Beirut. I arrive at about three in the afternoon. I'll take a cab and go to the campus and report to the Admissions Office."

Angleton rose. He approached Tony Crespi, the handsome young American with the Italian face and the bright brown eyes and the engaging smile. He came close to giving him a fatherly embrace, but all the forces of conventional restraint mobilized within him . . .

He extended his right hand. "Good luck, Tony."

"Thank you, sir. And thank you for ... everything."

Tony turned and opened the door to the hall.

He stopped, turned around, and gave way to his nature, fastening both arms around Angleton's shoulders. Angleton returned the manly embrace.

Chapter Twenty-Four

Anatoliy Golitsyn called out to his wife, Irena. He had set a rule: They would talk to each other only in English except on Sundays, when they would treat themselves to using their native language. Katarina was now eight. She was taught at home, by her mother. "I know, I know, Newton," he told the FBI agent who argued that it was safe to send Katarina to the public school. And that was three months ago. "I know," Golitsyn demurred, "that she is using different names and that school records give wrong histories of Katarina's parents. I know all that. But I know better than you, Newton, about KGB. You are FBI and FBI are a wonderful people, but the KGB they are amazing-awful."

While fully sympathizing with Golitsyn's concern for the safety of his family, Angleton had attempted to reassure him about his prospective relocation. The FBI's Witness Protection Program had come up, in October, with this little farmhouse in eastern New York State, a farm community which was never in the news. No famous people ever lived in Millerton, New York, or went there, Newton had told Golitsyn when briefing him on his new home. The FBI had agreed, at Golitsyn's insistence, on round-the-clock surveillance (three agents, doing eight-hour shifts), but only on the understanding that, after six months, protection would diminish to one agent if during the trial period there had been no evidence of threatening action.

"Do you know when Trotsky left Russia?" Golitsyn asked FBI agent Newton Ehrenback.

"Yes, I know it was way back, Mr. Golitsyn, back in the twenties—"

"It was the year 1929! Now, Newton, do you know in what year Trotsky was killed?"

"It was a lot later, Mr. Golitsyn. Can't remember, er, like what year exactly—"

"It was the year 1940. Where was Trotsky? He was not near to Moscow. He was much further than Millerton, New York. Trotsky was in *Mexico*. In a big house, with neighbors all around him. Where you are keeping me is only isolation."

"Mr. Golitsyn, we've come up with a comfortable house for you and your family which it would be very, very difficult to trace. We really are doing the very best we can. But you have to understand, the FBI could not give you twenty-four-hour protection, like the Trotsky situation—from 1929 to 1940 . . . that was eleven years—"

"You are saying, Newton, that you will not protect me until I am killed?"

"No, Mr. Golitsyn. I am *not* saying that. I am saying that . . ."

Ehrenback was a professional, with thirteen years' experience in the Bureau. Enough experience to know that some people can't be reasoned with. *Here was this—Russian KGB agent. No, ex-KGB agent!—assuming he's going to get FBI protection around-the-clock for the rest of his life; what else does he think we have to do?*

Newton Ehrenback decided he'd end the conversation.

"I will forward any protest you wish to make, Mr. Golitsyn."

"I deal only with the Chief of Counterintelligence of the Agency. And with Mr. Allen Dulles."

Ehrenback half smiled and left through the front door. He walked to the barn. One side of the barn had been reconstructed and was now a very small apartment with a bedroom and sitting room. The dormer window on the second floor looked directly out on the little farmhouse thirty yards away. An office chair and a table were propped up against the windowsill. On the table were the binoculars that the agent on duty would pick up every time somebody came to the door of "Dr. John Stone."

Professor Stone was on a sabbatical from Cornell to complete his book on Russia's Catherine the Great.

Golitsyn's intellectual and political interests were highly developed. The postman who came to the house regularly arrived with a package containing one or more books, furnished by the FBI contact at the New York Public Library. Indeed, there was nothing brought in from the post office except books and magazines and Golitsyn's cherished *New York Times* and *Washington Post*, which arrived the day after publication. The Russian material — copies of *Pravda* and reports from Tass and assorted other publications collected by the Soviet Division of the CIA — arrived weekly, and once every week or so Irena would drive to a neighboring post office — never the same one. She would go as far south as Pawling, as far west as Albany, to mail her husband's communications to the address given by Angleton. When she drove back to the house, the FBI agent was especially vigilant with the binoculars. She had been instructed not to drive right up to the door, but to leave the car a few lengths down the driveway, giving surveillance ample opportunity to examine who stepped out of the car.

Golitsyn spent several hours every day reviewing the material. And several hours every day analyzing it in reports he would submit to James Angleton. Once every few weeks after dark, and after surveillance had been advised, Professor Stone left the house.

Irena at the wheel, he would drive to Pawling and take the late train to Grand Central Station. An agent met him and took him by taxicab to Pennsylvania Station. There he boarded the sleeper train to Washington, locking the compartment door and telling the porter not to wake him. He stayed in the compartment, after the train arrived and the other passengers had left, until the special knock was heard on the door.

The FBI agent would take him, by car, to the safe house, where Angleton would meet him in midmorning. They would share a lunch brought in by the Filipino steward. Golitsyn elaborated on the events of the week or the month, driving home his thesis. The Golitsyn Epiphany: the United States Government continued unaware of the lengths to which Soviet policy was based on persistent, systematic, dogged disinformation and deception.

BOOK THREE

Chapter Twenty-Five

Tony Crespi had spent only three days in Beirut when he went there on his college tour. He was excited at the prospect of revisiting, this time to live there for up to one year, perhaps more, the city whose architecture and glamour had struck him and whose modern pulsations he had felt so distinctly in his first visit.

It was mid-May when he arrived. The old prewar airport was the same, including the seemingly endless messages in several languages that blared in through the loudspeakers. What was new were the posters. The entire airport, it seemed, was papered with advertisements. It wasn't only the tourist bait or conventional international commodities — Coca-Cola and Sony and *Time* magazine. Sites of interest to tourists were now featured in what seemed life-size posters covering the walls. Secondary attractions hung down from girders and were tacked onto ticket counters. Pictures and photographs and street maps and road maps were affixed to guard against a square inch of nudity.

The bustle confirmed what Tony had learned from reading the most recent travel bureau information and guides, as also from information he had got from the Lebanese Embassy: the tourists were coming in larger and larger numbers to the picturesque, bulging, prosperous seaside city of nearly a half million people. Twenty percent of the Lebanese population lived in Beirut and its outskirts. Behind the baggage claim area, a tourist poster called attention to the Omari Mosque, another to the imposing Parliament Building, another to the racetrack. In his pocket Tony had the guidebook crammed with advertisements for hotels and theaters, waterfront restaurants, and sports facilities.

After twenty minutes' wait for his baggage he thought to sit down. There was no prospect, in that crowded room, of finding a public bench. But he knew what to do—he had often done it, at railroad stations and airports and once or twice when traveling as a reporter for the *Yale Daily News*. He propped up his Royal portable typewriter case endwise and sat down on its hard, stable surface. Tony was nearly six feet tall but his legs were limber and he stretched them out for better balance. He found his eyes nearly closing, in mute defiance of the general commotion in the area. The Egyptian woman's ample pleated skirt brushed against his head, tickling his right ear. He heard her complain in English to a fellow Egyptian about the baggage delay. The complaints were now widely voiced.

Finally!

He stood up and reached for the handle of his typewriter case. He had spotted his two large suitcases on the baggage floor and nodded to one of the porters. The man closest by, a short heavy Lebanese with a large mustache, wearing blue overalls and a T-shirt, had been leaning over his trolley seeking a moment's rest. He acknowledged Tony's nod and made his way through intervening figures in various native dress, some of them seemingly rooted to their places in the hangarlike area, without apparent purpose, neither pressing to enter more deeply into the airport or to leave it nor moving to another section. They were lightly clad against the rising temperature of the room, which easily surpassed the relief intended by the large electric fans. The air was ruffled, too, by the kaffiyeh headdresses worn by many passengers over Western shirts and trousers. Some wore the full Arab aba gowns. It seemed to Tony that half of them were smoking, the smoke from their cigarettes thickening the musty, noisome air.

"Abdul?" In his three days in 1960 he and Alistair Gorman from UPenn, traveling with him on the student tour, had bet on the probability that the next service-connected person they encountered — driver, waiter, porter — would answer to the name "Abdul." Alistair had put his stake on one out of three, and won. Now Tony risked it, but the porter said he was Emil, placed the bags on the trolley, and after hearing the word "taxi," motioned Tony to follow him.

They went through the framed entrance door into the blistering sun. Emil hailed a faded-yellow cab. Tony guessed it was, or once was, a Fiat station wagon. The conformation of the car was familiar. He and his fellow students had been taken about in similar cars during the crowded visit, twice to out-of-town Byblos and Baalbek, and every day to organized events and historical sites within the city.

But this morning he was headed for the American University. He spoke with the driver. Like most urban Lebanese, Emil could make his way in English, and the car drove off through traffic much denser than Tony had remembered, moving west and then north, emerging at the promontory of Ras Beirut.

Now they had a view of St. George's Bay and drove slowly through university property. He had studied a map and spotted College Hall, the cornerstone of which had been laid in 1871 by the missionary order that founded what until after the First World War had been called the Syrian Protestant College.

That was many years ago. Now the thriving university had five faculties, including a school of engineering and architecture. At College Hall he would be directed to his dormitory. But first, of course, the dean.

Eldridge Dodge, trim and businesslike, greeted Tony Crespi with dispatch. Tony asked whether it would be wise to tell the waiting cab driver where to go now with the bags.

"Yes, yes, that's the thing to do. Then you can come back here and we can confer. Now let me see, you need to know where your quarters are." Mr. Dodge, dressed in rumpled, seamed white linen, turned back to his desk. The back of his head was shaved, as if a tonsure was his purpose. He leaned over to a file in a cabinet behind his aluminum desk. His back still turned he said in accents distinctly not American, "Yes. You are in Bliss Hall." He turned, smiled. "Follow me. I can point the house out to the driver. It is easily seen from here at College Hall. I think you will find your room comfortable. As a college graduate you qualify for one of the newer rooms. You have your own shower and toilet, though you may have to share it with the next room down when the fall semester begins."

Tony thanked him and said he would return as soon as he unloaded his bags, grateful to the unknowing dean not only for helping to get him established, but for establishing his identity.

Chapter Twenty-Six

Tony Crespi gave the assistant librarian, Gabriela Semenenko, the list of books he had been handed by Mr. Dodge. Miss Semenenko's desk was to the right of the library's entrance door. There were books on a dozen shelves behind her, to her right, and to her left. Others were stacked neatly in the corners of the alcove. The area was crowded, but a chair at the side of the desk was reserved for students who needed help from her more protracted than what she could give them, standing, on the fly. When Tony told her what he wanted, she beckoned him to the chair.

"You are taking 203—Are you with Mr. Amil or with Miss Hepa?"

"I don't know." Tony looked down at the sheaf of papers Mr. Dodge had given him. Semenenko rose, leaned over, and took the folder from his hands. Tony was momentarily exposed to the crease of her robust breasts. He whiffed a pleasant, unfamiliar scent. Seated again, she leafed through the material in his folder.

"Here is the course description if it is taught by Miss Hepa. 'A thorough course in basic literary Arabic, with emphasis on the vocabulary of modern literature, the press, and current affairs.'" She continued patiently. "'The grammar and structure taught enable the students to read, understand, and translate, from and into Arabic, within a tightly controlled syntactical milieu.'"

"You mean the other professor describes the course differently?"

"Mr. Amil is set in his ways. He's seventy years old. Miss Hepa is very young. My age. Mr. Amil insists on adding to what you have heard: 'Students will be required to exercise the language in recorded conversations with each other and to spend two hours every week outside the university practicing the use of the language.'"

"Well, that sounds fair enough. I assume I can sign up with either professor? Maybe I'm safer with Miss Hepa."

"Yes. But what else are you taking?"

"The dean recommended 101, Readings in Arabic Heritage."

"That's Kamil. Muhammed Kamil. He is very inspiring. I took his course when I first came here, eight years ago."

"You are . . . Russian, Miss Semenenko?"

"Call me Gabriela."

"Call me Tony."

She nodded her head. "All right, Tony. Well, I very much recommend Mr. Kamil. He is fluent in Arabic, obviously, and, obviously he teaches his course in English. But he is also fluent in French."

"How's his Russian?"

"He can read in Russian, but not speak it. When we first came to Beirut—my parents are from Kiev—he and my mother and father—my mother and father were with the embassy, the Soviet Embassy—made an arrangement. Kamil would come to our apartment. He would coach them in Arabic three days a week and they would coach him in Russian three days a week."

Gabriela is making this very easy for me, Tony thought, recalling his auxiliary mission, to get to know and to size up Gabriela Semenenko, double agent.

He decided to press more quickly than he had intended.

"It is just noon. Where does one eat lunch around here?—

Gabriela, I have an idea ... don't tell me *where* we eat lunch, just take me there and coach me on how to eat lunch in Arabic."

She looked at him inquisitively. She liked his spontaneous manner. *His teeth are very beautiful,* she thought. *Also his shiny brown eyes.* How would he look, she wondered, in native dress? It flashed through her mind to describe his appearance if he suddenly went Arabic — *... his arms protrude from loosely open sleeves of the shirt which muffles his pronounced shoulders, framed now in a blue Oxford button-down shirt, a thin blue-and-yellow tie coming down from his neck.* She smiled to herself and said simply, "Why don't you loosen your tie? Everybody does, or else they just don't use them."

Tony looked about the desks in the reading room. He could make out only tieless students.

"Good idea." He loosened his tie. "You didn't say anything about lunch."

Gabriela was suddenly very formal. "You came here for the books for 203 and 101. The two books, *Readings in Modern Arabic* and Richardson's *History of the Middle East,* you can find here" — she scrawled out the citation numbers on a three-by-five card. "These" — she ticked six books from a larger mimeographed list — "you will, I think, want to buy, as you will get a lot of use out of them. You can buy them from the AUB bookstore, which is" — she pulled a sheet from her copious drawer, a map of the campus — "here." She drew an X with her pencil.

Then she smiled and all but winked at Tony.

"Yes, that would be nice. I will be ready in a few minutes. You'd probably like to look around. We have a very fine library."

"*Don't hurry,*" Mr. Angleton had warned. "Deep-cover explorations take *a great deal of time.* Philby left Washington over ten years ago and he has been six years in Beirut. There is no urgent timetable on your mission there."

Yes, Tony thought as he chatted with Gabriela, opposite, at the spartan refectory table they shared. Yes, and Gabriela Semenenko, in the opinion of Mr. Angleton, had made an overture to a U.S. official when she was—most probably—a Soviet operative, pretending to be worried about her parents' recall to Moscow. Tony Crespi was moving much faster than by the tempo Angleton would perhaps have approved. But now she was questioning him.

"What about my parents?" He looked up at her, sipping an iced tea through a straw. "Well, my parents were—are—were Italian. My father died during the war, in Milan. My mother was taken to Milwaukee—do you know where that is?"

"In the State of Wisconsin."

"Very good. Anyway, she remarried, to a very nice man from Wisconsin—"

"It is very important in this part of the world to speak different languages. On the monthly museum tours I do, I can conduct them in four languages. Do you speak Italian?"

"My mother used to talk to me in Italian. After a while she stopped. When I was thirteen or fourteen I was embarrassed to be overheard by my classmates talking in Italian. But I got over that, and we still talk, when alone, in Italian. Where did you learn your smooth English?"

She arched her head back, her shining brown hair bunching up on her shoulder, her small jade earrings catching the light that came in from the large oval window of what was once, Tony learned, a church. "Last year I was in a play here at AUB. I had the part of the proud English lady in *The Barretts of Wimpole Street*. It was reviewed in the *Beirut Times*. I remember the reviewer's line about me."

"OK, Gabriela. I'll play—with pleasure. What did the line say?"

Her smile consumed her entire, exuberant face. "It said . . . 'The part of Lady Arabel was played by AUB's librarian, Gabriela Semenenko. She is rumored to be a native of western Siberia. This critic charges fraud. She is obviously a native of England.'"

"Well," Tony said. "You can't get better than that! How good is your Arabic?"

She fiddled with the tea glass, long-since emptied. Her answer was slow and deliberate. "Good enough to give you anything Miss Hepa—doesn't give you."

Tony suppressed a smile. He fancied a report to Mr. Angleton:

Met mark 11:50, Library, AUB.
Took mark to school cafeteria for lunch, 12:30.
Spoke with mark, general conversation.
Mark suggested sex, 13:45.
Question to mission director: Am I moving too fast?

Chapter Twenty-Seven

October, 1962

Nothing else, anywhere, mattered. The only news was Cuba. The CIA had discovered the missiles. The Soviet Union was decamping nuclear missiles into Cuba.

It was after eleven at night that McGeorge Bundy, National Security Adviser to President Kennedy, was shown the photographs at the Pentagon. Scientific analysts extrapolated from the tiny nipples showing on the photographs, extruded from what seemed mountain caves. Arthur Lundahl, Director of the National Photographic Interpretation Center, summarized the situation: "There is enough destructive power, I'd say, to eliminate urban America."

Flanked by eight experts and advisers, including the Navy, Army, and Air chiefs and the Deputy Director of Central Intelligence, Bundy pondered what to do.

"Are you going to wake the President?" asked Defense Secretary McNamara.

"No," Bundy said. "What's the point? We couldn't bomb Cuba tonight even if he decided that was what he wanted to do. I'll tell him tomorrow morning at eight."

The following day the President and his consultants met in the Cabinet Room.

Six hours later the critical perspectives had crystallized.

"We have the questions here," Kennedy addressed his special, ad hoc advisory group. "What we need now is the answers.

"To the question, What cities can be reached by the intermediate nuclear bombs the Soviet Union now has in Cuba, I understand that the answer is—am I right, General Taylor?—every city in America except Seattle?"

Kennedy managed a smile. He turned to Deputy DCI Marshall Carter. "I am informed that the Director of Intelligence, Mr. Mc-Cone, is on a honeymoon—in Seattle." Every one of the eighteen persons present exploded in laughter; such had been the tension, so welcome the least relief from it.

"He's en route back by military jet, sir," Deputy DCI Carter said, his voice meek.

Kennedy went on. "The next question is how many strategic nuclear missiles does the Soviet Union have?—at home. Though as I view it, what would it matter if they had none, given what they have right now, in Cuba? . . . Well yes, of course I understand: They couldn't risk annihilation in Cuba unless they had supplementary bombs outside of Cuba." The President, at this point, was talking to himself. "We could, after all, destroy the Cuban installations with one—two?—three?—hydrogen bombs? And incidentally kill one? two?—three?—million people?

"Anyway, they have thirty-eight long-range missiles within the Soviet Union. We have, I am told, two hundred thirteen missiles. In a plenary exchange we would have the advantage. A redundant advantage, no?"

Nobody interrupted, or raised a hand.

"The next question is: If the Russians decided to move against us, they would need, with only thirty-eight missiles and without a proper guidance system, to aim their bombs at our cities. They do not have guidance systems sophisticated enough to take out our command centers. What this means, gentlemen, is that the Soviet Union's deterrent capability is only defensive. They can threaten retaliation against us by threatening the urban civilian population. But they do not have an offensive potential because they cannot aim at our—what is it, eight?—"

Secretary McNamara nodded. "Yes sir, eight."

"—eight command centers. Well, we are on full alert now. It would take how long for our bombers to reach Moscow, General Taylor?"

"Six hours."

"Six hours. Mac?"—he pointed to McGeorge Bundy, who had raised his hand.

"A question has been raised, Mr. President, on the matter of Soviet guidance systems. The CIA seems to have some idea that our assumptions are based on a telemetry scramble—"

"Scramble? You mean we aren't getting reliable signals on Soviet missile capability?"

"It's not quite that they aren't reliable," Llewellyn Thompson broke in, "it's that it looks as if the Soviets have been engaged in deceptive missile testing."

Kennedy bit his lip and stared wordlessly past the eyes of the Joint Chief's Chairman, seated opposite.

Suddenly he stood up. Everyone in the room immediately rose. "It's late. We will convene formally at ten tomorrow morning. All of you are on a standby basis in the event I need you. Mac, Bobby, Carter, please come into the Oval Office."

The President led the way out of the Cabinet Room and climbed the flight of stairs. The guard opened the door to the Oval Office.

The door closed behind Marshall Carter, McCone's deputy.

Kennedy moved to his desk and sat down in his chair, leaving his aides standing.

"What the fuck is going on?"

James Angleton answered the hot line in his office. It was Mc-Cone, his voice coming in from the Air Force jet.

"Angleton"—the DCI had never before addressed him by his last name—"I'll be at National Airport at 8:05. I'll be in my office, then, at... 8:45. I want you there and also Carter. And have with you the files on Bernon Mitchell and William Martin. Jim. Your memo on the Soviet telemetry scramble: Did you send out copies of that to the Pentagon?"

"No. But I did send a copy to NSC. To Bundy."

"Find out, before I get in, whether Bundy made copies and sent them out. They're not supposed to do that, are they?"

"Not without notifying us."

"There was no such notification?"

"No."

"Does that mean we can assume only one copy of that memo is outside our office?"

Angleton puffed out the smoke in his lungs and smiled into the telephone receiver. "Well, boss, any such assumption is unsafe. If we found one or more copies in the Pentagon, that would mean only that NSC neglected to tell us that they sent them out."

"All right. I'll see you in a couple of hours. The President wants me in the Oval Office at eight tomorrow morning."

Carter addressed Angleton. "Since the defection of Martin and Mitchell, have we had any word of them?"

"Yes. We picked up their trail at—a reception party at Novaya Zemlya. A rare photograph, that: the Soviet missile development team celebrating something or other, with our defectors joining in the celebration."

"I'm reading this paragraph from your memo of last September, Jim. When McCone comes in he's going to go over all this ground and I want to make sure I have it straight myself: You wrote, uh, you wrote, '... Among the telemetry which our antennae in Turkey, Iran, and Pakistan picked up early in 1960 and 1961 were data from each of the nine accelerometers used by the Soviet rockets. These analyses showed striking variations between different accelerometers supposedly measuring the identical value. Why were the Soviets using nine accelerometers where three would be enough? — one to measure each of the three axes' ...?

"—You mean by that"—the Deputy used his fingers—"right-left, out-in, down-up. Three axes?"

Angleton nodded.

Carter continued. "'For some time, we have assumed that the reason for using multiple accelerometers is that the Soviet guidance system is primitive.'—But, Jim, you have argued that inasmuch as there has been no change in our readings, we reasonably assume that the Soviet Union is not concerning itself to increase the accuracy of its nuclear missiles. We should consider the possibility that only systematic biasing of telemetry by the Soviets would produce the apparent large errors in guidance. Correct?"

Marshall Carter needed help. "Well, let me stop there. An accelerometer—am I right?—is the key to accurate guidance because it exactly measures the force of gravity at any point and therefore can instruct the missile when to drop its payload which, guided by gravity and the knowledge of exact locations, will land the warhead how close?"

"If they have achieved our own sophistication, one thousand yards," Angleton answered.

"And of course that's close enough to target every command center we have."

"If I have analyzed it correctly, the answer to that is yes, Marshall."

Carter paused. Angleton said nothing.

"This has a direct bearing on the President's deliberations," Carter said. "If the Soviet Union could tomorrow demolish the eight locations from which we are equipped to send out instructions to our own missiles to launch and find and drop, we are, hypothetically, powerless."

"Not quite," Angleton said. "Our submarines, under such circumstances, would fire."

The door opened. John McCone walked in.

Chapter Twenty-Eight

Allan Taylor was a mathematician by training and now he used his skills at the NTM laboratory at Fort Meade. "NTM": National Technical Means. The abbreviation was used throughout the industry—or, better, fraternity. It described the work of the team of scientists and technicians engaged in enhancing U.S. missile technology and in discovering and analyzing the achievements and the technology of others. Concretely, the Soviet Union's.

"Jim," Taylor asked over the phone from NTM, "how extensive is your file on Bernon Mitchell and William Martin?"

"They were National Security Agency," Angleton said to his old acquaintance, who as a young man had worked with Angleton in London, on Enigma, "not ours."

"I know that. And of course they've been gone since their defection in 1960. We never found out how much they actually took with them or what link they might have handed over. What I'm wondering is whether you people have picked up where they are actually working right now. That could be a clue... Say, Jim?"

"I'm here."

"How about driving out here sometime. Sometime sort of, well—soon. I'd like to try something out on you. It's important."

"What my friend showed me"—as ever, out of habit, Angleton did not mention the name of his security-shrouded friend—"was a re-creation. We have antennae in the Middle East—in Pakistan, Turkey, and Iran—and they regularly pick up Soviet satellite and rocket signals. These are interpreted by NSA and tell us a great deal."

"How does it all work?" Esterhazy, ever curious, asked as the second course was served.

"How does *what* work?"

"Picking up Soviet signals."

"That is pure radio transcription, though very sophisticated. The Soviets send up their test missiles. These send back signals to Soviet ground control. The NSA intercepts these signals. What the antennae focus on is the rocket's direction and speed. And of course the Soviet scientists want to achieve control—more control, more control, more control—over guidance. What they need to accomplish is what we've pretty nearly effected, which is the elimination of the wobble."

"The wobble?"

"That's not a technical word. But here is what—my friend, the man I'm talking about, Hugo—here is what he and his people did. They re-created the scene at the last five Soviet rocket firings, over a period of six years, 1955 to 1961. In order to stabilize a missile on course you need to pull out any wobble, if your goal is pinpoint accuracy. In order to measure the wobble the missiles carry accelerometers—" He raised his hand, stretching thumb and forefinger in opposite directions. "That's about how long they are. Say, three inches. What they accomplish is to give out signals accurate to one one-thousandth of a centimeter. They give you the speed of acceleration and of deceleration and the gravity pull. The more vagrant the missile, the more accelerometers you need to keep it going in the right direction."

Esterhazy chewed on a breadstick. "I think I follow you. And...?"

"What made my friend itchy was that over a period of five years *the wobble hadn't diminished.* The Soviet rockets—and he pictured this for me on a big screen with graphical effect from the computer re-creation—continue to have just rudimentary accuracy. That would mean Soviet science had not advanced in missile guidance since 1955."

Hugo Esterhazy commented that he would need to be told why that was so extraordinary. "I mean, automobile technology hasn't really advanced all that much, has it, in five years? Except maybe another mile per gallon, or whatever?"

"Has golf technology advanced in five years?" Angleton countered.

"Fair enough. Let me think. They're always coming up with reasons why we should buy new golf clubs or new golf balls." Esterhazy, as he sometimes did, fanned his hand furiously left and right to blow away Angleton's cigarette smoke. "Well, let me say: No. I don't think it has. If it had, we'd be hitting the ball further and further. But we aren't doing that. The record is still 473 yards."

"What would you have to gain from telling me it *had* advanced?"

"Nothing. Unless I was a sportswear salesman trying to sell you something."

"What advantage would the Soviet Union have from not reducing the wobble?"

"None, obviously. That would mean just that they weren't getting any extra accuracy from their missiles."

"No. There is a very important second advantage, and this is what began to weigh in the mind of my friend. The other advantage is to deceive us on what progress they are actually making."

"I understand... So what do you do to find out?" Esterhazy peered out at the driving range, as if tracking a golf ball soaring up and out.

"The first thing to do, my friend said, was to try another reconstruction. What did the two defectors, Mitchell and Martin, *know* about how we go about measuring the wobble?"

"Did they know it?"

"They knew a great deal about the techniques we used. What the Soviet Union would need in order to deceive us is the results of our tests. It's one thing to speculate on the transmissions of the accelerometers, but you can't tie it together unless you look face-to-face at the data you are reading, the data they are creating."

"Did the two shits walk away with a trunkful of data?" Esterhazy's voice reflected growing indignation.

"No. But we get packets of data flying in on transport planes from Pakistan with some frequency. One of those transport planes overflew the Soviet Union and was forced down. In 1957."

"They got the stuff?"

"One has to guess so, Hugo. We got the pilots back after a couple of years. But they didn't come back in our Herc-130, with the same cargo they had going out from Pakistan."

Angleton raised his hand to the waiter.

"So what did you and your friend decide to do?"

"I've believed for a long time that we underestimate the extent of Soviet reliance on disinformation. My Soviet defector protégé, about whom I have spoken with you, feels emphatically that that is the case, but there is great resistance to accepting this presumption of unbelievability. 'You make it hard to believe,' John McCone complained to me last week, criticizing my approach, 'that when *Pravda* comes out tomorrow dated July seventh, it really *is* July seventh in Moscow.'"

"Well, he has a point, doesn't he?"

"Yes. But his point is itself based on a hypothesis, which is that what you see is what you ought to believe unless you have contrary evidence."

"And you're saying?"

"Assume it's wrong if, were it true, the Soviet position would benefit from your thinking it. The Heisenberg principle is relevant."

"Who is Heisenberg?"

"The man who invented quantum mechanics, is a crude way of identifying him. What he said was that before you let yourself believe what you want to believe, you must inform yourself what is it that it is necessary to know."

Esterhazy smiled cheerfully. "I'll remember that, Jim."

Chapter Twenty-Nine

White House, Oval Office

It had been a very long day, October 30, 1962. He rehearsed it in his memory, events 1-2-3-4-5, culminating in his live broadcast.

That's when I said, just now, *Leave me alone* here. Don't pass through *any* calls. The idea of taking Khrushchev's second communication as a de facto deal even though that communication flatly contradicted communication Number One was a good idea. A very good idea. First Khrushchev demands the impossible — that we abandon our Guantánamo Bay rights, terminate the economic blockade against Cuba, renegotiate Berlin arrangements in such a way as to cut out Konrad Adenauer... Then, as though he had *never sent* that first communiqué, he demands — in exchange for withdrawing his missiles from Cuba — just two things, that we withdraw our own missiles from Turkey and that we pledge not to invade Cuba.

I heard them — Bobby, McNamara, Rusk, Bundy, the generals — *staring* the proposals in the face. There wasn't anything else to say except: *Go with it!*

Speed was the thing. *No point* in waiting for Khrushchev Number Three, in which the drunken bastard might come up with a whole other set of choices/ultimatums/threats/proposals.

That was the fastest stretch of prose put together in the history of the National Security Agency, my response to Khrushchev Number Two. What it boiled down to was: *OK, Nikita, you shit. We go along*—then repeating the terms of Khrushchev Number Two, to make sure they hadn't blended in his mind with the terms he was insisting on only yesterday in Khrushchev Number One.

I had to place calls to the alumni. Funny term Bobby uses for living ex-Presidents of the United States, "Alumni." Tedious, calling up the alums, but a necessary chore. How many times have I done it, in office about two years?

Not that many.

After the Bay of Pigs. And when the Berlin Wall went up. And this time. That comes to once a year, that's not so bad. Hoover is always good, asks one, maybe two questions; then says I'm the president. Harry Truman is a little long-winded. Like he wanted to know what percentage of our firepower is forfeited if we pull our stuff out of Turkey. So what do you say in a situation like that? I mean, the whole world is on countdown while we're speaking.

I just made it up.

"Just four percent, Harry," I said. I haven't any idea what *percentage* it is for chrissake, the Turkish bombs. The fact of it is we can blow the Soviet Union to the ice age with half of what we've got in Omaha. I didn't know whether it was *four* percent, for goddsake, or seven — eight? — percent. I knew it wasn't fifty percent because if it was, Max Taylor, my general, would have screamed and yelled.

Ike. Dear Ike. He sounded like Mr. St. John, my headmaster at Choate. That patient, attentive sound—I could see his face working. Ike really does have — was it Ted who said it? — the most expressive face this side of the covers of the *Saturday Evening Post*. His questions were good—What would we tell the Turkish P.M.?

Had we agreed on the means of checking to see if all the missiles had been removed? I told him—I knew he'd like the sound of it—that the details, before we were done, would have to be satisfactory to Max Taylor and to McCone—Ike really likes and trusts Mc-Cone. It was Ike got him in to head up Atomic Energy before I put him in as head of CIA.

Then came the Oval Office broadcast.

Ted Sorenson said it went well. It was after that when I said: *I've got to be left alone and think.*

And what I sat down and asked myself was: What in the *hell* did Khrushchev *intend* to do?

So he's got twenty-four—is it?—missiles in Cuba with his technicians standing by. They can hit every big city—except Seattle! *Is it possible he'd do this?* I keep asking myself.

What is the answer to that?

That first day—God, was it only fourteen days ago?—I'm tipped off to some high-wire thinking by Jim Angleton. He says we can't *prove* Moscow doesn't have pinpoint missile capability. What does that mean?

Just that our conceptual strategic thinking has been not only pointless but grossly, dangerously misleading. If Angleton and the people at Fort Meade are right in their suspicions, it's possible that Moscow could pick our command centers off one by one—the eight places we send out signals from. That means he could leave our cities intact, just take out the command centers. If he did that, target just the command centers, where would we be?

Well, presumably, I'd be dead, since I am not only a command center, I am the Number One command center.

What would Moscow have to worry about? Ah, our submarines, Bob says. Moscow doesn't know, unless another spy has told Moscow, what the arrangements are if our subs get zero commands from us, if we're incommunicado. Do they stop at a pay phone and call the *New York Times*—"Give us the city desk...What's up?" The *New York Times* is not a command center, therefore presumably in this scenario it's still there; New York is still there. The submarine commanders are supposed to ascertain that the President and his command centers are no longer there, we are nuclear ashes — so our submarines send up a few missiles for old times' sake. Exit Moscow.

But Moscow has a message for the submarine commanders which is, "*Da,* you have no more command posts but you've got a whole lot of undisturbed cities. Do you really want us to send up our nuclear reserves and eliminate New York, Boston, Chicago, Dallas, Denver, San Francisco, and Los Angeles?"

Jesus it's awful. Step One means you got to go to Step Number Two, means you got to go to . . .

What did Khrushchev have in mind, putting those crazy missiles in Cuba?

It's hell to admit it, but I *do not know.* And you can do the if A then B then C then D business and no matter where you stop you're talking about catastrophe. Herman Kahn told Mac sometime somewhere that there was one thing the Soviets would never risk: The city of Moscow. It's like the Jews risking Jerusalem. Moscow, Kahn said, is the heart of Russia. Without it, all the rest is parasitic tissue. So if the Russians thought there was *any risk* of losing Moscow, they'd have to flinch. That's why half the scientists in Russia are working on a missile defense system, McNamara says. But meanwhile, what if one submarine commander lets one missile go into Red Square?

The Russians are not going to risk that, Mr. President.

So what the fuck are they doing with twenty-four missiles in Cuba?

They're certainly risking *exactly that,* if those missiles were used. And are those missiles really fine-tuned to take out all our command centers?

How come no one at the Cabinet Room meetings said: "The most important thing, Mr. President, is for you to get out of town. Uh, and we'll go with you."

I've got to get some sleep —

The phone rang.

He looked over at it in surprise. His instructions had been icy clear: *No interruptions, no phones.*

He picked up the receiver.

"Sir, Premier Khrushchev is on the line."

Chapter Thirty

At his desk in his office Angleton brooded over the terms, now published, that had brought an apparent end to the missile crisis. We
would (exact dates weren't fixed) pull our nuclear reserve out of
Turkey, Khrushchev would bring his weapons home from Cuba,
and the U.S. would pledge not to invade Castro's Cuba.

Angleton told his operator to get Golitsyn on the phone. The protocols were observed—Angleton gives the operator the phony name
of the person he wants to talk to, the operator dials the number that
corresponds with phony name, a computer decrypts the actual
number, call goes through, and phony name is asked to come to the
telephone because phony name is calling. All of this resulted in,

"How are you today, Anatoliy."

"I have much on my mind—Caspar."

"Yes, I'm calling to suggest we accelerate the schedule. Can you
come down tonight?"

Arrangements were concluded.

Angleton went to lunch with Hugo Esterhazy.

"Well, Jim, before you tell me the President made the wrong

deal with Khrushchev, permit me to say that I feel a lot better today than I felt last week."

"Yes. The tension got pretty high. Here *and* in Europe."

"You can say that again. I had the first telephone call since she skipped away with Lord Whats-his-name from my former wife. Dear Henrietta said she was worried about me. She wanted to know if I had my own bomb shelter. But tell me some juicy secrets, Jim. You know you can trust me. If I had been unfaithful to you, relaying all your secrets, Khrushchev would be in the White House now instructing us all in what to do."

Angleton cringed a little. He enjoyed the hyperbole, but it also reminded him of his formal indiscretions past and, he sighed, prospective.

"There was some vivid disagreement at the final meeting in the Situation Room, I've learned. Dean Acheson, Paul Nitze, and the Joint Chiefs wanted to strike at Cuba, strike hard and decisively."

"Am I right in speculating why JFK ruled that out?"

Angleton hesitated. Then, "I think the White House hawks hadn't weighed the consequences of our failure to act on Soviet disinformation. My own opinion is that JFK weighed, at that meeting, the full implications of the memo McCone questioned me on. It was simply unsafe for us to proceed on the assumption that the Soviet Union couldn't proceed to eliminate our command centers."

"So where do we go from here?"

"Castro has face to save. So does Khrushchev."

"Don't we also have a problem? I mean, half the Soviet nuclear missiles were parked just around the corner."

"Yes, we do." Angleton didn't want to pursue the point and went immediately on to say, "Did you see Castro's speech yesterday?"

Esterhazy shook his head.

"He gave Khrushchev hell."

"Asshole. Castro would have preferred Havana to look like Hiroshima?"

Both men were tired. They forced themselves to talk about other subjects. Richard Nixon has been defeated in his race for governor of California. And Mrs. Roosevelt had died.

Golitsyn was eager to talk. "I have seen and heard nothing since I took myself on the train last night."

Angleton filled him in. Castro had said that he ("and Cuba") had been "betrayed" by Khrushchev.

"Did Castro mention Mao Tse-tung?"

"Well, yes he did, Anatoliy."

Golitsyn's face was transformed into a single, eager ear. "What? Explain to me."

"He made three references to Mao and speculated on the question of leadership. Maybe Peking, not Moscow, should be thought the center of the world Communist revolution."

That, Golitsyn grinned eagerly, would drive Khrushchev "cuckoo-mad." He reminded Angleton, who did not need to be reminded of it, that the last time Khrushchev heard devolutionary opinion of that kind was from Imre Nagy in Hungary, who for a few golden moments in the fall of 1956 registered his belief that nations could find their own way to socialism. Khrushchev settled that problem by sending in Soviet tanks to quell the students, and executioners to take care of Nagy. What Golitsyn now counseled was to observe Khrushchev. He would act, Golitsyn predicted, to seduce Castro back to orthodox compliance with Soviet leadership. Two things needed to be done: "Khrushchev, he will need to bring his Castro back into his Bolshevik fold. And you? You, Jeem? What will *you* do? About Castro? Now that you have passed along—passed away—ignored the chance to—the opportunity to bomb him away?"

They spent four hours together.

Two weeks later Khrushchev invited Castro to Moscow on a state visit. He was treated like Karl Marx. Returning to Havana, he reaffirmed his loyalty to Moscow's leadership. But what would President Kennedy do about Castro?

The *New York Times* published, after several days, the diplomatic exchanges that had been held back during the final tense hours of the negotiations. Angleton read the text closely. He read, "Assuming this is done promptly"—the removal of the missiles in Cuba by Khrushchev—"I have given my [UN] representatives... instructions that will permit them to work out an arrangement for a permanent solution to the Cuban problem."

I do not believe it!

Angleton very nearly laughed out loud at the unintended irony.

On May 31, a few months earlier, Adolf Eichmann had been hanged in Israel for his role in attempting a "permanent solution" to Hitler's Jewish problem.

"And your people—our people—are doing nothing about Castro?" Golitsyn had asked at the end of their session.

Angleton walked now to his safe, withdrew his journal, sat down in his comfortable armchair, a glass of Madeira at his side, and opened his fountain pen.

I didn't say anything when Golitsyn asked that. I just nodded.

Hugo tells me that I have mastered the art of nodding my head in such a way as to leave the person I am talking to absolutely ignorant of whether I am agreeing with him, disagreeing with him, expressing doubt about what he has to say, or curiosity to hear more. I don't think I am all that inscrutable and in any event my intention was simply to say to Anatoliy that I agreed that Castro was a massive Soviet fist lodged in the underbelly of the West and, yes, something should definitely be done about that. My intention has always been to get from Golitsyn everything he knows. Not to tell him everything *I* know.

My problem sometimes is to feign ignorance and to try to reason through to a theoretical reconciliation of the highest problem of counterintelligence: When and under what circumstances does duty direct you to *deceive your superiors?*

I have discussed these matters in theoretical and hypothetical terms over the years with Esterhazy. I am every now and then tempted to be more concrete by way of illustration. After all, he and I have exchanged information at a top security level. But whenever my thoughts edge toward revealing some of the special knowledge, I always interject a reservation I have coached myself to observe when drinking. It is: *Do not discuss,* beyond the plateau I had predecided to venture into, *anything* that goes further.

I am convinced, after years of experience, that drinking does not alter my judgments. But I have admitted the hypothetical possibility that drink does encourage candor beyond what is intended — or is prudent. And since Hugo and I like to drink together when we dine, I always restrain myself when edging up into territory I hadn't already planned to invite him to explore with me. It would have been gratifying, but quite quite wrong, to have answered Golitsyn's question, *What are you people going to do about Castro?* by telling him that two days ago, Attorney General Robert Kennedy, shrouded obviously in utter secrecy, commissioned the assassination of Fidel Castro.

Chapter Thirty-One

June, 1962

It was June. The day before yesterday there was a hint of a break in the weather. The Lebanese, Tony Crespi had come to understand, think it menacing whenever the temperature drops below eighty, which on that blessed day, a Sunday, it did: a great protective hand, holding back the lingering summer heat.

Tony took Gabriela sailing. He was prepared to pay the 220 pounds advertised by the WaterSports annex of the Normandy Hotel as the half-day rental price for a fifteen-foot Snipe. Six bucks was fair enough for that comfortable, springy boat, the same model he had got used to sailing on Lake Michigan, serving as crew on his classmate John Aubrey's boat. Not entirely to his surprise, the beach manager, bowing his head in the direction of Gabriela, said, No—returning Tony's proffered money—the boat was his, courtesy of Normandy WaterSports.

Gabriela Semenenko, Tony was convinced, after benefiting from her ministrations for only two weeks, knew everybody in Beirut. And everybody was evidently disposed to do Gabriela favors. This included the here-and-now favor of Kassim. That was the WaterSports steward's name, imprinted in red letters on a yellow name tag fastened on his T-shirt.

Gabriela recommended the two-mile sail to Plage Long Beach, close by the Ras Beirut promontory of the American University. She had prepared an elaborate picnic. Getting there required a little upwind work against the lapdog seas, kept alive by the fifteen-knot wind. The Snipe made "anything possible," he reassured Gabriela, who had never sailed before. "And by the way, how come you know Kassim, if you haven't sailed before?"

"I called the manager and told him I had a friend who was taking me out."

"Who's the manager?" Tony asked, one hand on the tiller, the other on his beer bottle.

"He is Nassar Sadek, a very important gentleman. A very nice gentleman."

"Is he nice enough to let me win at the Normandy's casino?"

Gabriela moved her arm as if to slap his face for his impertinence. "You are very silly, Tony. Now tell me how to say in Arabic, 'Can I win at the Casino?'"

Tony accepted the challenge. He strung out a series of vowels and consonants, mostly vowels.

"That is very good. Are you enjoying your classes?"

"I am, as a matter of fact. I am up to my keister in Arabia. Do you know what 'keister' means?"

Gabriela was put out. She didn't know, she said.

"Don't worry. It's half slang. It means your rear end." Gabriela instructed Tony on how to say rear end in Russian and in Arabic.

"Duck! We're coming about." The boat was now on a port tack headed for the little beach. Tony noticed Gabriela's swimwear. It was the very latest zebra style, launched by Jackie Kennedy only last year, if he remembered correctly. He had seen it advertised at 3,800 pounds, in the fashion section of the *Beirut Times*. A fair amount of money.

It was a lively afternoon. The beach snuggled in a narrow bight, sheltered from the wind when it came in from the east. They could eat their smoked salmon and caviar and Bulgar bread and pickles and cheesecake, and drink their vodka and wine without any buffeting from the wind. Though the beach was substantial, only two other couples shared it with them, with three children who delighted in creating sand pies to throw at one another. The two women wore antediluvian swimsuits, reaching down to midthigh and high on the body. Even so, they did not enter the water. They spoke to each other in Arabic, as also to their husbands, who wore long trunks but stayed out of the water as well. They acknowledged Gabriela and Tony with only a ritual bow when they crawled up on the beach after anchoring their sailboat.

"They're Egyptians," Gabriela said, opening the lunch basket. "There are thousands of them, refugees from the revolution in Egypt." She was speaking of the overthrow of King Farouk by Colonel Nasser and its continuing reverberations, even after ten years. "Those two couples are probably second cousins of the king, or whatever. They are very clumsy with their picnic, notice. Probably they never had to wait on themselves until after the revolution."

"Were your parents born before *your* revolution?"

"Well, yes, but they were very young. The blessing is that they were not from the farm in the Ukraine. They were city folk, Kiev."

"You mean because, as city people, they were spared Stalin's starvation of the kulaks?"

She nodded. She looked around at the lonely beach, with its proud girdle of palm trees on the bluff, swaying from the unfettered breeze that arrived only anemically on the sheltered beach. "It takes practice to mention 'Stalin' critically," she said, lowering her eyelids. "For twenty years I never mentioned him within earshot of anybody who might report what I said."

"You've told me your parents are in gulag. But you didn't tell me—you changed the subject when I asked—why they are detained?"

Gabriela started to speak. She stopped suddenly, got up from the blanket she had spread out for the picnic, and rushed into the water, her arms high, her breasts exuberant, shouting, "First one in! First one in!"

Tony Crespi dashed in after her. Under the water she thrust one hand inside his trunks and, with the other, grabbed his hair and brought his lips to hers. When they broke through the surface, Tony was panting from more than the want of air.

Tony was surprised when at sundown he followed her avidly into her apartment on the Rue Khalidi. But he did not pause, following her lead into the shower and letting the salt wash off, catching in the mirror the dimming light as Gabriela drew the curtains. Tony flicked off the light in the bathroom and went to her, finally discharging the passion she had aroused underwater.

A very long silence follows. And then, finally, she speaks. "I can open the curtains now. It is now dark." She put on her nightgown and turned up the bedroom lights, and then drew aside the curtains.

By the standards of his own cubicle — as he referred to it — at the university, Gabriela lived luxuriously. Tony had been given by AUB a room with a single bed, a narrow desk, bookshelves, and a narrow closet. Gabriela had two rooms, the bedroom and the sitting room bordered by a small tiled terrace looking out over the sea. Both rooms were exotically decorated, the lithographs nicely displayed. Disagreeable, in the judgment of Tony, but then he hadn't got used to Arabic design. The curtains were of Lebanese damask, the cushions on the sofa and armchairs bulging full, in several shades of red. The apartment lighting was from sheltered bulbs resting in wooden sconces of Egyptian style.

"You are certainly comfortable here, Gabriela." He rested one arm on the pillow; with the other he stroked her breasts.

"This was my parents' apartment. I lived at AUB, in quarters very much like yours. When they were called back to Moscow they left money to pay the rent on this apartment — for a long time. I suspect they used up all their savings. Do you have savings, Tony? All Americans are rich, I know."

"All I have is the promise of a job with ARAMCO after I can translate into Arabic 'That's a pretty pot of pickled peppers.' I'm not saying my stepfather is broke. No, he isn't. But my monthly check is for $150. Sure, Mum will send me a little check besides — she's already started. She got into that habit when I went to college, and I guess never got over it when I graduated. I hope she never does!"

Tony reached over and kissed her, sprang out of bed, and drew up his shorts. "That was very nice of your parents, Gabriela, looking after the rent for you." He thought quickly to change the subject. She had twice resisted talk about her absent parents. "Where shall we go to eat?" He turned to her and smiled brightly, showing the teeth which, in bed moments ago, she had ecstatically acclaimed as "very beautiful, very beautiful, Tony, like your face, very beautiful." "I'm hungry. Your picnic was splendid. But that was quite a while ago. *Hours* ago."

She was combing her long brown hair. She dressed now in a sleeveless striped cotton dress that pulled her breasts up tightly, emphasizing the narrow waist. And then there were her long fingers, which Tony knew to be prehensile.

Tony didn't believe his telephone was bugged. He had learned something of the mechanics of the eavesdropping science and had searched first the telephone, minutely, then other features of the little room's landscape.

He remembered with excitement the tense days after the Soviets shot down a U.S. spy plane. Ambassador Henry Cabot Lodge was on television live, speaking at the Security Council, answering the latest charge of the Soviet representative complaining of America's "diplomatic aggression." Lodge had brought in a facsimile of the huge wooden eagle that decorated the office of the American ambassador in Moscow. A pointer in hand, he outlined the eagle's beak. He then leaned forward theatrically and, with his index finger, raised the beak, which rested on an invisible swivel. It was as though the eagle had opened its beak for food.

"There," Lodge had said, "there, ladies and gentlemen of the Security Council, was hidden this microphone." He brought it from his pocket. "Ambassador Dobrynin, your agents, in violation of the basic rules of diplomacy, were eavesdropping in the very office of the U.S. Ambassador in Moscow. Now what is it you were saying about aggressive U.S. surveillance practices?"

Tony Crespi had got a big bang out of that. He and Gabriela had discussed it that night at dinner.

Tony did not find a bug, not even behind any of the score of superannuated volumes that reposed on the bookshelves, passed on from one occupant to the next, unwanted any longer. Some of the books, Tony discovered, had been published before the war. Books of history, geography, Arab myths. *The Birds of Mesopotamia* was one volume. Nothing there especially useful, no Arab-English dictionaries. But neither was there surveillance, as far as he could see.

Yet Robert Matti was very experienced. He told Tony to be careful nonetheless. Their first meeting, ostensibly to welcome a matriculating American student, was all business. "You must assume," the cultural attaché had whispered in his own office, "that you are bugged. Nothing is to be spoken over the telephone that might jeopardize your security or that might attract special attention to you. In your dealings with Gabriela, tell her something untrue and unique. That's a useful technique, in case you or I ever hear it back. Let's agree on it.... Tell her your Arab language teacher at Georgetown committed suicide."

"I understand," Tony said, perhaps a little curtly. He had, after all, been schooled over a very long period on the proper deportment of a covert security operator. Bob Matti quickly used up the twenty minutes he normally allotted to matriculating American students. "Here is the one telephone number you can safely call. It is ARAMCO headquarters in Dhahran, Saudi Arabia. You are to call that number in any case, once a week, and ask to be put through to your sponsor. As you know from the correspondence, he is John Gaylord. He will come on the line. Or his secretary,

Samira Shabaan, who will relay any message. He might say he would like to see you, to discuss your progress. That means *I* wish to see you. He will say 'Meet me at my hotel.' Until further notice, that message translates: Go after six o'clock on the same day to the Cedar Tower Hotel on the Rue Makdissi. You are to knock on number 4-B. When we decide to change the safe house, you will in your mail receive a letter with the new address. You will without any difficulty be able to discern that address from the contents of the letter in which it appears. In the event you have an emergency need to meet with me, you are to telephone Gaylord. His home telephone — you can write this down, no problem — is 879-924. Tell him you have the information he wanted on Earl Stephens, whom he is trying to recruit."

Two weeks later, Tony got the message. Matti wanted to see him. This was Tony's first visit to the safe house, a small apartment on the fourth floor of a modest six-story hotel for transients. People came and went to the hotel, men (exclusively) of all ages and nationalities, staying usually for a few days or weeks. Robert Matti had arrived in the room just before six in the evening. At 6:23 Tony knocked on the door.

Matti was in shirtsleeves, without a tie; very different from the Mr. Matti of the U.S. Embassy, Special Aide on Cultural Affairs. But this afternoon he was in no hurry. He motioned Tony to the other armchair in the room and approached the little refrigerator in the kitchen nook.

"I keep here some beer, some tomato juice, Coca-Cola, and the native wine, a Ksara Syrah."

"I'll have a beer, thanks."

Matti opened two bottles.

Without further ado: "Tell me what you have been doing. First, your studies."

The first few weeks had gone well, Tony reported. After talking with one of the graduate students, he had decided to transfer from Miss Hepa's class to Mr. Amil's. "His special writing assignments suit my purposes. Beginning next week I am to go to all press conferences, to the Lebanese Information Office, and to our own, and write a weekly story as though it were a dispatch from a *Time* magazine correspondent."

"You will certainly run into Philby on that assignment."

"Well, of course. That's the idea."

"I have some intelligence for you. But before we get on that, what else have you been doing, besides your studies?"

"I've spent a fair amount of time with Gabriela Semenenko, but she diverts talk about her parents. She has made bitter cracks about Stalin, but nothing, well—nothing generic about Communism. I can't yet make out, on Mr. Angleton's question, whether she is reliably in our service."

"Maybe I will know before you do," Matti said. He took a drink from his glass of beer. "I've been scratching around for the last few months trying to come up with another assignment for her, something to give her a workout and to see how she performs. I've come up with one."

"Oh? What assignment did you give her, or should I not know what it is?"

"I told her to investigate you."

Tony looked up. "Me? What is she supposed to find out about me?"

"That is what we'll find out. If there is an exposure there we haven't been aware of, maybe she'll trip over it."

Tony's voice was tense. "How can she find out anything about *my* past? I mean, she doesn't presumably have a personal security apparatus in New Haven or Washington. Or Milwaukee—or does she?"

"That is her challenge, to work without an apparatus."

Tony's lips were set.

He spoke slowly, resolutely. "Her resources are—me. Me here in Beirut. Who else is she going to turn to to find out about me? You have to have known that."

"Yes, I knew that."

They were both silent.

"Remember," Matti counseled, "you're not, as a student at AUB, supposed to have very strong political opinions."

Tony forced himself to smile. Was he expressing political opinions when he asked Gabriela about the liquidation of the kulaks? Surely not. That was old hat—everyone deplored Stalin's liquidation of the kulaks. Even Khrushchev, he thought wryly.

Suddenly the clinical aspect of the relationship intrigued him. He would have to reflect carefully on *everything* Gabriela said. He thought it amusing, even. Was her lunch conversation that first day an exercise in her mission? What about the pillow talk?

But it was important not to fall for Gabriela Semenenko. She was bewitchingly beautiful. Forget that.

She is an agent, doing an agent's work.

Chapter Thirty-Two

In the aftermath of the attempted coup of December 14, 1962, the Lebanese Minister of Information suspended press conferences. The hundred-odd reporters and stringers in Beirut had to ferret out newsworthy information on their own. A month later, the official schedule was revived: two press conferences every week, Tuesdays and Fridays at ten in the morning.

Tony Crespi was there at the first conference. It was understandably crowded. The scholarly old Lebanese press director, Naddim Jabhour, put on his pince-nez and began reading the prepared press statement in English.

"The attempted coup backed by the Parti Populaire Syrien has been completely foiled. Moreover, intelligence information permitted the government of President Fuad Chehab to anticipate the attempted coup by the insurgent populist-fascists, and critical arrests have been made. Abdullah Saadah, president of the PPS, has been captured and is in detention —"

"Where?" — a voice from the rear of the room.

"We are not giving out that information." Naddim Jabhour looked down at his notes.

"What will Dr. Saadah be charged with?" a woman's voice broke out.

Jabhour, an elderly and self-composed former academician was accustomed to unruly questions only from students, and answered with a touch of frost in his voice. "The penalty for participating in revolutionary activity is death. Next question?"

"What support does the PPS have from the Lebanese people?"

"Mr. Philby," said Jabhour, "the PPS has no support from the people. The PPS are fascist revanchists. Their idea of a Great Syria incorporating Syria, Lebanon, Jordan, and Iraq, goes further than irridentism it is neo-imperialism."

Tony stared at the man seated in the third row who had asked the question. He wore a tie and an unbuttoned pink shirt. Harold Adrian Russell Philby, at fifty-one, was not an old man. Tony had studied Philby's background with intensity. He was looking at a man born in 1912, at a face deeply tanned by the sun, visibly older than two years ago. A little of his excess weight showed up in a jowl he compressed with his chin, bending his head as he wrote on his notepad.

There were other questions for the press director. Press conferences in Lebanon had evolved into a cumbersome routine. First there was the "official" conference in the Parliament Building; followed a half hour later by successive press briefings at the British Embassy and fifteen minutes after that, by a press conference at the U.S. Embassy. Getting around for these was more easily accomplished by those reporters who had their own automobiles.

Most reporters in this part of the world, Tony quickly concluded, had cars as a matter of necessity. He was preparing to rise and get a bus when the Dutch reporter leaned across him to address the woman on Tony's right. "I'm going to skip the Brits and U.S. press sessions and drive to Tyre. Want to come?"

She shook her head.

Tony was not afraid to reveal his ignorance. He asked her what was it that made Tyre a place to go to?

"That's where the headquarters of the attempted coup was, in the Tyre garrison."

Tony didn't reveal that he didn't know where Tyre was. He learned that it was forty miles south of Beirut.

Pocketing his stenographic notepad he walked out. He knew where the two embassies were and knew the bus routes. It would require two bus rides to get to the British Embassy. He was relieved when an olive-skinned elderly woman, observing him at the bus stop, asked, "Do you want a ride to the embassies?" Tony gratefully accepted and learned in the ten-minute ride that she was a reporter from the *Cairo Times.* On turning the steering wheel right, into Rue Yamout, Beirut's embassy row, she added, "As long as I don't write anything that offends Colonel Nasser, I'm OK. If I do, I'll just be one more Egyptian refugee in Beirut."

Arriving at the long rectangular room used by the British Embassy for press conferences, Tony spotted Philby, already seated; again, in the third row. The seat next to him was empty—they were early. The information officer would wait until those traveling by bus arrived. Tony nodded his thanks to the woman from the *Cairo Times* and walked forward, taking the seat next to Philby.

Tony anticipated the need to take the initiative. He smiled, extended his hand, and said, "I'm Tony Crespi from AUB."

Philby turned his head and returned Tony's greeting with a half smile. "I'm Kim Philby. *Observer.* London."

Tony would exploit his relative ignorance, perhaps even expanding on it. "This is my first time out. I'm taking a course in Arabic that requires me to attend press conferences and write about them."

"You mean you're not being paid to be here?" Philby's voice expressed mock incredulity.

"No, sir. Actually, no. I'm being paid by ARAMCO."

Philby looked at him with interest. "Paid to do what?"

"To learn Arabic."

"Can you stay here for the rest of your life learning Arabic and bill it to ARAMCO?"

Tony laughed a little, as if to say that he enjoyed the caricature of his own situation. "Actually, I have one year. If I don't measure up, they send me home."

"To do what?"

"To tell you the truth, I'm not so sure. But I think I'll do OK at AUB."

"Why not. You're just a kid, it's easy to learn foreign languages."

"Actually, Mr. Philby, I'm not *that* young. I'm twenty-three. When you were twenty-three you were already active, in Austria, in a political movement."

Philby put down his steno pad. "What's going on? How is it you know that?"

"I interviewed you here two years ago to do a piece for my college newspaper."

Philby thought back. The young man who stood out, in the company of his traveling companions. The bright expression, the oval face and striking eyes and teeth. "Yes. I think I do remember. I don't remember that you ever sent me your article. Perhaps it was intercepted by the CIA."

Tony laughed. "I thought you and the CIA had zero connections anymore. At least, that's what I wrote."

"For whom? Remind me."

"For the *Yale Daily News*."

"Well, you're right. I don't keep track of the CIA. Probably they keep track of me. But if so, they're doing a good job—because I'm not aware of it. *You're* not by any chance working for CIA?"

"Not unless CIA owns ARAMCO."

The information officer up front cleared his throat, and the hubbub died down.

"Ladies and gentlemen, the British Information Office has nothing to add to the official Lebanese reports about the attempted coup..."

And so it went, for twenty minutes.

As the reporters rose, Philby turned to Tony.

"Would you care to dine with me?"

"Yes, sir—"

"Kim."

"I would really like that. When?"

"Tonight?"

Tony drew on intuition. If he said yes, that would suggest inordinate anxiety to be with Philby. That didn't fit in with the impression he wanted to give.

"Damn, not tonight. I've got a date. Any other night this week?"

"Call me. I don't carry cards. Do you want my telephone number?"

Tony wrote it down and extended his hand, his face engagingly animated.

Chapter Thirty-Three

Tony often took lunch at the AUB cafeteria and almost always shared a table with Gabriela Semenenko. After learning from Matti that Gabriela had been given the task of exploring Tony's background he started paying meticulous attention to what she said. He was now noticing questions she asked and remarks she made which earlier he'd have passed off as conversational banter.

"Were there any professors in particular at Yale that made an impression on you?" — that was one of her questions at lunch on Monday. Suppose he had replied, "Yes, Norman Holmes Pearson." Was Gabriela Semenenko supposed to know that Professor Pearson had been an important U.S. intelligence official during the war? And that after the war, Professor Pearson had helped to recruit promising students for careers in the CIA?

He resolved to bear down on exactly that subject. At lunch the next day he said, "You were asking yesterday, Gabriela, about my professors at Yale. But are you aware of *any* professors at Yale?"

Her answer was wary. "Well, there are some famous professors at Yale."

"I know there are famous professors at Yale, Gabriela. But I don't think you know who they are. Why should you?"

If she had had a design in asking the question about professors, she now retreated. "Oh, I would not have expected to recognize their names. I just like to hear people describe special professors. The way I take pleasure in hearing about, oh — Ihsam Faour or Samir Tarraf or — especially — Adnan Youssef at the University of Cairo. I have, of course, read their work but I have never met them and I like it very much when students here who have studied with them talk about them."

Tony decided to give her the juiciest bait he could. "Do you recognize the name of Professor Norman Holmes Pearson? I studied English with him." He eyed her closely.

"No. I do not know his name." And then, "At Georgetown, did you have any interesting professors?"

It was the same thing all over again. His answer was dismissive. But also he had the opportunity to plant the little tattoo. "Gabriela, when you are at Georgetown the way I was, you are there to study the Arabic alphabet. Nobody who teaches that to you is famous, though one of them did commit suicide."

She accepted this, but her curiosity was persistent. Her mission, he reasoned, was obviously to accumulate material to give over to Matti — who had his own reasons to want to know what a persistent questioner could get out from this freshly arrived student about his past, his tastes, his interests. And of course one object of the exercise was to be alert to whether the material she gathered went elsewhere than merely to Matti.

He turned the conversation to local figures of interest. "I spoke with Kim Philby yesterday." Again he watched her face carefully for reaction to that word.

"Well, of course. Kim Philby is a well-known figure in Beirut. I take it you know of his background?"

"Oh yes. When I was here two years ago with the student group there was a joint interview. We were told by our guide that Philby was a bright and incisive expert on this part of the world, and the Lebanese folder we were given to read had two pieces on the Near East by Philby, taken from the *Economist*. But I knew also about his career with British intelligence — they call it MI6 — so for an article for the college newspaper I wrote about Philby."

"The whole business about his friendship with Maclean and Burgess? That chapter in Philby's life?"

"Oh sure. I mean, it was pretty dramatic back then. Philby was yanked out of Washington — you can find accounts of that in a 1951 story in the *New York Times*. And remember, those were the golden years of McCarthyism. And besides, the discussions about Philby's loyalty went on. Harold Macmillan gave a speech to the Commons in 1955. Do you know about that?"

"Oh yes. It got big notice here. A year after that speech Philby arrived on the scene as full-time correspondent for the *Observer*."

"Macmillan said nothing had been proved against Kim Philby, that there was no record of him having betrayed Western secrets. Did that disappoint you, dear Gabriela?" Tony continued in his teasing tone, "When Philby arrived, did your father attempt to get him back to work for you?"

Gabriela flushed. "I don't think it's . . . fair, what you say. My father is not KGB. He is a professional diplomat. He was not engaged in recruiting for British spies. Besides, we've known ever since the Macmillan speech that Philby never was a spy."

"I'm going to have dinner with him tonight."

Gabriela began to say something, thought better of it, drew a lipstick from her purse and applied it with some deliberation.

"That's nice," she said. "Well, I have to get back to work."

Tony got up. Carrying his emptied lunch tray to the conveyor railing that led back to the kitchen, he smiled at her. "I'll pop around tomorrow, or give you a buzz."

"Please do." Her attention was apparently elsewhere.

Chapter Thirty-Four

"Let's eat at the Cloche d'Or. I like that. But maybe that's too expensive for a mere ARAMCO trainee. I, on the other hand, can go there and charge it as expenses to the *Observer*."

"I can handle the bill for one night; thanks for worrying about it."

"I'll take you as my guest and put you on the expense account. But to justify that, I'll have to interrogate you."

Tony reacted quickly. "You'll have to buy a very expensive meal to get out of me all the secrets I have about ARAMCO."

"I'll be there at eight-thirty."

Tony Crespi arrived at 8:20. The Cloche d'Or was a medium-sized restaurant that evolved into something like a nightclub as the evening wore on. At first there was just the rebab, the Middle Eastern violin, under the light at one side of the small stage. What gave the sense that headier things were to come was the spotlight that shone narrowly on the musician. It changed its colors but managed never to reveal in any detail the face of the player, dressed in his white aba. The effect was to encourage a sense of mystery, and of mysteries to come. Tony could make out to the right, onstage, an upright piano, a black cover hung over it and, to the side, a set of drums and cymbals.

Tony had given Philby's name and was led to a banquette. He eased himself behind its thin table, already prepared with its dinner settings. He would be sitting with Philby side by side, not opposite. The design was to permit a view of the stage. A second banquette tier, with its dull-ivory velvet cover, angled off toward the restaurant's center. Behind it was a busy bartender working, again, in soft lighting, shaded red. Tony let his eyes accustom themselves to the light and distracted himself by looking at the menu. It was written in Arabic and in French. His work had made him fluent in Arab names of foods and dishes. He was exercising by contrasting the French and the Arab descriptions of the menu when Philby suddenly materialized alongside.

"Evening, Crespi. Have you ordered a drink?"

Tony had not. But instantly he intuited that Philby had had a drink before arriving.

"Good evening, . . . Kim. No, I'm behind. I'll settle for the Chablis they have down there on the menu."

"I suppose you have tried arak? Native stuff, granted, but surprisingly potable. I will have one and I will order one for you, and if you do not like it I will drink it. I will also order a bottle of Chablis."

He beckoned to the waiter and gave his order.

"Well now. If I remember correctly, you were going to divulge to me the secrets of ARAMCO."

Tony laughed. "You know, what you say is especially provocative. If I make out at AUB, probably pretty soon after that I'll know some ARAMCO secrets that really *are* valuable."

"Like where they are going to route the ancillary pipelines?"

"Oh dear. You're already over my head. I didn't know —"

"Try the drink," Philby interrupted.

Tony looked down at the amber liquid in the squat glass. He

raised it to his lips. He felt the scorch of the arak but it was protected by a sweet envelope and he discerned immediate and agreeable compliance by his stomach.

"Very interesting." He looked up at Philby.

"I'm glad you like it. Though also sorry in a way. If you didn't drink it I would have. I'll just have to order another one."

He motioned to the waiter.

Two hours later Philby had drunk a great deal. He had gone from the arak to wine, which he drank copiously during dinner, before ordering the cognac. He spoke of the recent attempt by the Parti Populaire Syrien to stage a coup d'état. "I know Abdullah Saadah, know him pretty well. Did you see my piece in the *Observer* a month ago? I said that Saadah was not a Fabian, willing to wait two or three generations for his Great Syria to emerge. His temperament is Bolshevik. Get the damn thing done."

"Yes. But it didn't work. Will he hang?"

"Oh yes. Summary justice."

Tony decided to take the opportunity to orient the conversation. He turned the rudder ever so slightly in the direction he was, after all, in Beirut to explore. "Are you saying executions are wrong?"

"Depends w-who's being executed." Philby smiled with satisfaction at his crack, sipped again on the cognac, and put a fork into his dessert.

Crespi didn't let go. "This—Abdullah Saldi—"

"Saadah. *S-a-a-d-a-h*. Born in Baalbek, Lebanon, fought the French, then the Germans, then the Israelis. But he managed, while young, to take the full course in political science at Cairo—"

"Sorry. Abdullah Saadah was spoken of as a 'fascist' by the ministry on Monday, at the press conference. I don't get it. He just seems like an empire-builder type."

"Dear T-Tony"—Philby warmed to the conversation—"'fascist' is quite simply a word of disapprobation. The Communists, you surely have noticed, refer to anyone who disagrees with any ... any hemidemisemiquaver in the Communist line as a fascist. Or a proto-fascist. Or a neo-fascist. This has nothing whatever to do with the political disciplines practiced by Mussolini."

Philby was now slurring his words. Tony had taken a convivial part in the drinking but was certain he had practiced control enough to know exactly what he was doing. And he had decided he would have to approach Philby with some directness. He would use idiomatic language to encourage spontaneity. "What do the fucking Communists think they can gain by calling everybody a fascist?"

"What do the fucking Communists think they can gain? They think they can gain the whole world."

Philby had barely finished the sentence when the commotion began. Later, much later, Tony struggled to put in order what seemed to have happened all but simultaneously.

The tall corpulent Arab with the huge arms was drunk and was returning, with difficulty keeping his balance, to his seat. Making way for another guest coming down the narrow passageway, he bumped against Philby's table sharply, collapsing it into the diners. The wine, the cutlery, the chocolate mousse, the water glasses were on the laps of Philby and Tony. They sprang to their feet. Philby muttered a word in Arabic Tony did not make out. The offended Arab turned and leveled a body blow to Philby's stomach. Tony thrust his leg between the legs of the Arab, shoved one fist into his neck and doubled back the other leg, toppling the Arab to the ground. The orchestra stopped playing. Intense lighting was switched on. A companion of the stricken Arab approached Tony, his right hand disappearing into his aba, as if for a weapon. Somebody somewhere gave a signal and two immense bodyguards descended on the scene. One of them kicked Tony in the crotch. He lay gasping with pain across the body of Kim Philby. Suddenly the police were there. Philby and Tony and the large Arab were in a paddy wagon traveling down cobbled streets.

The Arab stared at Tony and uttered what Tony assumed were

maledictions. Tony had only barely recovered the ability to speak in even tones. He heard Philby say, "The drunk bastard is doubting your mother's credentials."

Philby, his white jacket and shirt sodden with chocolate, his tie wrenched almost to his shoulder, had recovered his poise. "It is an Arabic word he has directed at you. There is no known translation."

Tony still managed to say, "Just so he didn't call me a fascist."

Chapter Thirty-Five

Tony Crespi looked forward hungrily to letters from home. For all that Beirut was a cosmopolitan city, which it certainly was, it was also an alien city, exotic — un-American, if the term can be used to remark contrasts. Tony had never before lived away from his adopted country, the exception being his trip with the ASU. His manners were urbane, his reading informed. And he was not resentful about being here. His deeply felt commitment to the anti-Soviet cause had reoriented him from academic concern for political science to active concern to reject an insidious political ideology. He was not restless, though he let himself wonder, from time to time, where he would be sent after the current mission was completed. Somewhere else in the Near East, he assumed, given the time he was spending on Arabic and in learning about the regional culture.

His mother wrote punctually, once every week. Wrote in Italian, as ever. She was inquiring and affectionate and told of developments in his stepfather's life, the problem there being that there were no developments in Lester Crespi's life, other than his

increasing activity in the local John Birch Society. "Your father" —
Maria always spoke of her husband as Tony's "father"; indeed Tony
hadn't known that Lester Crespi was other than his own father
until the real story was told him when he was twelve — "Your father
is very pleased that Mr. Allen Bradley has become a member of the
national board!"

Tony had tactfully avoided any discussion of the John Birch Society with his stepfather. He had read the two semi-secret books
written by the founder, Robert Welch. He was moved by the
founder's passion to prosecute the counterwar against the Soviet
colossus but entirely rejected the Society's operative assumption,
which was that the country's problems were owing to divided loy-
alties in Western leaders. He found especially alarming, at first —
then, amusing — that Mr. Welch had named President Eisenhower
as a covert Communist sympathizer.

He so very much wished it were possible to receive a letter from
Mr. Angleton. Tony Crespi felt a special warmth for his former
landlord and current overseer. He remembered mentioning the
John Birch Society in one freewheeling discussion in those last
days.

"Those people don't know what the situation really is," Angleton
said about Robert Welch and his associates. "But I'll say this for
them, their instincts are good. We wouldn't be so screwed up except that our leaders sometimes permit screwups to happen." Angleton's most interesting point, Tony thought, was that if any
normal, educated, well-nourished person could be a traitor, why
could that not be true of another, apparently normal person?
"What was it about Burgess? About Maclean? About Mitchell and
Martin? What happened to them that couldn't — didn't" — Angleton had pointed at Tony, who flinched — "happen to you? That's
one of the reasons why the search goes on for the Fifth Man. If you
use conventional figures, that means Burgess and Maclean and
Cairncross and — *their* accounting, remember — Philby. But there
must be someone else, because our secrets continue to drip out,

giving information from very high reaches of secrecy. The Fifth Man doesn't mean that he had to have gone to Cambridge, or been a fellow—or compatriot—of Burgess and Maclean. But it does mean this, that he has attained their level of infiltration in Western councils."

A good question, Tony thought. Did it happen that he, Tony, inherited the passionate political blood of his father, Emilio Valerio? He had given his life to resisting Mussolini. And what sweet vengeance he had, firing the bullet into the dictator's head. Imagine — he imagined—a historical turn of events that would put Tony, Emilio's son—Antonio Garibaldi Valerio—standing, pistol in hand, opposite Khrushchev, the leader's back against the wall, wrists behind his back, Tony raising his own gun and giving instructions to his firing squad: "*Pronto. Attento. Spari!!*" Tony fantasized that one day he'd find himself ending Khrushchev's life head to head.

The letter the next day was from Melinda Carrothers. As usual, one typewritten, singled-spaced page, leaving not a sliver of margin on top, at the bottom, on the right or on the left. When he first received one of these, his first week at AUB, he wondered how Melinda contrived to come to the dead end of her message exactly at the end of the page, leaving room only to squeeze in by hand, "Love, M." "If you were composing a sonnet," he commented in frustration, "I'd understand the discipline of stopping at the end of the fourteenth line. But now I've had four letters from you and the funny thing about it is that when you get down near the end you don't seem to be in a hurry. The reader isn't expecting you to slide into the telegraphic mode ('Last night S. came over, said he was through/through with Kitty. Permanent? W/knows.') Your thoughts continue at a leisurely gait and then they just ... happen to end, at the bottom of the page.

"But I promise to cut it out. I love your letters just as they are."

The current letter spoke of her progress at the Foreign Service School, Tony *must* meet Professor Emerson Haight as soon as he got back to Washington, he was the most colorful history teacher she had ever listened to. Grades had been handed in the week before and Melinda had gotten all As except for one C — "that was in Middle East studies, so you'll have plenty to do to catch me up when you get back." At Union Station she had spotted "our former landlord, James Angleton, carrying a briefcase, heading I don't know where, but heading there with great purpose. And anyway, I wouldn't have spoken to him, as per instructions when you were boarding there." Tony knew immediately: He'd have to destroy this letter. Nothing could be in his possession that mentioned that august name.

You can put a lot of words on a tightly typed page, and Tony felt that he had got from her a full and certainly indignant account of President Kennedy's speech to the ransomed Cuban freedom fighters, returned now to Miami eighteen months after their humiliating failure at the Bay of Pigs. Melinda had managed to underline the sentence in the Kennedy speech that especially offended her: "'*I can assure you that this flag will be returned to this brigade in a free Havana.*' What a hypocrite JFK is! In October he pledges to Khrushchev he will not invade Cuba. In December he is promising a free Cuba."

That word closed her letter. Tony wondered how she'd have handled it if Kennedy had said... "returned to this brigade in a free Cuba — in your lifetime." No room for those three extra words on Melinda's letter. Or in Kennedy's mind, Tony thought.

He put the letter down. He was feeling a little disloyal to Melinda, with his near-weekly nights with Gabriela, fully consummated nights, not to be confused with sharing a *schawarma* sandwich with her at the AUB refectory, which he did two times a week, sometimes three.

He could not help it — his mind fastened on comparative pleasures. The hour with M. compared with the hour with G. Melinda was still the college senior, affecting experience; beautiful, eager, aggressive, dominating. She probably read how-to books. If so, she had certainly mastered them. And she had given him reason to suspect, those last months in Georgetown, that she had developed ecumenical habits; certainly she was not taming her appetites pending his return to Washington. She was inexpert, but more than willing, as he knew. Not that he was himself affecting the savoir faire of Don Juan, Tony insisted on reminding himself. But he had, as his contemporaries put it, "been around." Jack, his roommate at Yale's Silliman College, had added, "and around the world." Well, Tony said to himself, Antonio Garibaldi Valerio Crespi, you have an Italian father and an Italian mother, why should you *not* be naturally . . . expressive?

Gabriela was really quite different. Both were equally nourishing, Tony reflected. But Gabriela approached the great moment differently every time, her use of her mouth was transfixing, the mouth and the hands operating in total synchronization, bringing on an agony of pleasure—and then she would stop him cold, nibble fiercely at his nipples and soon, just in time, return to advance another stride up the mountain. When he reached its top what came after was rapturous. There was nothing more to see, nothing more to experience; the whole of it to be remembered, indelibly.

And he felt a whole other attachment gestating. Is this what happens when on the way to knowing that you are falling in love? Observing her at the library desk, fingering her food delicately at the refectory, leaning over to close the shade in the bedroom, profiling her breast against the falling light, stimulating in him not only lust but possessiveness. He loved her. Yes. Had he ever loved more? He went to sleep trying to answer that question.

It was time, nearing 9:30 in the morning, to catch the half-hour AUB bus into downtown Beirut. He wondered whether, after his ordeal the evening before, Philby would still be doing press-conference duty.

He was. He motioned to Tony to come down to where he sat. Philby had reserved the seat on his left.

Tony sat down.

"That was a hell of a night," Philby said.

"You have a good way with the police." Tony grimaced, then smiled.

"And you, with Arab aggressors."

They had a bond now, the two men.

Chapter Thirty-Six

December, 1962

The DCI called Angleton and two principal aides into his office. The missiles the U.S. had embedded in Turkey would, pursuant to the agreement with Khrushchev, have to be removed. Moreover, removed under the scrutiny of Soviet monitors. Easily enough done at a command level—the Commander in Chief would simply hand down the order: *Remove the missiles.* But doing so satisfactorily required coordination with CIA contacts in Turkey. Men charged with intimate levels of supervision of the missile sites and personnel, three men who answered not to the Turkish government, but to our own.

"You're taking care of that, right, Ray?"

Raymond Rocca nodded his head.

"Now, we can go to the big news, Jim. What are you doing on the Blake front?"

George Blake had been sentenced, that day in London, to forty-two years in prison. The longest sentence ever given in British penology. McCone's lips tightened as he scanned the dispatch. "Here. Here is what the judge—Lord Parker—said about what Blake had done. A good summary, I'm afraid you'll have reason to believe." He found himself injecting a whiff of British flavor in the sound of the words. "'Your full written confession reveals'—he is addressing the prisoner—'that for some years you have been working continuously as an agent and spy for a foreign power. Moreover, the information communicated, though not of a scientific nature, was clearly of the utmost importance to that power and has rendered much of this country's efforts to protect vital national interests completely useless.'"

There was silence in the room. Four men charged with protecting the nation's secrets and ferreting out those of the enemy had just heard it said that "much" of the UK's efforts to safeguard their work had been useless.

To Hugo Esterhazy, that evening, Angleton said that hearing those words spoken was to be compared to a scientist's learning that the research he had done for the past ten years was useless.

McCone wanted to know what would be done to learn from Blake's experience and to weigh the damage he had done.

Angleton puffed on his cigarette. "I'm going over to London, look after that myself."

"Did we have a bead on him?"

"He fitted a profile Golitsyn gave us three months ago. We sent that material over to MI5—to SIS. To Nick Elliott."

"Do you have from the Brits everything they got on Blake? Or that they hope to get from Blake?"

"Yes to the former, no to the latter. A prison sentence of forty-two years says to me he's still got something MI5 wants. They nailed him on a single lead—from a Polish Soviet agent behind bars in Berlin—plus a massive accumulation of circumstance. Four people knew about Operation Gold, which was betrayed; one of them was Blake. Six people knew about the East German circuit breaker. One of them was Blake. Three people knew the secret address of the key East German defector. One of them was Blake. After a while plausibility loomed, and then we got the word from the Pole."

"When did the Brits decide to move?

"Six weeks ago."

"Where was Blake?

"Studying Arabic."

"Where?"

"Lebanon."

McCone read more of the dispatch, to himself, thinking: The MI6 people add it up to forty-two Western agents blown by Blake, most of them executed. Says here he knew Burgess. And ... he studied in Cambridge. "Did he go to Cambridge with the other people? Did he know the other people at all?"

Angleton spoke weightily. "It is established that he knew Philby."

"Well, I don't suppose that's anything new. Every traitor I can think of knew Philby."

Angleton made no comment.

"When you getting back, Jim?"

"Depends on how useful the material is over there. I might have to go back again in a few weeks; depends on Blake. And other things. Thank God for the jet airplane.... John, this guy Blake is bad stuff. But he's not the Fifth Man."

"I never suggested he was. But remember, Jim, it's you who insist there is such a creature.... And yes, I agree. They've made travel a little easier in the last couple of years. Thank God."

Bob Matti received his instructions and flew to London.

"Do you know anything about the Middle East College for Arabic Studies?" Angleton wanted to know.

"Yes. It's in Shemlan, nice little town. In the mountains outside Beirut. Are you going to tell me something interesting has happened in Shemlan?"

"Yes. George Blake was there with his wife and children."

"Studying Arabic?"

"Apparently."

"According to the *Economist* he already knows Russian, Korean, German, and French."

"So he learns languages easily. The SIS tells me they don't know about any contacts he might have made there in Shemlan. But it would be a good idea to send Crespi out there, look in fraternally on the people who tutored Blake. Just look around—an obvious place for Crespi to visit... Has he been useful on the girl, the Gabriela woman?"

"He's gotten very close. He's sleeping with her."

"Devotion to duty."

"He thinks she's on the level with us."

"But she might also be on the level with the Russians."

"She is certainly on the level with Philby."

Angleton looked up. "She's also sleeping with Philby?"

"Yes. Our gal Gabriela is a cosmopolitan lady."

"You saying she's a whore?"

"No. Something less than that."

"If she's sleeping with Philby, I assume you've pressed that button on her."

"Yes, but very cautiously. We don't want Philby telling Moscow—," Matti interrupted himself. He remembered Angleton's persistent doubts about the disloyalty of Kim Philby. "We don't want Philby acting in any way that has the effect of withdrawing Gabriela's working visa. After all, she's a Russian citizen, and Russia has to approve her staying here to work."

"You got her that visa in the first place, didn't you? It *was* you, wasn't it, Bob?"

"Yes. On your instructions."

Angleton changed the focus. "Is Tony doing OK?"

"Yes, he even got into a bar fight with Philby."

"He fought with Philby?" Angleton's voice was sharp.

"No. He fought alongside Philby, against some Arab drunk, no sweat."

"Well," said Angleton, lighting another cigarette, "these things take a lot of time. Blake was working for the KGB since what was it, 1953? Took eight years to trip him up. But... those are individual enterprises. We need to know more about the general picture. Specifically, more about the failed coup in Tyre."

"The arms came in from Syria. And the Syrians got them from the Soviet Union. We don't know whether the PPS president had any direct ties with the Syrians or whether the Soviets ran the whole operation."

Angleton pushed his chair back from the table. "Let's get some lunch. Roger Hollis will be waiting for us at the Tipperary."

"I'm surprised Hollis hasn't been — 'sent down,' they call it. It took him forever to catch on to Blake. And last year it was the Portland navy people he had let get by. And then Conon Molody, operating four years —"

"Six years —"

"— as a Canadian businessman. It's a long list of traitors working on his beat. Lona and Morris Cohen, the Krogers. And Henry Houghton and Ethel Gee. Molody was caught red-handed, as I remember."

"Conon Molody," said James Angleton in the voice of a sentencing judge, "was arrested carrying a shopping bag full of top-secret naval plans, including the plans for the Brits' first atomic submarine."

"That's what I call being caught red-handed," Bob Matti confirmed.

Chapter Thirty-Seven

Gabriela Semenenko had other male friends. Not many; she was choosy, which trimmed the clientele at the seller's end; and expensive, which tamed the list at the buyers' end. Only a select few would feel free simply to walk up to her apartment with her in plain sight, hand in hand, coming in after a dinner or a party. Kim Philby, for all that he was open and self-confident in manner, preferred a little formal discretion when visiting at Abdanal Nasir Towers. Accordingly, the date having been arranged, she left the Normandy restaurant at 10:30. He left with her and bade her good night at the front entrance to the apartment-house door. He lit a cigarette and walked around the block, giving attentive appreciation to the radiant moon under which the sparkling city with its multicolored lights throbbed. He felt the start of his passion pressing.

He followed the usual routine, using the rear entrance with the tenants' key, climbing a flight of stairs to avoid being seen in the lobby, and getting into the elevator on the second floor. He got out on the fourth floor. The hallway was attractively lighted, well enough to see, not well enough to encourage loitering.

Philby was accustomed to the endemic fragrance of "Araby." He hummed, "Well, I'm the Sheik of A-ra-BEE / Your love belongs to ME," and inhaled the understated, musky sweetness of—well, of Ara-bee! Why not?

The lightest knock brought Gabriela to the door. She had had to draw the curtain halfway, to give the rooms shelter from an aggressive moon. He hung his linen jacket on the back of the door, accepted the liqueur and a slow preliminary kiss, and went to the sofa opposite the bed, where he liked to sit while Gabriela disrobed.

"You have cut too much of the moon out, Gabriela."

"You think so? Well then reach behind you and open the curtain as much as you wish. Don't worry. There's isn't a mirror there that will force you to look into your old face—"

"*Vous vous moquez de moi*—you're making fun of me." He laughed, downing his arak. "I'm the youngest fifty-year-old in Ara-bee. And in bed, I am not yet eighteen."

She refilled his glass. She was now naked. Gabriela stroked his hair. He kept her standing until he had removed his trousers, then brought her to sit on his lap, put the glass to one side, and quietly stroked her soft and malleable vulva. With his left hand he readjusted the curtain slightly. He had the moonlight now just right, sending its mother of pearl down between Gabriela's breasts.

They made love silently and he lifted her then to the bed, where she stretched out, he over her. After a period she squeaked.

"Kim! The moon has moved! It is staring at us again!"

He rose, amused, walking over to the curtain. She was seeing his back, profiled against the moon, and then as he swiveled his body with the curtain, she saw the placid remains of his ardor. She knew that it was safe to light the tiny little protected night-light at her bedside. She now spotted her nightgown, grabbed it, and went for the carafe, to refill the glasses.

"I'd like a beer."

"Of course."

"And a cigarette."

"Do you want your own, or mine?"

"I'll take yours. Light it for me."

Philby drew up his shorts and moved to the half-lit sitting room, perching down on the green-felt card table, used by Gabriela as a dining table. He drew on the beer.

"Let me see your stomach in the light."

He stood and lowered slightly his underpants. "The big wog landed his punch right there. And it's still plenty sore."

"Yes, Tony told me he landed a very solid punch."

"You heard about it from Tony Crespi? Ah. Is that what you were talking about at lunch today at the Hirondelle?"

"I often lunch with Tony. You say he struck a good blow?"

"Tony is a pretty fast man on his feet."

"Tell me. What exactly did he do?"

"He maneuvered his legs, grabbed him by the neck and collapsed him like a building wrecker. I watched him with some curiosity. There was an element of professional finesse about it."

"Maybe he took wrestling or something in college."

"That's not exactly what they teach you in wrestling. More like judo, what he did. I don't know anything about his background, except that he went to Yale and is studying for ARAMCO." He sipped on his beer. "What do you know?"

"Not very much; he doesn't talk so much about his family, who live in Milwaukee. His father was killed fighting in the Resistance toward the end of the war, killed in Milan. He is adopted by a stepfather."

"How's his Arabic?"

"Very good." Gabriela intended a genuine tribute. "He works hard, takes every opportunity to use his Arabic. He got good training at Georgetown, though maybe he was held up"—Gabriela smiled as she reached for the ashtray—"when one of his teachers committed suicide."

"What else did he do, in Washington, besides drive his teachers to suicide?"

"He had a girlfriend."

"How do you know?"

"At lunch — we lunch often, you know — "

"Is that all you do 'often' with him?"

She affected indignation and shock, then smiled, then resumed her narrative. "At lunch he brings his letters, when he has letters. The post office is just the other side of the refectory."

"And you offer to mail them for him?"

"Well, why not! You make that sound like a sexual act of aggression. The library has its own office, so I just mail them there."

"And that's how you discovered about his girlfriend?"

"It isn't a big deal to look at the names of addressees."

"There is a lady in Washington?"

"Yes. Her name is Melinda Carrothers."

"And another girlfriend in New Haven? Milwaukee?"

"Milwaukee. Yes. In fact he has talked to me about his Milwaukee girlfriend. She is Maria Crespi."

"Ah, dear Gabriela. You become coy. You do not need to tease me about Tony's writing to his mother. Now let us turn on the television. They will be announcing at any hour the sentences today on the PPS people."

"Yes, I know." Gabriela's tone of voice had changed sharply.

Philby played with the dial. The omnipresent Nina Makdisi came on. She was giving the sports scores but interrupted herself. The military justices would be pronouncing sentences on the revolutionists, she said.

They watched together, in silence, as the names and sentences were read out. Fifty-one persons sentenced to death. Seventeen to life in prison. Seventy-six Lebanese, tried in absentia, received varying jail sentences. Twenty of them were sentenced to death.

Among those sentenced to die was Abdullah Saadah, the president of PPS. He and three other rebel leaders, Captains Shawki Khairallah, Fuad Awad, and Ali El Haj Hassen.

Philby clicked off the set.

"It will be a heyday for the executioners."

Gabriela spoke tersely. "I know Abdullah Saadah."

"Well, you will soon have one less customer."

She slapped him in the face, walked into the bedroom, shut and locked the door noisily.

Chapter Thirty-Eight

She had expected a body search before being led into the solitary detention quarters. This was the death house. She was there to visit Abdullah, who along with fifty of his subordinates, had been sentenced on Friday to hang. The case had gone automatically on appeal.

The government had been embarrassed by the escape of Fuad Awad two months before, a young captain in Abdullah Saadah's organization. That was just weeks before the attempted coup. No chances were now going to be taken, Gabriela was made to know, when the matron leaned her over, raised her skirt, and proceeded with a strip search. No prisoner would escape from Bhamdoun.

Seeking an appropriate basket of surprises to take to a prisoner, Gabriela thought back to the list her mother had sent her of desirable and scarce supplies at her own rehabilitation camp at Katyla, which family friends in Kiev attempted to supply her with. Gabriela's impulse was to duplicate that list exactly and take it to Abdullah in the shopping bag, its exact permissible size specified in the prison pass. But the demands of a working prisoner in gulag were very different, she paused to reflect, from those of a prisoner in a Lebanese jail. In gulag one might desperately want coffee, hard bread, and tobacco. In Beirut a prisoner would probably have as much coffee and bread as he wanted. His needs would shade over into delicacies. So she brought four pounds of chocolates, and a fruitcake, a jar of pine nuts and raisins, six ballpoint pens, and two large pads of notepaper.

The examining guard cut the cake in half, then placed it and the other goods in the X-ray cabinet. When its doors were open, the X rays automatically turned off. After the material to be inspected was put on the closet tray, the switch was turned on, activating the radiographic instrument.

The corporal found nothing to complain about but, for good measure, drew a knife across the fruitcake. He might, Madame Najm, the library head, had told her in a whisper, be looking out for a packet of poison. That is very easy to hide, Gabriela conceded, a few grains of poison.

The lieutenant came in. He reminded Gabriela that she was strictly limited to fifteen minutes, that her conversation would be audited, and that if she engaged in any forbidden exchange, the monthly visiting right she had applied for would lapse for a punitive period of an additional month.

The lieutenant was reading what he said from a prison script. He delivered the last line but then suddenly laughed uproariously. But he said nothing to explain the merriment.

She was led through the relatively neat and clean passageway, past heavy-duty cells, four prisoners sharing each cell; through the massive door to the single cells in which the most prized prisoners were guarded. She followed the guard, who stopped at the third door. He opened the lock, motioned her into the cell, and spat on the ground.

The Bhamdoun prison was only a few years old and the cell she was shown was not dingy. It was small, with a single bed and a toilet and a washbasin. On a hanger was one shirt and one pair of pants. They hung over a bookshelf. A square board served, presumably, as a writing desk and a table to put his tray on. There were no windows. A single fluorescent light illuminated the entire room.

Abdullah Saadah — Dr. Abdullah Saadah, the swashbuckling scholar so rapidly elevated to head of his young political party — had never grown a beard, at least not when her father introduced her to him as a rising young professor interested in political theory. In twenty evening meetings, designed by her father before his sudden recall to give the promising young leader an opportunity to learn Russian, she had exchanged with him much more than language training. She blessed her stars that they had had no written communication over the months he was hidden, the months of planning for the coup, she supposed. It was only three days ago that she received his appeal to come for a visit.

Now she saw him with a coarse mustache and a growth of beard at least three months old. He grasped her hand intensely. His agitation was complete. He said nothing until the door had closed.

He came to within an inch of her ear and in a whisper said: "Gabriela! *It is going to be at noon tomorrow!* The appeal has been denied. No ninety days. No nothing. They told me one-half hour ago —"

The lieutenant swung open the door. "The technicians says you are not talking loud enough. You, Abdullah, to that corner. You, Semenenko, you to this corner. Now when you talk to each other you will be talking so that we can hear what you say."

Abdullah's eyes showed desperation. He spotted the pads in the bag she had brought in. He reached quickly for one and one of the pens. He turned his back to the window of the cell door and spoke to her in a perfectly audible voice. Spoke meaningless sentences . . . pass his regards . . . mother . . . father . . . Rima . . . Rita . . . Saadah's attention was on the pad he was writing on.

The door swung open.

"Time!" the lieutenant said. And then — the concession. "You may embrace." It would be the final embrace, after all.

Abdullah clutched her. Their lips together, with his right hand he slipped the folded piece of paper into her sleeve.

Gabriela wept copiously and hugged him again and again until the lieutenant, finally, inserted his bayonet between them.

When she left the door, she was weeping, as was Abdullah Saadah.

Chapter Thirty-Nine

Gabriela left the prison gate in bewilderment and anxiety, and now it was dark outside. What was she to do? What *could* she do?

She needed to talk to someone. Someone in authority. AUB President Burns? No—she wasn't on close terms with the formal, reclusive president of her university. She walked along Rue Brazil until she came upon the restaurant, a dozen customers having their dinner outside, under the canopy. Where was the telephone? The waiter pointed.

She would try to get through to press official Naddim Jabhour. He had been a friend to her father and had once come to the apartment—her own apartment!—for dinner.

She knew the central government number. She dialed through. *Why did they take so long to answer?* It wasn't yet nine o'clock!

"Capitol, your request?"

The operator spoke in Arabic.

"I would like to speak with Monsieur Jabhour. Naddim Jabhour."

"That office is closed."

"This is an extreme emergency. Can you let me have his home telephone number?"

The line went dead. She took out another five-pound piece from her purse and dialed the number again.

"This is Mademoiselle Semenenko, from the American University. I just called, just now, and asked for the home telephone number of Naddim Jabhour."

"We don't give out home telephone numbers."

This time Gabriela hung up.

She would call the Associated Press! She warded off a young man who wanted to use the telephone. He was in Western dress. She spoke to him in English. "You will have to wait. This is a matter of life and death."

She found the number. A man answered.

Thank God, thank God. She recognized his voice. "Mr. Brewer! This is Gabriela. Gabriela Semenenko. Library, AUB."

"How you doing, Gabriela?"

"I need to know..."—her voice trembled—"I need to know about Abdullah Saadah. I have just been—I am wondering—I heard—"

"Abdullah Saadah is going to swing tomorrow, at high noon."

"What happened on his appeal?"

"Obviously the Big Man—President Chehab—decided to hell with the appeal. Very unusual. You know something special about Saadah?"

"I've just been with him at Bhamdoun."

"Gabriela. *Where are you?* I want to talk to you right away. I can come in a car to any place you want. Exactly where *are* you?"

Gabriela blurted out. "I will call you."

She hung up on Sam Brewer.

She yielded the telephone to the young man and sat down at a table. What would she do?

The waiter approached her.

She would have coffee.

He brought it. She opened her purse to pay him and noticed the paper she had secreted as she left Abdullah's cell. She got up, left the coffee, and sat down again at a table nearer to the light.

The message had been scrawled in English.

"Philby. Tell Colonel xxxx X"—Abdullah had started to write out the colonel's name, but then thought better of it, running the ink over the letters he had written. The scrawl continued—"our people still on location. V. strong. But need OK to resume, plus fresh supplies. The rev. will succeed, Comrade. Farewell."

She struggled to understand.

She went back to the telephone. Philby's telephone didn't answer.

When, soon after midnight, Kim Philby returned to his apartment, Gabriela was sitting outside his door, Abdullah's note in her hand.

"I want to know what this means," she said simply.

Philby helped her up, opened the door with his key, and escorted her in. Gently, he pried open her hand and lifted the piece of paper from it.

Chapter Forty

"The colonel Abdullah mentioned—he is the key figure," Philby said, pensively. "I don't know exactly what he meant by... 'Colonel X' and the business about 'location.' When he wrote, 'The rev.'—presumably he meant to write 'The revolution will succeed.' He is clearly talking about the PPS revolution for a Greater Syria." He turned to Gabriela. She was listening intently.

"Quite obviously he thought of me—thinks of me—as a fellow revolutionary against the present government. 'Comrade'! Abdullah should not use such language loosely—"

"Abdullah has more to worry about than loose language." She spoke acidly.

"Of course. Of course, Gabriela." Philby's brow was furrowed. "Of course. He was thinking of me as a comrade in his attempted coup."

"Why?" She reached out and retrieved the note.

"I certainly gave him no reason to think that. I was acting as a journalist. I actually penetrated his headquarters. Did you read my piece in the *Observer*—about Abdullah—a month ago?"

Gabriela confessed she had not. "But—" Her tone was impatient.

"—Of course. But our concern is for what is to be done at this moment." Philby got up and stared thoughtfully at the bookcase. "What matters in Abdullah's communication, I repeat, is— Colonel X. I *do* know who he is. And"—he looked at his watch— "if I leave immediately I can be where he is at dawn."

"What can he do to save Abdullah?"

"That will be a matter for hard bargaining. What Colonel X *can* do is disclose where the PPS reserves of arms are hidden."

"Will you ask him to disclose, also, the names of hidden supporters?"

"I don't know Azzam—Colonel X—that well. But I would guess that he would rather himself be hanged than give out the name of a single hidden confederate."

"So it is: the arms in exchange for Abdullah's life or—or nothing?"

"No. If I can begin a negotiation with Chehab—more critically, with General Salibi—I am sure it was *he* who put the pressure on Chehab to execute Abdullah without delay. General Salibi doesn't easily forgive, and twenty of his soldiers were killed during the fighting. . . . If we can *entice* Salibi with the possibility of getting the PPS's arms depot, certainly he would—they would—postpone the execution."

Gabriela was losing control of herself. "Well goddamnit, Kim, why don't you go!"

"I will, Gabriela." Philby spoke calmly, but with reassuring resolution. "But whether I left five minutes ago or leave a half hour from now does not matter. Where Colonel X is—is not that far. There would be no point in my raising him from his sleep."

He motioned to Gabriela to get up.

"We will go together to the cars. You go home. I will go—to my destination. But I must travel with this." He opened the drawer under the bookcase and drew out an automatic, putting it into his pocket. "And I will need Abdullah's note."

Gabriela looked down at her purse. But she didn't open it. She clutched it to her bosom. "No no no. I will keep the note. You have all the information in it."

Philby spoke patiently but forcefully. "I will need that note. Otherwise how will they believe me?"

"Why would you make it up?" Again she paused. Then, decisively, "I will keep the note."

Philby managed a smile. And then said he would be leaving.

"Will you call me?"

"Of course."

Chapter Forty-One

Gabriela fell to sleep. At seven, her telephone rang. She remembered it all with a start... and rushed to the receiver.

"Kim?"

"No, Gabriela. This is Sam Brewer. I'm on campus, at the Union Building. I'm sorry about this but—this is my business, you know, and New York wants more on Saadah. Could I meet you at the dining hall? Or the library? Or the Union lounge? *Anywhere?*"

Gabriela paused. She should oblige Sam. He was critically situated and might be able, somehow, to help. But she could not leave her quarters. Not until Philby called. She would have to ask Sam Brewer to come to her apartment.

"Sam. I can't leave the phone. You can come in fifteen minutes and we can meet here. I'm at 41 Rue Khalidi."

She rushed to bathe and dress, walked into the sitting room, and turned on the little television set. There might be news. There was a knock on the door. She turned down the sound level, leaving only the image. She walked over to the door. "Come in, Sam."

He nodded and sat down. Sam Brewer was in his forties, middle-sized, gray-haired. He wore a tie, but it hung informally around his neck. He had been a foreign correspondent for many years, she remembered. She remembered also being impressed when hearing him, in fluent Arabic, question Colonel Nasser's new ambassador, who was meeting with the students at AUB and knew no English or French. He took his recording machine from his pocket.

"I don't want a recording."

"The radio people are very anxious—"

"I do not want a recording."

Brewer repocketed the unit and turned to his steno pad. "Can you tell me how come you were with Abdullah Saadah last night?"

"He was a friend of my father's and he sent a message, he would like a visit from me. Of course, I went. But..."—there were tears—"he didn't know the appeal had been canceled until just before I got there."

"How did he tell you? Or did the guards tell you?"

"No, it was Abdullah who told me. He was very... overwrought."

"How did he look?"

"He looked very... very ill-kempt. He hadn't shaved and he was thinner than the last time."

"When last did you see him?"

"In September."

"So you continued to see him even after your parents left town?"

Sam Brewer had obviously prepared for this meeting. She must proceed cautiously.

"I had absolutely nothing—*nothing*—to do with his political movement, with the PPS. We... diplomats... are taught to keep our hands very far away from the political affairs of our host countries."

"So you know nothing about where the PPS got its garrison of arms? There has been much speculation on that question."

"I told you, I know nothing about politics and he didn't mention politics."

"So your relations with him were purely personal?"

"Well, yes. We were friends."

Sam Brewer paused from his notebook to look up at her. Her

head was turned slightly to one side. Her eyes were avoiding his. Her large breasts appeared in profile.

"Did he say anything, express any hopes, give you any message?"

"No. No."

"Why did he ask you to visit him, if he had nothing to say to you?"

"We have to assume"—there was starch in her voice—"that he was lonely. I brought him a bag of various things."

"What did you bring?" Sam Brewer was back with his notebook.

"Oh God. Does that matter, Sam?"

"Readers like details." Sam paused. "Gabriela, have you ever been to an execution, here in Beirut?"

"No."

"Well let me warn you—"

"I am certain there will be a reprieve."

"I certainly hope so. But you should know"—he looked over at the television set—"to stay away. The prisoners are hanged in Martyrs' Square. Traditionally the executioners wear white hoods and a white—cassocks, I'd guess you'd call them. Abas. The prisoner is left swinging for—"

"Sam! Stop! Sam, please leave. I have given you everything you asked for . . . and I have to get ready for the museum tour."

"Of course," he said, getting up. "I'm very sorry, Gabriela. Let's hope there will be a reprieve."

She waited until eight to call her office. She told Madame Najm that she regretted she could not be at the library at 8:30. She was sick to her stomach.

The telephone did not ring until just after ten.

"Oh, Kim. Did you see him? What did he say? What is happening?"

"I have seen him. I have relayed a message to the Palace of Justice. The message will be seen by General Salibi — perhaps he has it as we speak. I have absolutely no doubt that it will result in a reprieve. Absolutely no doubt, even if it is at the last minute."

"Why do you have absolutely no doubt?"

"Because I think Colonel — my contact — is in a bargaining mood and I cannot imagine he would not want to explore the possibilities here."

"How will you know whether it works?"

"I have a contact... here. He will call me. I am driving back to Beirut. I must sleep, at least a half hour. But I will sleep on the sofa in my office. But, Gabriela, I must have the note Abdullah gave you. It is a part of the bargaining process. I have arranged for an aide near to you to pick it up. His name is Farid. He will be with you any minute. Now I must leave to go back. I will be in touch." He hung up.

Gabriela went back to her bedroom, where, the night before, she had in her exhaustion dropped everything on the couch.

She took up her purse and pulled out the page with Abdullah's message. She read it again. She closed her eyes. Now she had memorized it.

She heard the knock on the door.

She spoke through the door. "Who is it?"

"This is Farid, mademoiselle. I have come for the envelope. You can slip it under the door, if you prefer."

She said, "I do not have the paper you want."

There was a pause. "Can I come in, mademoiselle?"

"No. I am not... feeling well."

"It would be just for a minute."

"No."

"Can you tell me where I can get the paper? It is a matter of life and death."

Gabriela closed her eyes and recited to herself the content of Abdullah's note. *How could those words help Abdullah?* No. It was not a matter of the words Abdullah had written. Philby knew those words. He had carefully studied them last night.

It was the piece of paper they wanted.

Why? What was there that would save Abdullah?

She addressed the man through the door again.

"The paper is in safekeeping and not available"—why not use the word?—"to Mr. Philby. Now please go away."

She went to the window and looked down on the entrance. In a minute she saw emerge the man who must have been Farid. He was a slight man of middle age. He was dressed in native garb and wore black-rimmed glasses.

He stood outside the door, evidently considering alternatives. After a minute, he walked away.

Gabriela looked at her watch—10:45. She had a sense of what would happen. A telephone call from Philby. He would tell her that he absolutely had to have possession of Abdullah's message. She wasn't ready to face that. And there was nothing she, Gabriela Semenenko, could do to affect whatever communications were going on between the Colonel and General Salibi.

She drew an envelope from her desk and placed the message in it. She put on the trim blue dress she often wore when working, opened the door, went down the elevator to her parked car. Eight minutes later she drew up alongside the library.

She went to the Office of the Librarian and told Madame Najm that she was feeling better and would resume work at her regular desk.

In the library's main room she walked over to a shelf nearby. She pulled out a nineteenth-century history of an expedition up the Euphrates River, inserted the envelope in the book, and returned to her desk.

She sat there thinking. Running the events through her mind, again and again. She looked at her watch. It was 11:50. She dialed the Associated Press.

"Is Sam Brewer there?"

"No. Who's calling?"

"I'm a friend. Gabriela Semenenko."

"He's gone over to cover the execution."

"It is ... still scheduled?"

"Yes. They always go on the button with these things."

Again she thought.

Then she picked up the telephone and rang Tony.

Chapter Forty-Two

After the lunch with Tony, Gabriela, who had not touched her tuna dish, sipping only on the iced tea, returned to her office. She kept the museum-tour material in a special drawer. After every monthly tour she would write down her own discoveries and those of inquisitive students. She noted which exhibits especially interested the students, or especially bored them. Most of the dozen young people who went with her in the bus to explore, or re-explore, the National Museum were AUB students, but usually there was also a foreign archaeologist or historian happy to have guidance from a librarian at AUB who, in the three hours devoted to the trip, would know to take her flock to points of special interest.

When first deemed knowledgeable enough to conduct the tours, Gabriela had been instructed on exactly what to do by Madame Najm. The ground floor featured the gallery of Ramses with artifacts from Byblos and the gallery of Jupiter from Baalbek. A quick visit to the basement to see the sarcophagi and the hypogeum of Tyre. The first gallery on the next floor held the Gallery of the Alphabet, with its early stelae, inscribed stone slabs, representing various stages in the development of writing. And, finally, the south alcove, with its collection of stone figures and stelae from Byblos. Madame Najm had counseled a variation in the museum-tour drill. "They should be given a half hour at the end of the afternoon to pursue their own interests or to buy postcards — or to sit down and rest."

Gabriela remembered the pride her parents had felt that first time. The consul and Mrs. Semenenko didn't get on the bus at the campus. By prearrangement they were waiting for the AUB tour by the museum entrance, where tickets and postcards and souvenirs were sold. They had brought school tickets and simply filed in with the students, as though they were academicians and members of the party. They were proud of the poise, the thoroughness, and the learning of their daughter. Nadim Semenenko was especially taken by her daughter's extensive knowledge of the museum to which, as a girl, she had frequently been taken, before marrying the young Russian sailor after the throbbing romance, nine months before Gabriela was born.

Now there was a mix-up at the ticket counter. Gabriela had fourteen tickets, but there were fifteen students. The clerk undertook laboriously to work out the discrepancy. Frozen in the line, she listened — she had to listen — to the man with the mop handle, talking to the clerk at the souvenir counter. "I was smart to go fifteen minutes early to the Square. It was very, very full. I had to watch from fifty meters away. They had to lift the prisoner up to get the noose around his neck. He's hooded, you know."

"Yes," the clerk said, he knew that, and continued to demonstrate his knowledge of such things. "And the executioners, they wear hoods, too."

"Well, they got set up, finally, and then somebody read something."

"Read what?"

"I don't know. I couldn't hear. The television said he was a revolutionary." He motioned to his throat and stuck out his tongue. "So much for revolutionaries. I wonder what platform he wanted?"

The clerk feigned a stern face. "Maybe free tickets for everybody for the museum!" They both laughed. The ticket agent motioned Gabriela and her students through.

Gabriela needed to clear her throat several times. She forced her mind back to the work at hand. She was relieved that for the next two and a half hours she had necessarily to fix her attention on other matters than Beirut politics and prisons and death sentences. She would look at and describe objects millennia old, some of what they would see — some of the artifacts, some of the sculpture — dating to a thousand and more years before Christ.

By the time she and the students got back into the bus to return to the campus she was very tired. She nodded good-bye as the students filed past, and set out eagerly for the little lot by the museum where she parked her Fiat. She took time to bring down the convertible's soft top, in deference to the heat.

She drove sleepily down the Rue de Damas, across the Avenue de l'Independence, and up the little hill to the second of the apartment houses. She came out of the elevator and turned the key, opening the door to her rooms. She only just succeeded in suppressing the scream.

She groped her way past the sitting room. The bedroom was similarly convulsed. Not a square inch of the fifty square yards of space had been left untouched. Carpets overturned, books on the floor, their pages torn through, her clothes on the floor, the lithographs on the floor, torn from their frames. In the bedroom the pillows were emptied, the sheets shaken and left on the floor, the bedside drawers overturned.

She went to the bed and lay down on the mattress. It was an hour before she could bring herself to get up and go to the telephone.

"Tony, can you come?"

"You all right?"

"I'm all right. But please come."

He was there in ten minutes.

"Oh my God."

He looked about him, took a shopping bag from the closet and stuffed some items into it from the bathroom, and one of the shirts from the floor.

"Come with me."

She followed him unquestioningly. He led her to her car and took her keys from her.

He drove her back to the campus, to his own rooms, and told her to lie down on his bed. From his medicine closet he took a phenobarbital from the little bottle Melinda had pressed on him at the airport.

"This will make you sleep."

He told her he would be back in two hours.

He locked the door on the outside. Back in the car he raged at what was being done to the woman whom he knew now he had come to love, completely.

Chapter Forty-Three

In three hours Tony unlocked the door to his quarters; it was just before eight. He found Gabriela sitting in the armchair next to the desk, a book on her lap.

"I am much better." She looked up at him, her expression composed. "I have bathed. And I have read a little bit." She held up a copy of the Bible. "It helps to read Job."

"I'm glad. I am so glad." He leaned, kissed her, then stood up. "Now—I have a reservation at La Terasse D'barbo, my favorite unflashy restaurant. I am friends with the headwaiter and he promises the table at the other side of the headwaiter's desk. It's private."

"But I must get back to my apartment."

"We'll worry about that later. You need a little nourishment. So do I."

They were in the car in seconds. Tony stayed at the wheel. It was dark, but the glow of the city surrounded them. He looked over at her, only just discerning her features. He extended his right hand to the back of her neck. "Dear Gabriela, you must not despair. We will work it out."

At the busy restaurant, six native waiters with little identifying red sashes on their lapels moved about busily, carrying their large menus and catering to a clientele mostly Lebanese. Salim, tall and authoritative in manner, spotted Tony and led him to a small isolated table. He brought quickly, as requested, the carafe of white wine and poured two glasses.

Tony drank his quickly. He poured another glass from the carafe and looked up at her.

"All right, Gabriela. What in the hell is going on? I want it, and I want it in detail."

She brought the glass to her lips and held it there. She appeared to be pondering, pondering the terrible twenty-four hours since leaving the Bhamdoun prison.

Tony was right. It was the only way—tell him everything. She looked up at his handsome face, at the dark hair that laced his forehead, at the inquisitive eyes, the slightly parted lips, baring the teeth she had first noticed when he came to her in the spring to ask her advice about the curriculum. How blessed she was to have such a man, at such a time. At any time.

Tony's thoughts went fleetingly to Melinda. He'd have deserted his undergraduate fancy, he now thought it, for Gabriela. It was easier, having heard from her in her most recent one-page letter that she would be married "by the time you get this long note, lover boy."

"Well," Gabriela said, "to begin with, Abdullah Saadah was my lover..."

"Well," he said, much later, "at least one mystery is solved. They want Abdullah's message."

She nodded.

"I take it it wasn't anywhere in your apartment."

She nodded again.

"Where is it?"

"Do you have to know? Do you want to know?"

"I think I should know."

"It is in a book. *The History of Euphrates.* Near where I sit, near my desk."

"Are you certain that you are giving me the text exactly? You are quite certain you have it in your memory?"

"I will die knowing that text exactly."

She repeated it, word by word, and Tony wrote it down. He began to write on a fresh page and stopped. He put the notepad back and withdrew his address book. He wrote out the words she spoke between names and telephone numbers of family and friends. No one else could make the message out. *"Philby. Tell Colonel XXXX X our people still on location. V. strong. But need OK to resume plus fresh supplies. The rev. will succeed, Comrade. Farewell."*

Tony thought back to the press conference at which the question had been asked, "Who supplied the arms for the participants in the coup?"

The answer from Press Secretary Naddim Jabhour had been suspiciously emphatic: No foreign government, not Syria, not Israel, not Egypt, not Iraq had been involved. The arms had been collected by the traitors, he said. Stolen.

Tony was deeply anxious to pursue the question—with Bob Matti. But he saw no purpose in exploring it with Gabriela. The intruders had not found, even after their convulsive search in her apartment, the document they so much wanted. By now, he assumed, the prowler had got into her desk at the library. He would discuss with her, then, only her own welfare, not the politics of the crowded day's events.

"Philby never did call back?"

"I don't know. I left for our lunch, went to the museum tour, and was in the apartment only when I called you."

"Well, Philby didn't get his precious document. He is not likely to try anything he hasn't already tried. I have to assume there's something in the document that goes further than the words you gave me."

"What?"

"You told me Abullah had begun to write out the name of the colonel who has the provisions and then crossed it out, right?"

"Yes, yes."

"A cryptographic laboratory would have no trouble seeing under the pen's scratches. He may have written out the whole name before deciding to blot it out. If the government gets the name they can identify the next-in-command revolutionary. Or at least the man in between, the man who is arranging the arms shipments. And Philby might have a very special interest in keeping his name from view."

"You think it was Philby who came into my apartment?"

"Probably not. But we can assume Philby has contacts. When he left last night to go to see Colonel X, he was saying he had—has—ties to the PPS, to Abdullah Saadah's movement."

Tony did not discuss his most private worry. It was that so long as Philby and company did not have Abdullah's message in hand and knew that Gabriela had it, she was in danger. There are painful ways, he lowered his eyes to Gabriela's graceful hand with the little jade ring on the index finger, to force people to divulge their secrets. Ways that hadn't presumably worked on Abdullah but may have been the reason why, at the moment of his hanging, he had not been able to stand up alone.

"I will stay with you in your apartment tonight. Tomorrow is Saturday. We will go to the beach and spend a day getting this creepy business out of our minds."

He didn't tell her about her apartment. He wanted to enjoy her surprise. She took out her key and apprehensively opened the door.

"Tony!" She embraced him.

Her apartment was all but completely restored.

Chapter Forty-Four

Tony didn't sleep well. He hadn't shared the bed with Gabriela, not this time. He insisted he would sleep comfortably on the couch in the living room and he kissed her good night. His intention was to leave the apartment early without telling her. He'd have been glad to use the telephone, but decided it risky to do so. Better wait until tomorrow.

He woke easily, without any need of an alarm clock. It wasn't yet seven. He dressed and walked quietly out of the apartment. He had her car keys in his pocket.

He didn't know how extensive Philby's resources were. Sufficient, he wondered, to tap Gabriela's telephone on a few hours' notice? What he needed was Matti. To get to him, on a Saturday morning, required a phone call to John Gaylord, technically his ARAMCO supervisor. He had Gaylord's home telephone number. It was listed in his little pocket phone directory as "ARAMCO #2, 879-924."

He drove to the campus and went into his own room. He waited until 7:30. He followed carefully the code instructions.

"Mr. Gaylord, Tony Crespi. Sorry about the early call. You

wanted to know about Earl Stephens. Well, I had a call late last night. He's going with Standard Oil, not ARAMCO."

Gaylord said. "Well, that's too bad. Stay in touch with him and let me know how it goes."

"Yes sir. Nice to talk to you."

"Your studies going OK?"

"Fine, thanks."

"Stay in touch."

"Thanks, Mr. Gaylord."

It was 7:45. Assuming that Gaylord connected immediately with Matti, he would be at the safe house in two hours, waiting for him.

At 9:45, wearing a sailor's cap and carrying a backpack, he entered the hotel. The concierge asked where he was going. To 4-B, he said. She went back to her newspaper.

Matti answered the knock.

Tony put down the backpack and his cap. "I think," he said, "there is evidence that Philby had a role in the PPS business and that there was a Communist angle in it."

He recited yesterday's events. "And here is the text of Abdullah's document. I'll have to read it to you—"

"You mean, you don't have it?"

"No. But I think I can find it."

Matti wrote down the words as Tony read them out from his address book. "*Philby. Tell Colonel* xxxx X *our people still on location. V. strong. But need OK to resume plus fresh supplies. The rev. will succeed, Comrade. Farewell.*"

Matti spoke out the words twice. He closed his eyes in concentration.

"All right. We have to build on a few assumptions. The first has got to be that Abdullah was not playing games. The poor bugger had only a few hours to live.

"The second is that the Philby he wanted Gabriela to contact is—Kim Philby. There isn't another Philby around."

He allowed himself to interject, "Thank God."

"The third is that Philby wants very badly to put his hands on that document. You told me that he read it. That Gabriela showed it to him that night?"

He didn't wait for Tony to confirm Matti's memory of what he had heard a mere ten minutes earlier.

"The fourth is that the forces of Abdullah are not fatally depleted. Now this assumption does rest on the reliability of Abdullah's estimate of what was left of the PPS after the coup was put down.

"Five. Philby is not entirely surprised that a communication to him was intended. He doesn't feign total ignorance when Gabriela accosts him. That means he is an accomplice in the uprising. Moreover, he undertakes to get in touch with Colonel X, whoever *he* is—"

Tony interjected. "He wrote out the name of the colonel but then crossed it out and put 'X' there. Conceivably the real name is decipherable by technicians."

Matti paused and made a little notation on his pad. "Of course, we have no idea whether, when Philby left Gabriela's apartment, he in fact drove off to see the Colonel, who clearly is not a fictitious figure. Abdullah would not have written down his name if he were. You say that at the meeting with Gabriela, Philby inadvertently gave an Arabic name in place of the 'X'?"

"Yes. But she cannot remember what it was. Remembers only that it was something like Aswan."

Again Matti paused.

"Here is what we do not know. Does the 'Comrade' business and the letters 'r-e-v'—do they suggest a simple Communist fraternal relationship? If Philby is an undercover Soviet agent, that will surprise nobody except our cherished and dear leader, Jim Angleton. But if he is now, finally, exposed, that is very big news. The CIA didn't succeed in identifying any delinquency attributable to him, even after Philby's three years in Washington. Nor did MI6 after his years of service to them. And was it seven years ago that Harold Macmillan talked about Philby in the House of Commons as though he was a faithful Brit?"

Matti got up and walked to the window. He peered about. "I don't suppose you were followed here. I should think it unlikely that you were subject to instant surveillance just because you spent the night with Gabriela."

He allowed himself another sally. "A lot of people do."

Tony said nothing. The night before, at the restaurant, Gabriela had said she would tell him everything. She had done so. There were no surprises now to be got from Matti's wisecracks.

"We have no idea what round-the-clock resources the Soviets here deploy. They can arrange anything ad hoc—anybody with money in Beirut can arrange anything up to, and sometimes including, murder. I would not hazard a guess whether the interval between the failure to find the Abdullah document and your accompanying her home last night was enough time to initiate surveillance. I repeat. I cannot hazard a guess whether that was time enough. I frankly doubt it.

"Which means," Robert Matti's face broke into a grin, "that I *will* hazard a guess, which I have just now done."

He sat down again. "So what do we do?

"One, I will get a report filed with Angleton. He will alert the Agency to explore possible ties between PPS and the pro-Communist Baaths in Syria—"

"And Gabriela?" Tony broke in.

"Two, I think she'd better get out of town. She can't go to Russia, for the obvious reasons. Italy. Let's pack her off to Italy. We'll arrange the whole thing. Her Soviet manager is hibernating. He hasn't asked her for anything—assuming she can be believed, and I believe her—for over a year. Let's try to put her on the flight

Wednesday morning. I'll get busy on that. Meanwhile, you'd better keep in close touch with her."

That, really, was all that was decided, though they were together for two hours. The message he had handwritten for Gabriela when she woke up was simply, "Don't let anybody into the apartment. I'll be back in time for lunch."

He was back by one, carrying a nicely stocked picnic basket.

Chapter Forty-Five

Gabriela was waiting. She delightedly drew his attention to her beachwear. The cotton leggings reached down to the tops of her knees and, in yellow-and-white stripes made their way right up to her shoulders and adorned the light jacket in matching colors. Her beach shoes were corresponding yellow, matching the yellow of her wide-brimmed hat. Tony whistled appreciatively. She addressed him: "Go get the trunks you left here a week ago. They are hanging in the bathroom. Did you remember an overnight bag in case we stay out? I've packed mine. I will check out your cuisine." Tony was back carrying his russet trunks and a towel, and walking on sandals with straps across the arch of his feet. As they spoke, the afternoon newspaper was fed through the mail slot.

"I don't want to see it." She shoved the paper away. "What beach are we going to? The Byblos Beach would be nice today. It is a good forty-five minutes, but it is never crowded. And there are tables. We could put our *feast* on a proper surface!"

Gabriela Semenenko bore no trace of the Gabriela of yesterday. Tony was cheered by her survival, it seemed, of the events. He would wait until after lunch to tell her about the trip to Rome she'd be obliged to make.

The day was accommodatingly bright as they drove off, Tony again at the wheel. Gabriela was so comfortable in the seat alongside, she gave the impression she would like it that way permanently, driving together, he at the wheel. But, after all, she knew the route better and now after leading him to the Tripoli highway, where they'd drive for forty kilometers, she could lean back on the car seat and enjoy the sun while Tony attended completely to the driving. "Get ready for a right turn, at the Coca-Cola sign," she told him, an hour later.

He found it and soon they were at the Byblos Beach. It was very nearly deserted, a mere half-dozen couples in view. There was the lonely kiosk tender, offering Coca-Colas, oranges, tomatoes, pineapple juice; crullers, biscuits, cheese, ham. No beer, let alone liquor. In the country, away from urban centers, the Muslim taboo got back on its legs.

They occupied one of the tables, depositing their basket of food and Gabriela's basket, with its sun lotions, paperback books, and cigarettes. "Catch me!" Tony called out, loping down the beach to the waterfront.

From a distance of a hundred meters, viewed through binoculars, it was one of those jolly portraits, the blue sea, the yellow sand, the pencil figure of a man with brown trunks followed by the pencil figure of a woman in yellow-striped swimwear running after him.

The man behind the binoculars was beefy, of middle build, wearing a heavy mustache. He put the binoculars back in the case and walked toward the car parked in the lot by the swimming beach. He stayed on the main road until he got nearer his destination. It was easier to walk on the road than through sand. He opened the back door of his old Volvo and discarded the binoculars, taking out a camera.

It was an old model but he knew well its peculiarities and its uses and had several times successfully worked with it.

He aimed it at one or two of the couples nearby, writing down their names and addresses in order to send them, for their approval, the prints he seemed to hope they would buy.

He came to the table where Gabriela sat taking the wrappers off the lunch.

"You are a pretty good provider, Tony. While I get the chicken and the potato salad, you open the wine."

"Miss, Mister, a picture please? You no like, you no take." He brought out a pad and a stubby pencil.

"Just your address, ma'am."

She dictated, cheerfully, "G. Semenenko, AUB, Beirut 8," and went back to her table setting. The photographer squatted down. At that moment Tony had the wine bottle between his knees, his left hand at the bottle's throat, his right straining to bring the cork up. At that moment the cork popped out and the muffled shot exploded and Gabriela fell face foward into the salad.

Tony grabbed the back of Gabriela's head. The bullet had entered above the ear. He stared at her. She was lifeless.

He reached inside the basket for a table knife and ran as he had never run before. He could see the photographer approaching his car, running fast for his size. He was fifty yards ahead. Tony prayed that the car would not start up quickly. But it began to move, though not yet as fast as its pursuer was moving. Then it accelerated. He shouted out and fastened his eyes on the license plate, which ended with the numbers 431. Her car — he could give chase!

But the car keys were in Gabriela's purse.

When he got back she was surrounded. One of the women bathers told Tony that her husband had gone to call the ambulance and the police. Another man climbed up on Tony's concrete picnic table and stood demanding silence. "Did anyone get one of the killer's cards?" He looked about him. No one raised a hand. The killer had not handed out cards.

The police came. The ambulance took Gabriela off. The police lieutenant told Tony he would be needed at the station for questioning. Did he have means of conveyance?

"Yes," said Tony, fumbling the keys in his pocket, retrieved from Gabriela's purse; yes, he had a car and would follow them.

Chapter Forty-Six

Tony was in luck at the police station because Inspector Kahlil Nazer was on duty. The slim, middle-aged Lebanese with the trim beard stood there while the police questioned him. They had detained one of the couples who were on the beach and had repeated, to others, to themselves, time and again, the sequence— the approach of the alleged photographer, the head bent for an ostensible camera shot of the girl, and then the explosion. Several picnickers had seen Tony running after the killer and returning a few minutes later furious and disconsolate. "He was torn apart by what had happened. The first thing he did," the elderly woman told the inspector, "was to grab a sash from me—I was glad to let him have it—to cover the poor lady's face. Such a beautiful lady. Who was she?"

The inspector murmured that she was a Russian and an employee of the American University of Beirut.

Inspector Nazer drew Tony to one side after the police had done their routine questioning. "Please come into my office."

Tony sat down opposite Inspector Nazer in the cramped room. No light worked its way through the old, dirt-stained little window, but two fluorescent lights overilluminated the interior. Nazer looked at the young man's pale face and reached up to move the focus of the standing lamp away from him.

"Mr. Crespi, the crime today classically asks investigators to look into the question of motive. There was no theft, no rape. I will, of course, be questioning the staff over at the university. But the person to begin with is, obviously, you. What motive can there have been?"

Tony hoped he wouldn't be subjected to a lie detector when he answered, "I don't know."

"Well, we have to begin with the most basic questions. Was Miss Semenenko married?"

"Not that I know of—" *Perhaps a good idea putting it that way.* It suggested a little distance between him and Gabriela. But he knew the hard questions were ahead.

Dead ahead.

"Did you have a romantic liaison with the deceased?"

A conjugation of answers to that question raced through his mind. He could say no. But if there were circumstantial witnesses—people who had seen him come and go to her apartment, one or more of the deliverymen who had brought in food during an evening—he could think of several times when that had happened . . . All he needed, he thought desperately, was to be held in a Beirut jail as a material witness who had lied to the police.

He looked up at Nazer. "Yes, we were in love."

"Was she, to your knowledge, estranged from a former . . . lover?"

"Estranged? No. I know nothing about that."

"Mr. Crespi, an examination of police files for the last two days reveals that the deceased visited Abdullah Saadah the night before his execution. The prison records have it that it was the prisoner who made the request that she be admitted, and that the visitor— Miss Semenenko—agreed to go. Nothing more than that. Was there a relationship there? Saadah and the deceased?"

Had the Inspector brought together random records of Gabriela's friends and liaisons?

There is no way they can hurt Gabriela, Tony said to himself, gripping one hand with the other. He was trying to force himself to take a clinical view of the investigation. He could say no. He didn't want to tell the police that Gabriela had been Abdullah's lover. Above all, he did not want the questioner to come up with the name of Philby. No, not yet, Philby.

"I know nothing other than that when she came from the jail she was terribly distressed that Abdullah was to be executed the next day. When he asked her to see him, he did not yet know that his appeal against the sentence had been rejected."

"Why should Saadah have wanted to see the deceased?"

"They were friends, she told me. Abdullah—Saadah—was a friend of her father, the former Soviet consul."

"Did she tell you anything about her visit with Saadah?"

Careful now, Crespi. "She said that he mumbled incoherent things." He had better say a little bit more, in case Abdullah's document turned up and could be useful in finding the killer. "And she said that Abdullah had scribbled out a note."

"What did the note say?"

"I glanced at it briefly, but couldn't make anything out of it."

"The AUB authorities complained that last night someone entered the library and broke open all the locked drawers in the deceased's desk. A telephone call from one of my agents who has been looking at the deceased's apartment reports there are traces there that show that a thorough search was made of her premises. Do you know anything about that?"

Tony understood why, in America, people sometimes refused to answer questions until they had seen a lawyer. In America, yes. In Lebanon?

"Yes. Someone broke into her apartment yesterday while she was taking students through the National Museum."

"After they completed the searches, they killed her," Kahlil

Nazer mused. "You cannot recall the wording of the message from Abdullah?"

"No," Tony lied. He then accosted the Inspector. "Mr. Nazer, you will perhaps understand that I am as eager to lay hands on the killer as you are. I reported instantly to the police who arrived at the scene that I had got the last three numbers of what looked like a Volvo and that they were 431. Surely it isn't hard to search out license plates that end in 431?"

"No, it is not hard and it has been done. A Volvo with the license plate 782-431 was found this afternoon, abandoned along the Beirut River. This morning the owner of the car complained that it had been stolen."

"Is the owner... reliable?" Tony was depressed at the choking off of that trail.

"I hope so. He is president of the Bank of Riadh al-Solh."

Tony attempted a smile.

"We do have," Nazer said wearily, "photographic files of criminals and suspects. They are extensive. I am afraid I will have to ask you to stay with us to examine them. I can order in something for you to eat, as it is getting late."

"Mr. Nazer, I think it would be a good idea for me to be in touch with our embassy. I happen to know Mr. Matti, because he interviewed me when I arrived to begin my studies. Can I call him up?"

Nazer hesitated. Then, "Yes. I will be waiting next door." He opened the door to the adjacent office.

"Mr. Matti, Tony Crespi. Hope you remember me. We had a session when I checked in at the University."

"Sure, I remember you. Studies going OK? What can I do for you?"

"Well, I'm in trouble. There's been a murder—Gabriela Semenenko. I was there. Lots of eyewitnesses, some thug-for-hire, I'd guess. They asked me about her, a lot of questions, and I told them I had been with her after she visited Saadah. Abdullah Saadah. I told them that Abdullah had given her a message on a piece of paper, that I read it but didn't know what it was all about."

Matti answered cautiously. "Was there any name mentioned in the message?"

"If so, I didn't remember it. Mr. Matti, I was very very close to Gabriela, you know what I mean."

"Yes."

"So I'm determined to do whatever can be done to track the killer."

"Well, as an American consular, I advise you to be careful not to engage in any activity without first coordinating it with the Lebanese police. Who are you dealing with?"

"Inspector Kahlil Nazer."

"Inspector Nazer. Yes. A fine man. But look, I wish to help you. You are a student in distress. So please come to see me as soon as you are free. When do you anticipate that will be?"

"They said there are a lot of mug shots I need to plow through. The trouble is, everybody with a mustache looks like everybody else with a mustache. Cancel that. I think I can tell. If I do, that bugger doesn't have a long life ahead of him."

Matti's voice was stern. "Crespi, I want you to report to me as soon as they release you. You have my office number. Here is my home number."

Tony memorized it.

"OK. See you later."

"I don't care what time it is, you understand?"

"Yes, sir."

Chapter Forty-Seven

It was after ten when he finally left the station. He had for four hours stared at and restared at mug shots of three hundred men. The first hour was spent dismissing persons unmistakably not the killer. In the second hour, he succeeded in winnowing the list down to fifty. But then he had to stop, he told Nazer. "I mean, I've reached the point I could accuse my own father of being the killer. I really do have to let my eyes focus."

"Come with me."

Nazer led him from the crime laboratory across the street to a little coffee shop. He detected a look of distress on Tony's face as they walked in. "Don't worry. They also serve beer and wine."

Tony gulped down on his beer and tried to nibble on the almond cookie. "One of those bastards had to be the one. Maybe when I go back I'll spot him. Tell me, Inspector, what do you do if I reduce it to ten people?"

"We try to find them. We bring them in. We ask you to identify the killer."

"But that could take days, weeks, no?"

"Yes, before all ten of them were brought in. We would round up as many as we could find in the next few days, expose them to you, continue to look for the others unless one you saw, you identified positively."

Tony tasted the cookie and took another draught of the beer. He wondered whether he should call up Matti. But he didn't know how much longer the photo viewing would take. His mind was clearing.

"OK, Inspector. I'm better now. Let's go back to work."

An hour later he was looking for the fifteenth time at the faces of six men. "Would it help if you read me something about their records?"

"We don't allow that. It is prejudicial."

"OK. Let's leave it this way: I would like to see those six people in the flesh."

Kahlil Nazer made the notation. "We will call you when we are ready."

"Thanks."

"Mr. Crespi, a word."

Tony looked up.

"If you know where Abdullah Saadah's document is, you are in danger."

"Yes, thanks. Yes. I see your point. Thanks very much. Well, I have to go and try to get some sleep."

He had said nothing about Gabriela's car and they had not thought to ask about it.

He needed a pistol.

Where, oh where, did Philby live?

It was probably too late to buy a pistol.

He had to go to Philby. Where did he live? *Gabriela!*

He turned around. He saw her car. On the backseat was her beach bag, clothes to put on after the swim. And next to it her city handbag. He felt with his fingers for what might be a little address book. He turned on the light above the dashboard. The convertible's top was still up. Yes! He looked through Gabriela's address book.

"Philby. 1142-101."

A phone number, no address.

He mustn't see Philby until he had a gun.

He drove without purpose down the Avenue de Paris. At a stoplight his eyes focused on the sign across the street. It was a parking lot. For the adjacent hotel. The Hôtel Méditerrané.

He suddenly realized he had to postpone everything. He was not thinking, he was not in control. He didn't have a gun.

He drove the car into the lot, went in, produced his wallet, and told the concierge he wanted a room for the night.

Chapter Forty-Eight

Daylight. Tony was muggy with yesterday's sweat. He looked at his watch. It was just after seven. He forced himself to think, and happily remembered. He put his hand into his pocket and felt the reassuring car keys. He walked out of the hotel to the car, opened the trunk, and gazed gratefully at the two overnight bags, his and hers. He pulled his out, and walked back up to his room. Then down the hall to a shower. His overnight bag had what he needed, a razor, toothbrush, a comb. Back in the room he put on fresh shorts and a shirt and the light seersucker jacket. Yesterday's trousers would have to do. He went back to the bag, fished out the tie he had packed, and put it on. He looked in the mirror and combed his hair. He was ready to go out. He had his passport. He hoped the gun dealer would not insist on seeing it.

But he did.

Hariks Débit de Sport opened its doors at eight. Tony walked in and greeted the huge man behind the counter, happily puffing on a pipe that gave off an odd odor. Tony said he needed a pistol; his apartment had been broken into while he was out of town and he wanted protection.

Mr. Harik did not need to know why a customer needed a gun. All he needed, if it was a foreigner, was to note down the passport number. He wrote down Tony's number and pointed to the gun selection on green felt, under glass.

"*Choisissez ce que vous voulez, Monsieur.*"

Tony picked up a .38 automatic and tested its slide. He asked for a box of cartridges and brought out the 3,600 Lebanese pounds from his wallet.

It was now 8:30. The Information Office would be open.

He called. "Is Mr. Jabhour in? If not, I'll talk to his assistant... This is Eldridge Dodge. American University. I need two home addresses. We are sending out our annual catalog. I need the address of Homer Babbidge—yes, *Christian Science Monitor*. And Harold Philby, the *Economist.* ... Thanks very much."

He knew the street. He drove to a block away, parked the car, and walked, pistol in pocket, with a steady gait to the gray concrete apartment house, its air-conditioning units pockmarking its broad front.

The lobby was unattended.

He stopped suddenly.

What did he intend to do?

Yesterday, the answer to that question was simple. Kill him. Kill the fucking traitor/murderer.

All right. He wouldn't kill him. He would knock him out, tie his hands behind his back, and force from him the identity and address of the killer. He would use his tie to bind him. He unknotted it and put it in his left-hand pocket.

He took the elevator to the sixth floor, one floor above Philby's fifth-floor apartment.

He had weighed what to do. Knocking on the door was excluded. Philby would not let him in. He would wait at the bottom of the fifth-floor staircase, only a few feet from apartment 5-C. When Philby opened his own door, Tony would charge into him and bang the door open. Then he would overpower him.

And the session would begin. He was steeled for it.

He waited. It was a Sunday. Philby would certainly emerge. If not early, certainly by noon. He never missed the Sunday horse races — Philby himself had told him that.

But noon came and went. It was now 1:30. Could Philby have left his apartment earlier than when Tony had got there? Before nine?

He walked back up the stairs, into the elevator and then descended, out into the street. He had noticed earlier the coffee shop at the corner.

There was no putting it off, he had to call Bob Matti. He would have to put off until later in the afternoon, or evening, his rendezvous with Philby.

"I told you to call me last night, goddamnit."

"I'm sorry about that. They kept me until very late. To tell you the truth, Bob, I'm outside Philby's apartment. We have some talking to do."

"Philby left last night — for Cairo, I've established. He probably wants to be out of town for a few days. Speaking of being out of town, I want you out of town. Come right away and I'll tell you what arrangements I've made."

Chapter Forty-Nine

Tony arrived at Matti's apartment dejected and confused. As he closed the door of Gabriela's car he wondered idly when he would be giving her car up, and to whom. When did Matti intend that he, Tony, should leave town?

Matti was waiting for him. He met Tony at the door and led him without comment through his living room to the study. Neither his wife nor children were there. Tony had seen pictures of them in Matti's study at the embassy. Perhaps they were out of town.

"Where did you spend last night?"

"At a hotel."

"How did you get there, cab?"

"I've been using Gabriela's car."

"What did you end up doing with the police? With Inspector Nazer?"

"We closed in on six pictures. I was pretty dizzy at that point. It was after ten. He plans to round them up and have me try for a positive ID."

"That will take time. Nazer is a good man, but he has to depend on police who aren't so good. Not that easy, rounding up six thugs and bringing them in. He probably wouldn't be calling you for several days. Meanwhile, you are hot. Philby's out of town for I don't know how long, maybe a week or more. But it could be that he is out of town waiting for Colonel X's people to come up with something—goddamnit I wish we knew who Colonel X was."

"I can't help you on that, Mr. Matti."

"You have the note. Or can get it. Maybe with spectrographic equipment we can make out the name he scratched over. Philby may be counting on this trusty aide, like maybe the nice guy you met on the beach, to pry that document out of you. Philby must be torturing himself, letting Gabriela walk off with it. We don't want you around waiting to be picked up and submitting to Arab ingenuity on how to get cooperation from unwilling people. I have to have that document. With it in hand I can do a little horse-trading with Nazer."

Matti opened the folder in front of him.

"*You* have to get out of town. I have booked you on a 7:00 P.M. flight to Cairo. You will connect with the 11:05 PanAm to New York."

"Tonight?"

"Tonight."

"What am I going to tell . . . the people at AUB?"

Matti paused. Then, "Have you seen the morning newspapers?"

"No."

"Well, you are as prominent in them as—as Beirut's soccer victory over Baghdad." He reached to the card table at the side of his desk and brought out the *Daily Star,* unfolded it, and held it opposite Tony's face.

"The *Beirut Times* and *La Revue du Liban* are every bit as much interested in you."

Tony stared in disbelief at the huge tabloid headlines.

"You know, Tony, it doesn't happen every day that at a municipal beach a killer claiming to be a photographer approaches a beautiful, twenty-eight-year-old woman and in the presence of her boyfriend and eight or ten other people shoots her dead with a pistol hidden in a camera and bounds off with lover boy in chase."

Tony was silent. He shook his head slightly. In the awful confusion and tragedy and despair, he had forgotten the photographers who squatted outside the police station and flashed away as he was led across the street by Inspector Nazer to the crime lab.

"There isn't one Lebanese over the age of sixteen who isn't right this minute talking about the AUB boyfriend on the beach and wondering what his role was in this murder. For you to just go away for a while will surprise exactly nobody."

"It will surprise Inspector Nazer."

"I told you, I'll take care of him when I have the Abdullah document in hand. What does that give him? It gives him Philby as the key figure. And it gives the government grounds for believing that the countercoup activity has a long way yet to go. And it suggests a tie-in with the Syrian socialists/Communists."

Robert Matti stood up. He was now the general, handing out orders.

"So. Concretely. Ivan Bloch, who you met when you came to the embassy for your briefing in June — my aide — is standing by. Of course he knows nothing about your . . . mission here. As far as he is concerned, you are a student who got mixed up in a hot Beirut scandal. He has been told that you will give him an envelope, sealed, with something he is to bring to me. And he is to stay with you until you board that airplane. Leave Gabriela's car in the lot. Give him the keys."

He went back into the folder. "Here are your tickets. You have some cash?"

Tony nodded.

"Some U.S. dollars?"

He nodded again.

Matti got up. "Calling me up for help was OK. I'm just a U.S. Embassy official helping out an innocent American student who got into trouble." He looked intently at Tony. "Good-bye, Crespi. I don't know whether our paths will cross again." He permitted a touch of resignation in his voice: "I hope so."

Tony rose. "Is Mr. Angleton up to date on all this?"

"Are you kidding? The answer is yes."

He was reintroduced to Ivan Bloch, the elderly clerk who looked after Matti's appointments and typed out his reports. He was waiting in the lobby of Matti's apartment house.

Another jolt was ahead for him. On reflection, Tony reproached himself; he had no right to think of it as surprising. His rooms at the university had been treated as Gabriela's had been. He sighed as he viewed the mess.

He had no time to lose. His first mission was in the library. Ivan Bloch reminded him that Matti's instructions were not to let Crespi out of his sight. He would accompany him.

They walked together to the library. Entering into the reading room, he saw a student look up. He recognized him and nudged a student alongside. Ivan went to a desk nearby and sat, a magazine shielding his face from the students staring at them. Tony walked over to the card catalog. *Euphrates . . . Economic value of E . . . E, as subject of Cairo conference . . . E, font of 2000 years of poetry . . . History of E.*

He jotted down the call number. After so many hours there, he was familiar with the library. He walked over to the 000·3191R section. It was close to Gabriela's empty desk. He scanned the shelf. His eyes froze on the quarry. He reached up and took down the frayed brown volume, closed his eyes with apprehension, and parted the covers. It opened to where the envelope was lodged. He unsealed it and stared down at the last words of Abdullah Saadah, sealed it again with the Scotch tape on Gabriela's desk, and put it in his back pocket. He turned to the shelf to hide the tears that flowed down his face.

Mr. Bloch motioned him. "We must move on," he whispered.

———

The packing went quickly. He had no concern for the disheveled room that was left after he had dumped his personal belongings and his books into the suitcases. He made no attempt to rehang the curtains or reorder the bookshelves. There wasn't time. Ivan helped him pack. There were three bags. He filled them with an intuitive sense of priorities. The library books would, of course, stay—they would be found by the cleaning woman and returned, unless the administration was given reason to believe that he would be back in a week or two.

It was fast work. He had bought two framed lithographs of Beirut done by a local artist he had taken a fancy to. They had been torn from their frames. One of them fitted into a suitcase. The other, a view of the mountains behind the northern profile of the city, was too large. He took a sheet of paper and wrote on it, "This is a gift for Madame Najm. With all best wishes, Tony Crespi." With his eyes he did a final sweep of the two rooms.

Together they put the bags in the back of Ivan's car.

At the airport a porter was there with a trolley. The loudspeakers were voluble, as ever. The sun had just gone down but Tony was sweating from his exertions and from the compressed hideousness of it all.

Ivan went with him to the check-in counter. They walked to the gate. There were only minutes to spare.

"Tony, Mr. Matti told me something about an envelope you were going to give me—"

"Oh my God!"

He reached into his back pocket, drew out the testament of Abdullah, and handed it to Ivan Bloch.

"Thank you, Tony."

"Thank *you*, Ivan."

The flight to Cairo was called.

Chapter Fifty

A short air ride, Beirut to Cairo. It was only just after eight when Tony had got through the baggage routine, escorting his bags through Cairo customs on to the PanAm flight that would take them to New York–Idlewild.

The Cairo airport was newer than Beirut's. A little grander. The posters were heliocentric: Colonel Abdel Nasser was everywhere. There were photographs of him meeting with world leaders in Washington, in London, Paris, Moscow, in Bandung giving a speech at the 1955 Third World conference. Mostly the pictures were simply pictures of Nasser looking grand.

Tony had two and a half hours to kill. Looking about for an eatery, he spotted something called the Ramses. He looked through a musky window into a dimly lit cafeteria and bar, windowless on the runway side, a portrait of Nasser at the center, against what seemed a red velvet background.

He entered, depositing his briefcase on a chair at a small table covered with a checkered red-and-white cloth. He slid his tray down the counter rail, looking listlessly at the foods offered. He made up a plate from hard-boiled eggs and what looked like an-chovy, some hard bread, some butter, and some cheese. He added a half bottle of French Bordeaux, paid the bill, and took the tray to the table.

He had begun to nibble on an egg when he heard the voice at his side.

"Hi. Can I join you?"

He looked up at a cheerful blond face wreathed in a smile. The young man had a tray in his hands and, on his shoulders, a con-siderable backpack.

"Sure." Tony pointed to the chair opposite. The traveler de-posited the tray and wiggled his way free of the backpack.

"Damn that's heavy! But not as heavy as it felt walking around Luxor! Oh my God, that was hot! I'm Andy, Andy Wharton." He proffered his hand with a smile exuberant with good humor.

"I'm Tony Crespi."

Tony was brought up short by the transfusion of lightness and happiness communicated by Andy Wharton in a half hour, as they ate their dinner. "Thanks, but no wine for me. In Ohio I'd be ar-rested if I had any. Got two years to go before it's legal!" — Tony was given Andy's rollicking story.

Yes, he too was on the flight to New York. "Can't wait, because coming in this direction all I did was make connections, went from La Guardia directly to Idlewild. Going back" — he beamed at the utter pleasure he contemplated — "I have two days in New York City. Two days! I'm going to see everything. I'm going to see the Metropolitans. The Metropolitan Museum and the Metropolitan Opera. Guess what! Tuesday night is Aïda! Imagine that luck! Going from the pyramids in Luxor and Cairo to the pyramids in the Metropolitan Opera in two days! Some people have all the luck."

Andy sipped on his Coca-Cola. "What about you, Tony? You've been in Beirut, you tell me. Going back for a vacation?"

Tony explained that his mother was ill.

Andy was very sorry about that. "I will say a prayer for her re-covery. My aunt taught me a special prayer. If you like, I'll write it down and give it to you. On the plane." Andy brushed his blond locks back from his sunbaked face and gave a blue-eyed look of concern. "That's actually my *late* aunt. In fact, that's how come I'm here!"

He explained. His aunt had died and had left Andy and his brother Jeff—"Jeff is a *really* neat guy. He's older. He's twenty-one." He chuckled. "He can drink wine, all right. I mean, he drinks beer, usually." His aunt had died and left an unusual will. "She was an unusual lady." The will, he explained, allocated one thousand dollars to each of her two nephews, with a very explicit provision. "I read the will. There was no way around what Aunt Eleanor spec-ified. The money was to use on only *one* trip. It could not be used for college expenses, could not be saved for future use. It could be used only to finance a pleasure trip.

"Jeff wanted to go to Venice. I wanted to come to Egypt. What a great lady, Aunt Eleanor. She was a bunch of laughs, too. She'd have had a hard time getting through this airport without asking somebody, for instance, 'Who *is* this Colonel Nasser?' If you can imagine!"

Tony felt the muscles in his stomach easing, resting, for the first time since he arrived at the beach. He was stimulated to contribute to the conversation and spoke of Washington, and before that of his time at Yale, of his fondness for soccer, about his experience on the wrestling team. Andy listened with rapt attention. "Gee, I wish I knew some of the tricks in wrestling. Maybe I can learn it next year, at Ohio State. *If I get in!* Taking two weeks off to go to Egypt in the middle of January of senior year isn't too good an idea, but what the heck; if I don't go to Ohio State, I'll go somewhere else, right? No place ritzy like Yale. On the other hand, Yale is fun, isn't it?"

Tony said that yes, Yale was fun.

Andy laughed. "Maybe somebody will die and leave me money

and say I can only spend it at Yale!" He tossed his head back and laughed at the delight of that thought, at the delight of it all.

They heard the first call for their eleven o'clock flight.

"It takes me a minute or two to put on my backpack. That's all the baggage I have. Right there"—he pointed to the pack at one side.

"Can I help you with it?" Tony asked.

"No no, I put it on and off twenty times every day."

They went out to the international departure section.

They were walking slowly, Andy remarking the sights they passed by. They were bound for Gate 34. The even gates were on the right side. They came to Gate 22. Tony stopped. He heard his name being called out.

"Crespi!" A man waved at him from the gangway.

He looked up.

The passenger, disappearing now into the airplane, wore a fedora, carried a raincoat over one shoulder, a briefcase in his right hand.

Tony stopped dead in his tracks.

Andy then stopped, concern written on his face. "Tony, what's the matter? You're pale."

Tony said nothing. His eyes fixed on the gangway. Other passengers were now passing into the Antonov 10.

His eyes darted to the flight panel. It read, MOSCOW, FLIGHT 778. DEPARTURE 2245.

"You know that guy, the guy called your name?"

"Yes," Tony said, his face still riveted on the gangway. The steward was now shutting the airplane door.

Andy just waited. He didn't say anything.

Finally Tony turned his head. He knew now what it was to feel absolutely helpless. Philby. On a plane to Moscow. Finally confirming his allegiances. Waving at Tony three days after effecting the execution of Tony's Gabriela. And Tony could do absolutely nothing about it. If he had a machine gun handy, he could do nothing about it. Philby was behind that door, beyond his reach, beyond the reach of the West, at liberty to forget Gabriela forever.

"We'd better get going," he said, his voice deadly flat.

Andy nodded and they walked on, toward Gate 34.

BOOK FOUR

Chapter Fifty-One

January, 1966

James Angleton turned off the television set. "Do you mind?" he looked up at Marina.

"I don't mind, Jeemee. Hugo, he's late. Maybe hees looking at the television in his bureau."

"Talk to me in Spanish," Angleton replied, in Spanish. She had trouble with English, though she had been almost six months in Washington, very much at home with Hugo Esterhazy, who had befriended her at a moment of high distress in Mexico City when, she averred, her husband had determined to kill her.

She complied. In Spanish, "What I am saying, Jeemee, is that Hugo hasn't called and I know he wouldn't want to miss the President's speech. So I assume he has watched it in the office."

Angleton looked at his watch. "It's 11:05. That has to be the longest State of the Union address in history."

"Our presidents in Mexico give State of the Union speeches that last two or three hours."

"Your presidents have captive audiences. What has it been, Marina, forty years since the president's party, the PRI, lost an election?"

Marina chuckled, lit a cigarette, and cozied herself in her silk nightgown into the armchair. At thirty-five she was still a believable Miss Mexico. "I am teaching Spanish to Hugo. He is very good. When he comes, shall we speak in Spanish together, like right now?"

Angleton got up. He said distractedly, "I'm not sure Hugo is quite up to that yet. Besides, it's bad for you. You have to buckle down and learn our language. You're not going to spend the rest of your life writing personals for *El Diario*." Marina Reyes had got work at the Spanish-language daily.

"I will learn, *poco a poco*." Angleton had started to dial a number when the door opened wide and Esterhazy blew in. He kissed Marina. "Darling, get me a drink. A strong drink."

"*Quieres un whiskey?*"

Hugo nodded. "Sorry about that, Jim. I was on my way out when the word got to me: the Secretary said he'd like us all to watch President Johnson's speech with him in the conference room. Couldn't very well say no, though there were twenty of us; he wouldn't have missed me." He accepted the drink with a nod and continued talking to Angleton. "What in the name of *God* did our chief executive forget to pledge the American people in return for their support on Vietnam?"

"He promised to do his best for the redwood trees," Angleton confirmed solemnly.

Hugo raised his glass in a mock toast: "Better redwoods than deadwoods."

Marina asked Hugo whether he wanted any food sent up. The Baghdad Bar and Grill doesn't deliver after midnight, she reminded him.

"Yeah, let's get something. How about a little rice and sweet and sour?" Without waiting for Angleton to deliberate the offer, he told Marina, "Order for three, *querida*."

"I will go myself and bring them," she volunteered.

He didn't protest.

"Coming down the elevator with Jim Ramsey"—Esterhazy pursued his conversation as he drew the cork from a bottle of wine—"he told me the *Washington Post* has scooped the story on the national draft. They're going after a total of *five hundred thousand men*. Obviously the President did some political planning in anticipation of a Vietnam buildup. What day are you going out to Saigon, Jim?"

"I was going on Saturday. But after tonight's speech, the DCI might want me to wait for him. McCone's in Buenos Aires, not back till Monday. Well, at least we've got some good news from that part of the world. Che Guevara has had his last fling at bringing bloody Communism to a Latin American country."

"The Bolivians didn't waste much time on due process. Did you hear about the exchange with the sergeant?"

No, Angleton said, he hadn't heard.

"Great stuff!" Esterhazy took a gulp of his drink and eased his long legs up on the sofa. "It came in from *Novedades*. The sergeant got the order to execute him and asked Che if he would leave him his corncob pipe.

"Che said, 'Are you going to shoot me?' The sergeant said, 'Yes.'

"'In that case,' Che said, 'I won't leave you my pipe.'"

The two cold warriors laughed a little over that story.

Angleton confided his suspicion that Castro had set up Che Guevara. "There was real rivalry there. I think Castro got word out to the Bolivian army about where Che was operating, where he and his little band were operating."

"Why doesn't somebody do something about Castro?" Hugo Esterhazy permitted himself a smile.

There was a great deal to engage the Chief of Counterintelligence in the days following upon the State of the Union address by President Johnson. And much had accumulated during his ten-day absence, long-postponed vacation. Among other things he had now to give attention to a letter from a covert agent.

It had been brought in unopened, retrieved at Angleton's daily examination of a postal box number. The letter was addressed to "Mr. James Cooper." It had been mailed in Cairo.

The letter was from Tony Crespi, in Riyadh. It observed protocols. No names except the addressee's . . .

"Dear Mr. A.:

I wanted to run this one directly through you instead of through—well, through regular channels.

I'm twenty-six, and as far as the world goes—the world that's interested in . . . Valerio's son—I am working year after year for an American oil company, getting nice pay and learning all about pipelines and oil and proper Islamic behavior. Would you believe, sir, I haven't had a drink since my vacation in Rome three months ago?

Well, you know, I know, and I know that you know, that I have been performing other services, and every six months or so I get a bleat from Up There saying I am doing good and valuable stuff, and as a matter of fact, even from my own perspective I know that's true.

But I really don't feel like passing out a fake word, now that all my contemporaries are being drafted to go to Vietnam, that I failed my physical. I'd have to say it was something pretty exotic in my offensively robust body, like maybe a Mesopotamian sexual disease.

I don't want to do that. When you were my age you faked a physical—in order to get *into* the war, not out of it. I don't have a bad conscience about serving my country by doing what I'm doing—I *am* serving my country. Anybody who thinks it's fun out here is welcome to come to live and work in Riyadh for four years and remind himself every week or so that he isn't

here on an assembly line that takes you to the pot of gold
ARAMCO offers real-time workers after twenty years. He's here
for the recondite interests of the good old USA.

I don't mean to sound restless, but I didn't want to do this
except through you, since you've been my godfather, in a way,
since I started. What I'm telling you, Mr. A., is that either I quit
and check in with my draft board or I give up the deep-cover
front and give out a CIA address to friends & family, and
people will know I'm doing work for the USA. I'll hope to hear
from you soon through the usual channels.

My warmest — S.

It amused Tony to improvise on the habitual seat-of-the-pants
device of encryption. T would be wrong, since a supersleuth inter-
ceptor would begin his excavations with the proper first letter of
the spy's real name. Use, therefore, U? — the letter that comes *after*
T? Oh no, Tony said to himself, he was much too sophisticated to
do that. He would go *back* in the alphabet: whence S. He thought,
correctly, that that would also amuse the director of Counterintelligence.

Chapter Fifty-Two

November, 1972

"You never mentioned Jay Lovestone to me," Hugo Esterhazy said. "Now you tell me that Deputy Director Colby's 'closing out of Lovestone' is a very grave decision."

"It is," Angleton said. "If Colby goes through with it...Have you noticed, Hugo—I don't think you ever do notice the orchids here. I remember your telling me that your late mother, Lady Lucinda?—do I recall?—was also an orchid freak?"

"You are correct. Dear mother loved orchids—"

"Well, if only as a courtesy to this lovely lady slipper here on the table, I formally call your attention to her."

"They are quite beautiful, Jim. And while we're at it, here's a toast to the beekeeper."

"Orchid keeper. Bees are other things."

"Sorry, I meant orchidist?"

"No such word."

"OK, orchid keeper. So Colby calls you in and tells you you have to liquidate the Lovestone operation. And you complain to him that that's a crippling directive—"

"You do know who Lovestone is, don't you, Hugo?"

"Sure I know. He was sacked by Stalin back in the twenties for something or other, came back to America, and restarted the Communist Party. Only that made *two* Communist Parties, the Lovestone Communist Party and the Josef Stalin Communist Party."

"Yes. Of course, Lovestone had to surrender on the nomenclature. Stalin vs. Lovestone, on which is the legitimate U.S. Communist Party, is a no-contest. They ended by calling themselves 'Lovestoneites.'" Angleton relaxed for a moment and chuckled. "Whence the wisecrack, 'Is Lovestone really a Lovestoneite?'"

"What was that about?"

"Lovestone became progressively anti-Communist—not only anti-Stalinist, but anti-Marxist, and, finally, anti- the whole shebang. He lingers nowadays in a kind of welfarist socialism, but he has really only one interest, which is to destroy Soviet Communism. What he still is, and always will be, is a labor-union militant. Jay Lovestone has been the center of our efforts to help the free labor-union movement in Europe."

Esterhazy interrupted Angleton to greet the stunning blond woman in a short white tennis skirt coming by. She wore a sweatband over her perspiring forehead and extended her left hand, her right hand gripping the tennis racket and one tennis ball.

"I'm not going to get any closer, darling. I'm all wet."

Esterhazy took her hand and blew a kiss at her. Then, "Melinda, this is James Angleton. Melinda Fletcher."

Angleton rose and bowed his head slightly.

Melinda Fletcher paused for a moment. Then, offhandedly, "Goodness. You are taller even than Hugo. I don't suppose you can beat him at golf, though?"

"I don't know," Angleton said, no hint of a smile on his face, "I never tried."

Melinda liked that. To Hugo: "I like your friend." And then in a whisper: "He dresses like an undertaker."

Hugo couldn't respond with a levity. He was standing too close to Angleton. Melinda tilted her tennis racket in good-bye and went off toward the lockers.

"Melinda was a ladyfriend of JFK." Esterhazy was back in his seat, stretching his legs. "Melinda Carrothers, she was then. She's something of a sport. This being man-talk here, and since we talk to each other with sacramental confidentiality, I can disclose that in 1963 Melinda and I watched the Oscars in bed together. It was the year *Lawrence of Arabia* won Best Picture. Who says the Oscar ceremony is too long?"

Angleton hesitated, but only for a second. "Well then, you—and JFK—and I—have something in common."

Hugo Esterhazy's eyes lit up in a smile. "Why you old . . . Why am I saying old?"

"I am fifty-five."

"So back then with Melinda you were . . . Hey, let's cut this out. I thirst"—he signaled the waiter at the bar—"for a gin and tonic, and some more information on Jay Lovestone."

Angleton told him about the valiant and resourceful ongoing fight waged now for almost twenty years, beginning immediately after the war ended, to keep the Communists from total control of labor unions in Italy, France, and Germany. "Nobody is better than Angleton at coming up with exactly what is right to say to union leaders—and to union membership. The AFL-CIO's Irving Brown has been his lieutenant-in-place. He lives in Paris. He's got a big problem now with the CGT and Mitterrand and the wage-price freeze. The Communists are playing a hard hand. The fight is never won, but Lovestone was critical as far back as 1948 in Italy, and has been ever since. The *Free Trade Union News*—a monthly, though it sometimes comes out with special issues—is all his: founder, publisher, editor. It examines developments in labor unions from the point of view of Communist penetration and—control."

Hugo Esterhazy confessed he hadn't known the extent of Lovestone's work. "Thank God for George Meany of the AFL-CIO."

"Yes. Thank God for Meany; he's done terrific work. But Lovestone is not his operation."

"Whose is he?"

"Mine."

"Why on *earth* does Colby want to shoot *that* down?"

"Because it's illegal."

Neither said anything. Then, from Angleton, "Are you familiar
with the French use of the phrase, *tout court?*"

"No."

"Well, it means 'That's it... Nothing more to say... Leave it—
that's the story.' *Tout court*. What I'm saying is that I don't think in
my line of work you can say, 'That's illegal' and then think, Well,
tout court, we've got to stop it. Counterintelligence is an art form.
It's against the law to contrive to assassinate a foreign ruler. So—
close your eyes and imagine: You are hidden in a grassy field but
within range. You are armed with a sharpshooter rifle and you have
a bead on—in our fantasy—Idi Amin of Uganda, one of the twentieth century's bloodthirstiest tyrants. He has got himself a theater
nuke bomb and it's being loaded onto one of his fighter planes.
Orders? Drop the bomb over Jerusalem. Question: Do you pull
the trigger? Remember, Colonel Amin is a chief of state and the
law says you can't assassinate chiefs of state."

Esterhazy was solemn in his reflection. "Lincoln asked himself
a related question, I remember. Along the lines of, Does it further
the aims of the Constitution to abide by it when doing so endangers, well, endangers the whole thing—"

"Here are his words exactly. You can understand why I have
committed them to memory. Lincoln said, 'Is there, in all re-
publics, this inherent and fatal weakness? Must a government, of
necessity, be too *strong* for the liberties of its own people, or too
weak to maintain its own existence?'... Well, Hugo, there's a good
case to be made for declining even to talk about quandaries like

that. It's best left that although the truth may make you free, something less than the whole truth, in some situations, is necessary in order to keep the fire lit."

"We've talked about everything else.... So what are you going to do? About Lovestone?"

"Do you have any ideas?"

"Yes. To order dinner. I'm hungry."

Chapter Fifty-Three

February, 1973

The little bell in his office rang three times. As rapid a sequence —
dot!dot!dot! — Tony reflected, when he began working as general
aide to the Counterintelligence Chief, as one finger of one hand
could hope to effect. "If Vladimir Horowitz wanted to tap out a
single note that fast," he told a delighted Marina Reyes at the State
Department's Fourth of July Party, which Hugo Esterhazy had invited him to, "he'd have to come down to Washington and take lessons from James Jesus Angleton." Marina, who was drinking vodka
on ice, said she was a pretty fast typist herself, and she did a scale
on Tony's wrist and said she would do it in five octaves on his
pechuga if ever he wanted. Tony laughed and looked over at his
host, chatting with the Secretary of State.

In fact, Tony's nervous system never got completely used to the
buzzer, even though there were days when it called for him as
many as six times. Sometimes that would be late into the night. Mr.
A. often worked late and simply assumed that Tony would be there
if needed. On hearing the summons, Tony would scoop up his yellow legal pad, walk out into the hall, pass by the two lithographs of

colonial Washington and open the unmarked door that led into the offices of the king of Western counterintelligence, J. J. Angleton.

It had been difficult, alike for Angleton and for Tony, to slip into first-name round-trip usage. Tony Crespi had been "Tony" since the day he moved into Casa Nogales, a freshly graduated young man embarking on a profession that required a full year of Arab studies at Georgetown and complete training in the craft of a covert agent. But that was twelve years ago. Now he had been back in Washington three years, preserving the traditional form of address.

One night he picked up a note in his box at the corner office that served intramural purposes. The familiar little initials on the upper left corner of the page were simply "JJA." The handwritten note, in the broad black brushstrokes he was so familiar with, read, "Tony. From now on, it's 'Jim.'"

That order was executed, Tony thought, with the singular crispness Angleton—Jim—could display when in his resolute mode. Quite the opposite of Angleton in the discursive mode, when he might spend an hour—or three hours—analyzing a problem or a personnel folder or a tactical recommendation. Complying with such directives could take weeks and months, especially if Golitsyn was involved.

Tony had never laid eyes on Anatoliy Golitsyn. He did not know where Golitsyn lived and did not know the code for communicating with him, neither by telephone nor by mail.

But after a few months a picture of Golitsyn had begun to distill in Tony's mind. And after a year Tony could feel almost palpably the influence of Golitsyn on Mr. A. Tony was not usually told whom Angleton was meeting with, if the meeting was to be with an agent who dwelled in a high-security sphere. But he reasonably suspected that those half-day meetings, once every month or so, were almost surely meetings with Golitsyn, from what he knew and what he had gathered about him; from carefully reading files given to him to study and to store away. The meetings produced an Angleton who was progressively consumed by the black cloud of disinformation that hung over his thoughts, words, and deeds.

Much of the past six months had been given over to the implications for Vietnamese loyalists of the American military withdrawal from Vietnam. Angleton had been frustrated, once or twice to the point of fury, over what he pronounced a straight-out betrayal of clandestine, cooperative Vietnamese, some of them left at the mercy of the Vietcong. He spent hours and hours, many of them over the telephone, attempting to devise ways and means of rescuing individuals. Angleton had met personally with several of the men who had penetrated the Vietcong and served as pro-democratic agents, passing information back to headquarters in Saigon for use by South Vietnamese and U.S. military.

But with the withdrawal of the American forces, contacts with such agents in the field were more direct. There were fewer and fewer American intermediaries. However beleaguered the South Vietnamese military, it was to them that information was now brought. Angleton's grip loosened, and contacts were fewer and fewer. Then, toward the fall of 1972 Tony detected a reorientation in Angleton's concern. Angleton's chief quarrel was with public policies enacted by the Nixon Administration under pressure — "pressure," as he put it one afternoon to Tony, "from allies, churchmen, editorialists, politicians, and poets," to get out of Indochina. Angleton was fatalistic about weaknesses in the Western will, while feeling a direct responsibility for collateral victims of U.S. policies. Now something else was the center of his concern.

"The great retreat," Angleton ruminated, "began with the fall of President Diem in 1963. Who was most directly involved in that fatal error?" Angleton was seated, as by custom, at one end of the little table used for conferences within his office. He was addressing today Raymond Rocca and Tony Crespi. "As far as the public is concerned, and the historians, it was a great mix-up that got him killed. Maybe some people in the field interpreting President Kennedy's instructions in one way, McGeorge Bundy's in another—this telegram, that directive, that special order, and so on. We know there was one critical transmission: *Let 'em kill Diem.* Question: Whose ends was that man serving, I'm talking as the man who said OK to the assassination?"

Rocca and Tony were familiar with the apparently endless historical accounts of just what exactly had brought on the events of November 2, 1963. The day before, President Ngo Dinh Diem had fled the palace in Saigon, anticipating a coup. He hid out that night at the home of a friend, gone with his brother to an early service in church, had been dragged from the church, put into the back of a truck, driven to the country, and shot.

"One of my most learned friends," Angleton went on—that meant Golitsyn. Rocca had known this for ten years, the particular inflection that went with a mention of one of Angleton's "most learned friends"—"has drawn my attention to an intelligence fragment he came upon in the last months he spent... in enemy territory. And now he finds an amplification of one clue in the ongoing decryption we have been doing of the Soviet wartime interceptions..."

At lunch Rocca didn't mention that part of the morning's talk with the CI Chief. "You'll find plenty to do in Saigon," he said to Tony. "You've got the three key figures we're counting on and hoping will be alive when you get there—and that you can get to them."

They talked about Tony's mission, designed to do what could still be done. "And you'll have to walk carefully around the Thieu military. We don't even want them to know who we're talking about." Tony nodded and ran his fork aimlessly through the pasta. There was silence.

Then, finally, Rocca broke the silence. "I'll see what I can do to get the boss to ease up on his current fixation. Now Golitsyn's got him persuaded that Averell Harriman is a Soviet agent, God help us. I think Harriman's hands were dirty on the Diem business. But I mean — Angleton's even given the Investigate Harriman project an official code name! Project DINOSAUR." Again, silence.

"Come on, Tony. We're not being disloyal. It doesn't help our boss, let alone our team — our joint cause — to do this kind of self-discrediting thing, to just sit there and take in what Golitsyn has got him thinking."

Tony said cautiously. "I see what you mean."

Rocca pushed away his plate of half-eaten salmon.

He let it all out. "You know, JJA is suspicious of Armand Hammer. OK, I'll give him Hammer. That greedy oil tycoon shit, old pal of Lenin himself, laundering money for Stalin, up to his ass in cooperation, quote unquote, with Moscow. Hammer would give them the Statue of Liberty."

"Yeah, I know about Hammer."

"And OK, there are reasons to be permanently pissed off with Olof Palme. There's been no situation in the United Nations, in NATO, anywhere, that he hasn't been on the other side. But does that make him a Soviet agent?"

"What do you want me to say, Ray? 'No, that doesn't make him a Soviet agent?' That's kind of obvious, isn't it?"

"Less and less to Jim, with that odd guy leading him around like a candidate for president of the John Birch Society. Sometimes, damnit, there is a thread of plausibility in what he comes up with. Take Willy Brandt. Angleton told Peter Wright in London that Brandt was a Soviet agent — no, a KGB agent! Brandt is Chancellor of West Germany!

"Then there's Lester Pearson. All he is is Prime Minister of Canada! Granted there's some stuff in the Pearson file that didn't originate with Golitsyn. Jeff Harrison brought in a ten-page overview, a sort of Deep Thoughts about Pearson's loyalty. The supersecret memo goes on the boss's desk. He does nothing. Then a month later there's a high-level meeting with RCMP officials, a top-security conference. Jim pulls out Harrison's ten-page draft and he is reading out loud unverified charges to the Royal Canadian Mounted Police, as if doing a résumé for the benefit of a jury: Pearson, he says simply, is a Soviet agent.

"Well, the Canadians said, thanks a lot; and as far as I know, they didn't do anything more, just let the whole thing go. What I don't know is whether any one of them got through to Schlesinger. Jim Schlesinger as DCI is meaner than McCone, and Colby, his deputy, is tougher than Schlesinger, in my opinion, and I've watched him closely. Schlesinger's been boss for what, six months? And he's just plain impatient with Jim. I mean, it shows. And then Jim's relentless search for the Fifth Man. The big man we've never caught. The mole in place, in our place. I could see him the other day looking Schlesinger in the face, all those wheels spinning in that mighty mind . . . *Is it maybe this guy?*"

Tony Crespi said yes to the waitress, he would take both cream and sugar with his coffee.

"Ray, did you read Philby's book?"

Philby's memoir, *My Silent War*, had been published earlier in England. Tony had requisitioned two copies. He left one of them on Angleton's desk. The covering note read, "Jim, a book by our Moscow correspondent." Angleton hadn't acknowledged it.

"No," Rocca said, "I haven't read it."

"He is one cool son of a bitch. Listen to what he said about Hoover." Tony pulled the book out of his briefcase. "'I cannot speak of the record of the FBI in checking crime in the United States. With that side of its activities I had nothing to do. But I had a great deal to do with its counterespionage work, and its record in that field was more conspicuous for failure than for success. Hoover did not catch Maclean or Burgess; he did not catch Fuchs, and he would not have caught the rest if the British had not caught Fuchs and worked brilliantly on his tangled emotions; he did not catch Lonsdale; he did not catch Abel for years, and then only because Hayhanen delivered him up on a platter; he did not even catch me. If ever there was a bubble reputation, it is Hoover's.'

"Spooky, when you think of it. It's conceivable—you'd only need to have moved a chess piece differently once or twice here, or there—that Philby might have ended up *head* of MI6. He was headed exactly there—experience, savoir faire, connections—when Burgess and Maclean ruined the show for him by bailing out at just the wrong moment. And even then we didn't know for sure—James Jesus Angleton didn't know for sure; Harold Macmillan didn't know for sure—that Philby was a Soviet agent. For the hell of it, imagine that he had made it to the top. And now Angleton, his American counterpart, confides to him that three Western European government elders, the Canadian prime minister, the former governor of what was America's most populous state, are—Soviet agents! What hurts is that the bastard would have been right to laugh and laugh and laugh."

"And," Rocca spoke sadly, "we find ourselves here undressing the man who did more than everybody else combined to give us a structured way of using counterintelligence to try to find out what the enemy has been up to for twenty years."

Tony nodded. "I know. In the trade, he's a hero. He's also *my* hero. Let's hope he gets over it. When we're through assassinating Castro, how about doing it to Golitsyn?"

"At the Castro rate, Golitsyn will have died of old age."

Chapter Fifty-Four

1974

CASA NOGALES

Except that Jeff Harrison has no sense of humor I'd have suspected that the device he dreamed up and handed over to Colby was actually *intended* to be funny. An elaborate — bureaucratic — joke. For five or six weeks Harrison had spent what I have to suppose is one hundred percent of his time locked in his office with all of those folders and calculators. I had to guess he wasn't playing Solitaire, though we'd all have been better off if he had been.

And then last week, walking over to my own personal library, I passed by Harrison's office and stumbled into Colby coming out of it. There was a trace of a smile on Colby's face. More accurately, a trace of a smirk. He managed to consolidate his workaday stern — boring! — features, after a fleeting second; but a fleeting second is all that I need, most of the time, to come to conclusions on which I am willing to act. In that bit of time I had some sense of what it was that Colby was conspiring with Harrison to do and sensed also that the whole enterprise had a serious purpose. That it was more than a joke. It was never seriously intended — and I don't care *what* some of my colleagues might say on this point in disagreeing with me — to *incriminate* me. Its purpose is to find a reason to jettison the counterintelligence edifice I have built up over a generation as CCI.

In the world of disinformation, the world in which the Soviet Union thrives, the first lesson to be learned (I have every year stressed this point more and more) is: *Do not take at face value the apparent credentials of anyone.* Do not be won over by the ostensible believability of anything you hear, or hear argued, defended, urged, that bears on the war we are engaged in with the Soviet Union.

If there is misrepresentation, there are misrepresenters. The whole Soviet team, of course. But their tentacles are very far-reaching. We had the defection of Burgess and Maclean, the subsequent exposure of Anthony Blunt, and the defection of Kim Philby ten years ago. It is true that along the way I have concluded that there is a missing person, an important—unidentified—operative, an agent of the KGB concealed in a critical security agency here in Washington, possibly the National Security Agency over in the White House, most likely, in the CIA.

When Philby left Beirut and went off to Moscow I was exposed to not a little in-house raillery. Some of it good-humored, some of it not. I actually overheard Henderson. I was in the men's room, cloistered in a stall. He was talking to Miler at the urinals. Henderson said—jocularly, of course!—"Angleton was so suspicious about everybody he became suspicious of everything, including the claim that Philby was a suspect."

Actually, the Philby episode pointed in a different direction. It wasn't suspicion of suspicion. Philby was a man who I believed to be *loyal*. I hardly need add that so did Harold Macmillan think him loyal, or at least he said there wasn't conclusive evidence to the contrary.

What I then did—in part to advance the thinking and to refine the practices of the Agency, in part to learn for myself where I had gone wrong—was to go back and restudy the whole story of the four Cambridge students who in the early thirties bonded together as Apostles and swore secret allegiance to the Soviet revolution.

That investigative study convinced me, not by any elaboration of what the future spies had said and done as Marxist undergraduates, but by a study of what they went on to do in their professional lives. I sensed a missing presence. I sensed that there was a—yes—a Fifth Man.

Maclean managed, with his continuing access to White House correspondence, to see dispatches between President Truman and Clement Attlee in the critical period after the Czechoslovakian coup in 1948. I have not laid eyes on that correspondence, but one needn't be a psychic to guess at the importance of it. More properly, what were the problems the President and the Prime Minister addressed? What contingent arrangements were agreed upon?

—What would the United States do if Stalin pressed the Berlin blockade of 1948 to the point of strangulation?

—What would we do if the Soviet military began to harass— perhaps even to shoot down?—the cargo planes we were using to keep the Berlin population from starving?

I did not see that correspondence between the two leaders of the West, as I said. *But Stalin did.* A brilliant feat of espionage. But as I labored retrospectively over the information assembled by our security people and by the FBI that the KGB had got hold of, I kept bumping into a loose end. Some of what the Soviets had hadn't been included in the packages Maclean sent. There was a missing human being.

Well, surely that would be Burgess?

But it wasn't Burgess. We were able to establish that it wasn't he—he was physically elsewhere, and under surveillance in those weeks.

Well then, had I finally come up with a concrete infamy executed by Philby?

But Philby, too, was physically out of the country.

Was it conceivable that Anthony Blunt, the fourth member of the Apostles, operating out of London, could have been the activating figure in the operation? I investigated even *that* remote possibility; and the answer was no. Blunt didn't fit. London could not have substituted for Washington. Whoever the agent was, *he had to be located in Washington.*

And that person tipped off Burgess and Maclean that they were about to be arrested by MI5. That wasn't Philby, because we were tapping Philby at that point—not at my suggestion, I admit—it was an initiative of the FBI. The FBI swore, and I believe them, that no communication of any sort went out from Philby between the hour that MI5 made the decision to arrest them, and the critical twenty-four hours later when they stepped onto the ferry at Southampton to arrive at Saint-Malo and board the train to Paris, and from there, on to the arms of the KGB in East Berlin, thirty-six hours later. But the tip to Burgess came from—Washington.

I freed myself of the assumption that the Fifth Man was presumptively, let alone necessarily, a classmate of Maclean, Burgess, Philby, and Blunt. Even so, in my world—and, by extension, the world that stretches to London and Paris, Berlin, Rome, and Jerusalem—the person we were looking for continued to live conceptually, in our thoughts and in our words, as—"The Fifth Man."

For ten years we have been looking for him. *I know he exists.* I do not know *who* he is. Golitsyn is equally convinced that the Fifth Man is loose and operating. I continue to hope that the infrastructure of Golitsyn's experience and of his mind will continue to generate valuable clues. Golitsyn has been twelve years a defector but still he manages, with his vast knowledge and deductive powers, to come up with critical insights. And of course we give him what data we ingest on our own, as does MI5 (with less than entirely commendable regularity) and his mind is always working on our problems.

So, soon after William Colby came in as the new director, and after the heated exchange I had with the outgoing director, James Schlesinger, I sensed that the new DCI would try to do more than merely overrule me on successive issues under contention. He doesn't like to overrule me on matters like that. On matters like Is Nosenko a genuine defector, or is he a plant? Such evaluations are traditionally the responsibility of Counterintelligence. On the matter of Nosenko, for instance, I ruled that his credentials were suspect. That left Mr. Colby very frustrated. He did not want to overrule me, technically his subordinate, on Nosenko; so he has set out to undermine me.

Enter Jeff Harrison.

Their big, secret plot, as I get the feel of it, is actually simple-minded, for all that its fireworks would cause (*a*) derision among most of my colleagues; yet (*b*) genuine suspicion in the loonier of my colleagues.

The exercise given to Harrison is, I admit — I have no problem in seeing through it — patterned after my own practices:

Harrison has been instructed to piece together judgments I have made over the past twenty years in individual evaluations; piece together positions I have taken on a hundred policy questions that have arisen.

What will come of this construction? A kind of psychic portrait. One that will give rise to a little cloud of unknowing about — James J. Angleton. And then, as the data pile up, the miasmic cloud's consistency darkens, and you know — suddenly, irreversibly — that cloud is not evanescent, it will not blow away . . .

That calls for a drink.

Yes, the cloud over that man's head, or that woman's head, is a cloud that warns, indeed *instructs* the security fraternity: Do not expose your nation's secrets to that person.

Am I carried away with bitterness? I am a rigidly self-analytical professional, and I explore my own psychological strengths and weaknesses. The answer to the question, Am I bitter? is yes. And I am despondent about lost opportunities for my country to fend adequately for itself against a continuation, by the Soviet Union, of the protocols of the Trust.

So Mr. Harrison will put into the pot everything he can accumulate about my background: I was engaged in intelligence work in Italy after the war when the Communists accumulated power. . . . I was a friend of Kim Philby and argued his innocence.... I sent a young agent to Beirut to lock horns with Philby, and six months after he arrives in Beirut, Philby, having been warned, goes to Cairo and defects, flying off to the safety of Moscow. And by huge coincidence, my agent is at the airport in Cairo when Philby flies off.... I befriend Golitsyn, who advises against taking on four different Russian defectors, saying they are phony. I agree. Two of those rejected defectors are caught by the KGB and executed, so indeed they were genuine.... Our Vietnamese assets sent over the word that the 1968 Tet offensive would be modest in scale and I endorsed that opinion. And what happened? The Vietcong's thrust was so massive they overran our own embassy.

Add one hundred items to these and spin the wheel...

Who is Angleton. What is he?

Answer: I am the Fifth Man.

Chapter Fifty-Five

Colby scheduled his meeting for ten that night. Only Harrison and Bill Nelson, Deputy Director of Operations, were summoned. No other member of the cadre was given any reason to guess that the meeting was scheduled, let alone its mission. Security guards needed no warning. They were around to do their duty at all hours. And officials with proper credentials could come and go at any hour.

At the appointed time Colby was sitting at his desk. He had decided he would officiate from his desk the next day, at the apocalypse. Bill Nelson came in, quiet, dressed in a light brown suit, his hearing aid conspicuous, his hands as ever holding down his notepad. He nodded at the DCI, said nothing, and sat down in the chair Colby pointed out with a gesture. Harrison came in from the back office and sat down alongside Nelson, his own notepad in hand.

"All right, gentlemen. I intend to dismiss James Angleton tomorrow." He could hear the breath drawn. "Yes. I know what you are thinking. This is a dramatic moment, dismissing someone of his stature." William Colby indulged himself in a wry comment. "Like dismissing General MacArthur.

"Now let's handle the easy part first. The Church Committee is meeting every other day and will probably do so through the month of October, perhaps even into November. The Committee's report to the Congress will be very damaging. We can't guess everything the senators and their staff will come up with, but political assassinations will certainly play a big role.

"Their general charge, I think we can safely surmise, will be along the lines of—contumacy. That the Agency is not operating within the prescribed limits of the National Security Act of 1947.

"Without running any risk of perjury I managed to deflect all interrogatories that might have led them to stare in the face at what we did for so many years with Jay Lovestone and that particular operation. But the raw material is there. I mean, that operation was financed by our agency. And not inconceivably, when the report is published, someone who knows the story will step forward and give Senator Church, or Senator Schweicker, or the chief counsel, the details. The wonder of it is that the Communists didn't do so years ago. We have only to thank for this the Communists' assumption that *every* anti-Communist impulse in America is generated by government—or Wall Street. But it matters a great deal, on the scales of Congressional-Agency relations, that we should at just the right time—and this is just the right time—hand over to Senator Church a scalp. A big scalp. James J. Angleton, Chief of Counterintelligence, who has taken liberties the Senate Committee has correctly identified."

"That's a hell of a large scalp, Mr. Director."

Colby turned to Harrison. "It's the biggest we've got. Unless we turned me in. I vetoed that." There was a faint chuckle.

"The Committee will view this as a genuine act of propitiation. Without knowing all the rules the Agency has ... dealt informally with, they'll have got out the master planner of extralegal activity.

Then, too, the senators and the staff will have some rhetorical satisfaction. It was, after all, Jim—of all people! He couldn't control his intellectual arrogance!—who said it was, quote 'inconceivable that a secret arm of government would always obey the law.'"

Nelson began to say something but stopped. Colby was not in the mood to be interrupted.

"All right. That, in a way, is the easy one. The tough one is this."

Colby went on to explain what he intended to say to Angleton. He then asked both men what they knew about Angleton's privately supervised physical resources in the Agency.

Nelson departed the room and came back with a sketch of the second floor of the building. He leaned over Colby's desk and marked an X on the diagram. "That's Angleton's inner office. Over there"—the pencil led the movement of the eye—"next to it is his outer office. That's where ongoing investigations and analyses happen. Then there's the reception room, where his three secretaries have their desks. Across the hall are his safes. Over there, across the hall, are two small offices. And in there"—the pencil pointed to a two-square-inch grid—"in there is his safe. A walk-in safe. Three people can stand up and work in it."

"You got the combination?"

"Oh *no*, Bill. *Nobody* has the combination to James Angleton's personal safe. Not even Rocca, his right-hand man. Only Angleton."

Colby's voice was impatient. "How long's that been true?"

"Ever since Langley became headquarters—1961. Back in Dulles's time."

"This is absurd. We're talking about government property." Colby looked up at his subordinates. He got no ideas from them; no sympathy, in fact. Nelson finally said, "Boss, this side of going to court I haven't any ideas how to enter that safe. And if a court order was issued, you know, and I know, that Jim Angleton would go to jail and stay there until he rotted before opening up that safe."

"There's got to be a safecracking expert could get in, obviously."

"He'd have to have been born after 1962 because Angleton's safe was designed to be invulnerable to any safecracking science anyone could come up with as of that time, short of dynamite. And Jim looked everywhere back then for the brainiest guy in the business."

Colby showed signs of extreme exasperation. He lit a cigarette, violating his own rules about not smoking in his office.

"All right. There's nothing more we can do on that front right now. I want you both here with me tomorrow. I don't expect to call on you to say anything. But I want two witnesses. Angleton knows things aren't going his way. But he doesn't know what I'm going to tell him tomorrow. God save us all."

He heard both men, in their own way, pronounce, *Amen*.

Chapter Fifty-Six

James Angleton walked into the DCI's office at 11:15. He was surprised to find Colby seated not at the conference table, where he was usually to be found when discussion was anticipated. Harrison and Nelson were in the room but seated—again, an irregularity—not at the conference table but in armchairs, one at either end of the DCI. Colby answered Angleton's puzzled look by pointing to the chair directly opposite his desk. "Sit there, if you will, Jim."

Angleton knew instantly: This was to be a meeting of some formal consequence. He took his chair and reached for one of the pads always distributed around the table. He drew his pen from his inside pocket and said nothing. If grimness in general tone was what the DCI wanted, he'd not get cooperation from the Chief of Counterintelligence, who doodled on the yellow pad. But Angleton permitted himself a silent smile: Who, if not the crowned king of counterintelligence, would know that there was design in the theatrical arrangements?

"Jim, let's get right to it." Colby's voice came in at a higher pitch than normal. But with a slight throat clearance he spoke with his usual well-regulated baritone.

"Effective at noon today you are relieved of all duties.

"There are grounds for relieving you for undertaking enterprises not sanctioned by the law, and it is immaterial who else at the Agency knew about these enterprises. Certainly you did."

There was a second of silence. Angleton could have broken in, responded, reacted, in whatever way. He did, said, nothing. Colby, his eyes fixed on a folder on top of his desk, continued.

"You are dismissed not because of these transgressions, though they would be cause enough." Colby cleared his throat yet again.

"The Agency does not wish you to continue your work here because," Colby let out the words with metallic intonation, "in our judgment, you present a loyalty risk."

Angleton shot up from his chair. He drew breath but the words did not flow. His occasional stammer was back. "You—you aren't *finished* with your preposterous ... *joke* about my loyalty?"

"I can only say this, that by the standards we seek to govern ourselves by, standards substantially set by you over the years, we cannot proceed, in my judgment, confident that you will place the best interests of the United States above all others."

Angleton remained standing.

Colby went on: "There are, of course, many formalities to consider, among them the access we shall have to have to your files. I don't think you would find it in your best interests to engage a lawyer, but if you do, of course we will deal with the situation using our own resources.

"But we need go no farther this morning than to advise you that a deputy of mine is instructed to accompany you any time you are on these premises.

"Other details you can take up with Bill Nelson."

Colby nodded his head and tightened his lips, brought together the papers on his desk, and put them into a manila folder. That meant that the meeting was over. There was no question of an exchange of handshakes.

Angleton turned his eyes briefly to Nelson, then to Harrison, both of whom had stayed seated.

He turned and walked to the door. He did not return to his own office but walked out in the brilliant fall sunshine to his Mercedes in the parking lot, at that special space reserved for the CI Chief. He unlocked the door of the car, got into the driver's seat, closed the car door, and wept a long while. He was frightened and lonely and — as his tears dried — his fury mounted.

He started the car then and drove off slowly to Casa Nogales. He had some hard thinking to do.

Chapter Fifty-Seven

At one in the morning Angleton woke up Guido Andreotti. He did this without compunction. Guido Andreotti once said of himself, in conversation with Angleton, that he "never like-a slep. There is always the emergency." The intricately tapped telephone was his specialty; another was devising defiant safe mechanisms. He had done one such for Angleton in 1962, shortly after the Agency called in its administrative diaspora and installed itself in the grandeur of Langley.

"Guido, I want to know something. If somebody wanted to get into my safe at Langley, could he do it?"

"You mean like-a a foreign agent?"

"No. Actually, I mean like somebody who has the authority to investigate anything on the premises."

Guido paused. "Would that person have-a authority to call Guido?"

"Yes, he would. Of course, Guido, you could tell them that you have no means of getting into the safe."

Guido laughed. "Guido can get into anything. Well... not

quite. Yours would-a be very difficult. But we are old friends. If you-a want, I tell them Guido can't do it, not this one."

"I'm not sure they'll ask you, but—there are things going on, Guido, that aren't so good."

"I am *always* your comrade. We a-fought Mussolini together and we've-a stayed together."

"Thanks, Guido."

Angleton weighed the information and reasoned quickly to the dark but probable contingency. If, as Guido had told him, it was in fact possible to open the safe, then Guido could be got to do it. He might stall, and he would certainly warn Angleton, but he would have no alternative but to open it.

Which meant that Angleton had to go in first.

He needed to retrieve one file in particular. One hefty file. It contained his personal conjectures about important suspects in five countries, including his own country.

Retrieve that file and the letter. The letter that had haunted him ever since its arrival, a month earlier. It was addressed to Casa Nogales. He had taken it for safekeeping to his vault.

He looked at his watch. It was almost two in the morning. Colby had said that beginning "immediately" Angleton could not enter the offices at Langley except with a security guard at his side. That could mean only one thing: a guard that would not permit him to remove anything from his office or from his vault.

Surely the security guard wouldn't be on duty already? Even Colby could not suspect that Angleton would return to Langley before morning.

And then, Angleton thought, as he opened his drawer and took out his small .38 pistol, it was inconceivable that he would not be able to maneuver as he wished in the womb of the Agency of which he had been the ongoing godfather for so many years.

He started the engine of his Mercedes with some confidence, and backed out of the garage.

At Langley there was the preliminary guard, protecting the broad, wooded premises. It would probably be someone familiar with his face, Angleton thought as he drove up. But he was prepared to exhibit his laminated credential.

"Yes sir, Mr. Angleton, good evening to you."

The barrier lifted, the car drove on.

He was apprehensive primarily about the guard at the main entrance. He parked his car and walked over to it, ringing the buzzer. He could see the silhouettes of two uniformed men, armed, one of them seated before a console whose red and blue lights flickered on and off.

The door opened.

Angleton lifted from his pocket the plastic identifier worn in the office by everyone with the single exception of the DCI.

"Yes sir, come in Mr. Angleton." The guard went over to his colleague — it was Sergeant Henry, an old-timer. Henry ran his fingers over the keyboard in front of him. His face crinkled with concern. "Mr. Angleton, sir, the directive here is that you have to... proceed... with an escort officer, sir."

"Yes yes," Angleton said. "Those are my own instructions. I am doing an important exercise."

"Well, sir, we aren't exactly a full staff at this hour of the morning. Would it be all right if Jimmy here" — he pointed to the guard who had opened the gate — "just keeps you on his monitor? That way we can report where you go. How long will you be here, Mr. Angleton?"

"Not long. I have to go to the cable office and check a few things there, then stop by my own office. Say a half hour."

Sergeant Henry was relieved. He handed James Angleton the monitoring device. "If you'll just keep that in your pocket, sir. We'll record the movements down here."

Angleton went up to the third floor and walked over to the cable office. The wires were banging away. A dozen clerks filed and made notations on the miles of paper that flowed stutteringly in from two dozen outposts in every corner of the world, advising the intelligence headquarters of the free world what was afoot, or perhaps afoot, or problematically afoot.

The clerks nodded at Angleton. He walked over to the British wire and gave it a cursory look.

He walked then down one flight to his outer office, using his key. Through the reception room to his inner office. There he took off his jacket, placing it and the monitor on his desk.

He retraced his steps and turned the key on the door that opened up into the room that held his vault.

He closed the door and walked to the safe.

He moved his fingers over the computer keyboard, and went then to the massive dial. The huge door swung open.

Without delay he went to the corner and got out the bulky folder. And then to the little metal box, with the envelope.

He wondered: Did Sergeant Henry's console require him to search the Chief of Counterintelligence going out, as if he were a common visitor?

If that happened, there'd be no alternative. Angleton would need to make an instant row and draw on his seniority. He would not use his gun, though he was always aware of it when it reposed in his pocket.

He closed the safe, returned to his inner office, put on his jacket, and walked down to the entrance.

Sergeant Henry detained him. "Mr. Angleton, it says here you can't take anything out of the building without it goes to G-11 for OK."

"That's the system we're going to be experimenting with beginning tomorrow, Henry. I may change that instruction a bit. I'm in conversation with the DCI about these new rules. But meanwhile I have here just the daily cables I have to get through before the ten o'clock meeting."

There was a moment of hesitation. Then, "OK, Mr. Angleton. You're the boss."

Angleton set off in the direction of Casa Nogales but did not drive there. He went instead to a small dwelling in Georgetown which had once been a safe house but was no longer listed in the Agency inventory. It had been an easy task for Angleton to contrive its administrative disappearance. It was now a modest alternative residence. He put the folder in the safe. Then he drove to Casa Nogales, reaching it just as dawn was breaking.

He went to his study and poured a large glass of brandy.

Then he reached for the envelope and studied, for the twentieth time, the typed return address. KYROMSKI 23. MOSKAV. He opened the letter and read it, as if he had never seen it before.

The blood surged into his face. He felt rage—and exultation.

He stared at the handwritten words:

"Jim, Why don't you give up? You'll never find him. Fondly, Kim."

But Philby was wrong. Angleton knew now who the Fifth Man was. The man who had fired him. The Director of Central Intelligence.

God help America, Angleton thought, finishing his drink.

READING LOG		
103		